# THE DESOLATE BOND

D.K. HOLMBERG

ASH PUBLISHING

If you want to be notified when D.K. Holmberg's next novel is released and get
free stories and occasional other goodies, please sign up for his mailing list by
going here . Your email address will never be shared and you can unsubscribe at
any time.

www.dkholmberg.com

# CHAPTER 1

*E*ris Taeresin stood in the shade, massive svanth trees stretching high over her head. Thick vines curled around the trunks of the trees, their near invisible barbs sinking into the bark. The teary star flower—the flower she'd claimed as hers—last bloomed six years ago and would not bloom for another year, but its energy surged through the vines already. One hand wrapped around one of the thick vines, unafraid of the barbs, she delved through the roots of the forest and listened.

The roots had taught her much during the months she'd spent within the Svanth Forest, the only place she knew where both svanth trees and the teary star flower grew. She learned from the first keeper, from the lessons twisted into the roots as the trees grew, and felt the power locked within the great garden. From those lessons, she felt a pressing danger from the south. Already the Conclave regained strength.

But she needed to know more. Every day she spent twisting through the roots of the forest, searching for the answers to what she was from the lessons woven there by the first keeper. Eris caught glimpses, but nothing more.

"You can't spend every day like this."

Eris turned to see Terran standing behind her. His dark hair hung about his shoulders, not pulled back as he usually wore it. Deep brown eyes matched the serious expression on his face, and his lips pressed tightly together. Stitches held his dark green jacket together, each mark a reminder of where thorns from the forest had tried tearing it from him. He wore it now like a shield.

"I know it's here, Terran."

He shook his head. "I'm here. The trees and the flowers and the *life* around you are here." He fixed her with a hard expression. "But you're not here."

She turned to him, trying to hide her surge of annoyance. "Where am I, then, if not here?"

"I don't know. Lost somewhere."

"I need to understand what I'm supposed to do. Why did the trees summon me here if not to learn?"

"And have you learned anything? Spending each day searching for answers—have the trees told you what you want?"

Eris sighed. Once, such a question would have seemed strange, but once she hadn't known anything about the keepers. The story woven into the roots had taught her some of the history but nothing about what had happened in the hundreds of years since the first keeper began this forest.

"The roots only reach so far."

Terran touched her hand. She smiled at his familiarity. The smile he'd once worn so easily had disappeared since she'd escaped from the magi, replaced by his steady determination to serve as the gardener he thought he needed to be. A protector, keeping her safe from the dangers of the forest. Eris had given up telling him that she sensed where dangers hid within the forest. Most she could defend against. The others could be avoided. Even after all the time she'd spent here, she still didn't know what they were.

"You can reach beyond the forest, Eris."

She nodded, sliding her hand along the vine as she released it. Here in the heart of the forest, sunlight didn't quite reach the base of the trees, but she still felt its warmth. Terran had brought her clothing, something other than the thin shift she'd worn when running from the magi, and today, she wore a plain yellow dress the color of a corinth. Nothing like the wild dresses she'd preferred when living in the palace, but there, she'd felt the need to show how different she was from her sisters, as if she'd needed her clothes to remind them of that. Her dark hair was reminder enough.

"And I *have* reached beyond the forest." The Verilain Plain stretched away from the forest, and she could follow the roots of the needlegrass growing throughout the plains, but the energy there was different than the near sentience she had within the forest. Still powerful in its own way, but different. "There's so much I can learn here, Terran. I just need more time."

Terran frowned at her. "And while you take time to listen to the past, you ignore what's happening around you. You isolate yourself from everyone."

She frowned at him. "I don't isolate—"

"Three elms on the north edge of the forest have rotted. Another oak near the southern border does the same. What if it spreads deeper into the forest and reaches the svanth trees here?"

Eris searched for the trees he described and found them. The three elms were beyond repair, rotted from disease. Eris sent a request to the forest to keep the disease from spreading. She could not find the oak.

How had she missed them?

She sighed. Maybe Terran was right. She *had* been spending most of her time searching for answers. That had been the summons of the forest, but since staying here, she hadn't learned much more than what she'd glimpsed that first night.

Terran took her hands. "You're avoiding returning. You know the Mistress of Flowers wanted you to return so she could begin

3

teaching you arrangements. And I'm certain your parents wonder—"

Eris turned away. "Lira will have told my mother what happened to me. I'm not sure they care more than that." They were probably happy to see her gone. After all the times she'd disappointed them, surely this would be another disappointment.

At least here, she felt a part of something. At home, she was only different.

Terran took her hand and turned her to him. He smiled, but it had a hint of sadness. She missed the lopsided expression he used to wear. "Your family cares about you. I saw your father after you'd gone missing, how distraught he was at what he thought happened. And your sisters—"

"My sisters will be pleased that I'm here."

Terran laughed lightly and shook his head again. "Your sisters will want to know what happened. You may be different than them, but they're still your sisters. Didn't you tell me about an aunt who was different?"

Eris glared at him. Of course Terran would remember her talking about her aunt Rochelle. "My father's sister. Rochelle." Eris hadn't seen her for years, since before Lira arrived in the palace. Rochelle had been gone so long most thought her dead. Before, she would come and go, spending much of her time in the library, studying something new. Eris remembered the way her mother and Rochelle would stroll through the palace garden together, before Lira had taken it over. Then, trees had filled the courtyard. Eris had never learned why Rochelle hadn't returned. "What's your point, Terran?"

"Only that you once told me how fond your father was of her and how he worried about what happened to her, even now. Why do you think your sisters would worry any less?"

She really *should* return to Eliara. Not for her sisters. Regardless of what Terran said, Eris didn't think they missed her at all. They were too different. Jasi, married to the prince of Saffra, intended to unite the kingdoms, though that union had proven a mistake, especially after how the magi betrayed her family. Then there was Desia, so much like Jasi in how she understood her role within the kingdom. Even Ferisa, pledged to serve the Sacred Mother since birth, had not fought her station. Only Eris pushed against what she had been born into.

Yet, doing so had helped her discover what she was *really* meant for. Would her sisters—and her family—understand? Wasn't it easier to remain in the forest and learn what she could about being a keeper?

She sensed an energy deep within the roots of the forest. It felt like a promise, there at the edge of awareness, some deep and powerful secret she could almost grasp.

Each day she tried but never quite understood.

But she *had* promised Lira she would return. As Mistress of Flowers, Lira was a keeper different than Eris, but she had to know something, certainly more than Eris managed to learn by delving into the roots. Maybe there were only so many lessons she could master from them. And the last thing Eris had said to Lira was that she would return to learn what she knew of being a keeper.

More than anything, Eris owed her that.

She sighed. If only she could learn faster. The trees had taught her how to follow the roots, how to learn what happened outside the forest, and she had stretched that awareness, sensing beyond the borders of the trees, past the Verilain Plains, until she found hints of a growing danger.

Along the plains, she could follow the roots of the needlegrass, roots that didn't delve nearly as deep as the forest but still carried much potential. A garden in its own right, one even Lira had not realized existed. And then, beyond Verilain, lay the open expanse of Eliara. The roots of the grasses growing around the city were too shallow to follow and learn much, but still she felt them.

Beyond Eliara, to the south toward Saffra where the Conclave hid, she felt nothing.

It was the nothingness she feared.

The nothingness continued to grow.

"You don't know enough yet."

Eris looked at Terran, frowning. "I don't know enough for what?"

"I see from your face what you think. You don't hide your emotions nearly as well as you imagine, Eris Taeresin. You aren't strong enough to take on the Conclave by yourself. I know how their attack angered you; how you think about what they did, wishing you can do more."

Terran looked around the forest, his gaze flickering over fallen trees lying around the perimeter of the heart. One, larger than the rest, had fallen. Age and time had felled the trees, but Eris knew how much it troubled him that he hadn't managed to save it. It was another thing Eris hadn't noticed in time. She'd been too focused on learning what she could from the roots.

Had she noticed, would there have been anything she could have done? Terran claimed responsibility, but wasn't her job to protect the trees of her forest?

"Can you blame me? After what they did?" she asked.

"I don't blame you, but there's only so much you can do."

"The Conclave failed when they attacked the last time."

He shook his head. "Not the Conclave. Only a few magi. And you know the Conclave managed to attack and destroy the Gardens of Elaysia."

"There was no keeper of the forest then."

Terran nodded. "And there is now. But she's untrained. You still don't really understand the power stored here. Until you do—until you can control it—thinking about the magi puts you at risk."

Eris sighed. Terran was right. She didn't really control the power of the forest. She borrowed it, asked it to help her, but didn't control it. In that, she was still as green as the saplings growing along the edge. While she could delve into the roots and listen to the histories written there, she had no more control over the forest than the wind did the trees. Enough to bend them at times but no real mastery over them.

Maybe she couldn't have done anything about the diseased trees—would her abilities have allowed her to do anything more than ask the trees for assistance?—but they'd healed Terran when he lay injured, bone sticking from his broken ankle, keeping infection from setting in as it surely would. If the power of the forest allowed her to help Terran, certainly it would have let her heal one of its own.

Thinking about what had happened the day the Conclave abducted her and Jasi always managed to draw out Eris' anger. It bloomed in her like a flower facing the sun. The Conclave had wanted her and her sister to destroy the forest, and their destructive magic had nearly killed Terran. Had Eris not been here—or had she *not* learned that she could be a keeper—would they have succeeded? What would have happened then?

Eris didn't want to consider it.

"I don't think I can confront the Conclave on my own."

Terran laughed. Like so much else throughout the forest, the sound faded, disappearing as if swallowed by the trees. "You think I don't know you? Working alongside you these last few months, you don't think I've gotten to know anything about you?"

She frowned at him. "What do you imply?"

"I imply nothing. The Sacred Mother knows you need help. More than just help, you need training." He took a step toward her. "Listen. I know the Conclave pushes again. When I see your face each time you connect with the trees, how can I not? But there isn't anything you can do, not all the way in Saffra. Remember Lira and the limits to her power. What makes you think you're so different?"

Eris considered him for a moment. He looked back at her with defiance in his eyes. For so long, she *had* been different. Now,

Terran reminded her how she was like Lira, and she hated that he was right. "I thought the gardeners were supposed to help the keepers," she pouted.

"You think I'm not helping?"

"I'm not sure what you're doing, but it doesn't feel like help."

Terran shook his head. "Just like Lira never tried to teach you."

She shot him a look and pulled away from him. "Careful. I might ask the trees to tear another hole in your jacket."

As she said it, she knew that was the entire problem. She would have to ask.

She sighed.

What she felt each time she followed the roots told her that she needed to fear what happened to the south, where Errasn met with Saffra, the way everything simply *stopped*. There should be something there. From all the time she'd spent in the library researching her flower, she knew that even the hot, arid climate of Saffra would have flowers of its own. Shouldn't she be able to cross over and reach them?

If only she knew more. The first keeper had likely hidden answers in the story woven throughout the roots, but Eris couldn't understand it. Maybe another day...

She shook her head. Another day wouldn't change anything.

But could there be another reason she didn't sense anything beyond the southern border of Errasn? Did her ability as keeper have limitations? That didn't make sense. A keeper's reach was limited only by the life growing across the land. Besides, other than the keepers, no one stood between what the Conclave wanted and Errasn. Already they had tried to destroy the gardens. Had the forest not still stood—and the plains—they might have succeeded. Then they would move on north.

Yet, she didn't *want* to leave the forest. For the first time in as long as she could remember, she felt a part of something. Her sister Jasi had always known she would play a political role. Desia had the same destiny and embraced it the same as Jasi. And Ferisa…she took to the faith as intended, filling her duty as servant to the Sacred Mother. But Eris never wanted any of that. Until she'd learned she could be a keeper, she hadn't known what she wanted.

Having found her place, she would do anything to keep it. If that meant battling the magi to keep them from destroying her garden, she would gladly do it. She only had to learn how.

She turned toward the south, where the subtle change from where Lira's gardens grew emanated.

Learning to use her ability meant returning to Eliara. Facing her sisters and her parents. Would they accept that she had changed? That she had a different place in the world than the one her father had assigned for her? Or would they try to force her to be more like her sisters?

She sighed again. They couldn't force her, not any longer.

"I see you've decided."

Eris frowned at him. "I've decided I'm ready to leave you here. I might have the trees keep you from following."

Terran shook his head. "You know they won't. And you know I'm right."

She glared before shaking her head.

Eris started to say something, but a low howl split through the calm of the forest, interrupting her.

Terran peered through the shadows between the trees, as if he could make out what was out there.

Eris touched the vine surrounding the svanth tree and delved into its roots. A stillness came through the forest, as if it were holding its breath. Birds sat motionless atop high branches. Squirrels and tree lions perched, waiting. Even the wind seemed to pause.

She searched for where the creature prowled and found it nearby. The forest had been unable to provide answers about what the creature was, and neither she nor Terran wanted to search for it. They were safe at the heart of the forest. But when they left, they were often followed.

She sent a request to the trees, asking for a barrier. It was little different than what she'd asked after her first night spent beneath the trees, when Jasi had been in danger from the tree lion. Then the trees had responded, pulling around her and keeping her safe.

This time, she felt indifference.

Eris didn't know how to explain it any differently, only that the trees didn't answer. The creature—whatever it was—prowled around the edge of the heart of the forest.

"It hasn't come this close before," Terran said.

Eris shook her head, pulling away from the sense of the forest around her. "But we're in the heart. We're safe here."

"I could hunt it—"

"We've talked about this before. You were the one who told me how dangerous this forest was, and we know it's because of that creature." Eris didn't think there was more than one but couldn't be certain. "Hunting it would be dangerous." And she had the strange sense that the forest wouldn't allow it. Another problem.

Terran frowned and pushed his hair behind his ears. "Leaving it out there is dangerous. What if the heart of the forest no longer contains it?"

"The forest tolerates its presence."

"I'd feel better knowing what it is."

Eris nodded. Not knowing anything about the creature bothered her as well, but short of tracking it, she had no way of discovery, if the trees refused to tell her. "You can see if Lira knows, when we return to Eliara."

Terran blinked as the words registered, and then he smiled. "Are you certain?"

She shook her head. "Not entirely. But you're right. There are limits to what I can learn here." And there was so much she wanted to learn. She needed to command the forest instead of ask. What would happen to them when they needed the trees to respond?

Would asking be enough? Would they care about Eris—or the same things Eris cared for—or would they simply ignore her requests?

Eris couldn't be at risk of the trees not responding if something were to happen. Not again, not like when she'd first tried to heal Terran. Had anything happened to him then...

She shuddered at the thought.

Terran nodded, studying her face. "When do we leave?"

# CHAPTER 2

*T*hey stood on the western edge of the Verilain Plains, past the burned remains of the magi's attack months ago. The grasses should have regrown by now, but Eris didn't take the time to stop and determine why they hadn't. The grasses couldn't help her, not like Lira could.

Eris felt exposed. It was the first time in months she'd left the forest. In the time she'd been staying within the trees, she'd barely left the heart where the towering svanth trees all around her kept her plunged in shadows. The bright sunlight streaming across the plains blinded her, making her cup her hand across her brow as she stared out. The trees loomed behind her, beckoning her back beneath the canopy.

Did she really need to leave? Couldn't she learn what she needed by delving into the roots, tracing the lessons the first keeper hid there?

Eris looked over her shoulder, knowing the answer as she did. Delaying wouldn't change it. The trees had been home for the last few months—more like home than Eliara often felt—only now she didn't know when she'd return. The connection to the trees was faint, drawing on her and never fully leaving her mind. Eris hadn't expected to miss it as much as she did.

The wide expanse of needlegrass waved in the whistling wind. The first time she'd gone through it, she was left with dozens of shallow cuts across her arms and face. Since then, her connection to it changed. Or maybe *she* had changed by accepting the mantle of keeper. Now the grasses parted for her, giving her a wide berth so she walked unharmed, leaving her deep green dress intact. Eris had an open pathway, nearly as comfortable as the Kingsroad, leading away from the Svanth and back toward Eliara.

Beyond the plains, the ground opened into wide, rolling hills. Trees dotted the land, but fewer than in the forest. Eris delved into the roots, questing toward the trees, sensing the energy available. Nothing like with the Svanth, but knowing it was there put her at ease. That sense faded as she traced across the rolling hills, following the roots through Errasn until they met Saffra. Then there was nothing more than desolation. Eris shivered.

"We could have taken the Kingsroad."

Eris shook her head. The wind caught her dark hair and sent it whipping around her. "It would take longer than cutting across the plains."

Terran looked at his jacket and frowned. "You need to see the Gardens sometime. What is left of them, anyway."

Eris didn't tell him that she'd seen the Gardens, at least through the visions the forest granted to her. From what she saw, she recognized how majestic they once had been. Had they been the same during Lira's time, or had time changed them, made them more impressive like it had with the forest? And now that was all gone, destroyed by the Conclave. Such potential wasted. What else would the Conclave do if threatened?

That was the reason Eris needed to return to Eliara. If she didn't learn what she needed from Lira, she wouldn't be able to help her family. "You think I need a reminder of what the Conclave can do?"

"Yes."

She shot him a look. Terran doubted her?

"You still think there's little to fear from the Conclave. I know what you experienced. I was there for part of it. But the Conclave —the *entirety* of the Conclave—is something entirely different. When you see what happened to the gardens, you'll understand."

"The magi showed me what they were capable of doing." She suppressed a shudder, remembering the one magi whose hand had crept up her leg, touching her in a way she'd never been touched. Anger coursed through her with the thought, and she forced it down. "I know better than to rush after them."

Concern wrinkled Terran's eyes as he looked at her. She offered him a half-hearted smile.

They made their way across the hills, speaking little. The closer they came to Eliara, the more anxious Eris became. Would her father welcome her home after the months she'd spent away, or would he push her back out, ignoring her? And what of her mother? Surely Lira would have told them what happened, why Eris remained behind. But if she hadn't? Would her parents have worried?

She kept telling herself that the only reason she returned was for the lessons Lira could offer. Another keeper—one still living and not simply a memory stored in the roots of the forest—would be able to provide a different type of instruction. Lessons where she might learn enough to counteract whatever it was she felt along the border and keep it from creeping forward into Errasn.

While in the forest, there was a constant connection to every-thing around her, a sense of *knowing*. The farther she went from the Svanth, the more disconnected she felt. Without that, she felt... empty. But as they made their way toward Eliara, the growing power of Lira's garden built until Eris felt it easily. She couldn't access it directly, not at this distance; she was not its keeper.

This close to the city, she was amazed at how much power the garden generated. Smaller than the Svanth Forest, this garden still had much potential. She could almost imagine dozens of similar gardens placed together like when the great Gardens of Elaysia had existed.

After cresting a hill, Eliara spread out below them.

Eris sighed. As much as she'd tried preparing for her return, nothing made it any easier.

Terran stepped next to her. For long moments they didn't speak as they looked down at the city. People moved about the streets. Carts and horses filed past the massive outer wall, spilling out onto the road. Smoke curled from dozens of chimneys; thick and dark from the blacksmiths on the edge of town, wispy and pale near the center where the bakeries would be located, and barely visible against the sky from hearths scattered other places in the city.

It was home, but no longer *her* home.

"I remember the first time I came here. How it seemed so much bigger than I had expected."

Eris looked over at him. "I always felt like the city was so small."

"You should see Helash sometime. We have a few taverns, a smith, a mill, but not much else."

"Do you miss it?"

Terran met her eyes. "Not any longer."

"You don't regret coming to Eliara?"

As they neared Eliara, he'd kept a greater distance between them, but now he moved closer and touched her hand. "I am a gardener. There are few keepers remaining."

"That isn't an answer."

Terran smiled. "Because it's a question you don't need to ask."

She took his hand and held it purposefully as she started down the hill toward the city. Farms dotted the outskirts of town, most smaller than the ones they passed farther from Eliara. As they neared, the sounds of the city washed over her. Voices and clatter and hooves—a cacophony of noise around her. After all the time she'd spent in the quiet solitude of the forest, the noise bothered her most.

The massive walls of the city rose in front of her. She sighed again, pushing back the conflicting thoughts she had about returning. If she didn't simply press forward, it would be all too easy to turn back, but doing so would change nothing. The nothingness—the desolation—pressing toward Eliara wouldn't stop. Her inability to control the power within the forest wouldn't change. She'd be keeper in name only, barely able to use her gifts.

She needed what Lira could teach.

Eris led them to the gate and through. A tingle of anxiety crawled across her as she did, leaving her stomach fluttering, but it passed as the familiarity with the streets returned. She followed the road as it led to the palace. There, she finally paused, forced to a stop by the closed gate at the inner wall.

She stared at the heavy iron with a frown. "That's odd."

"What?"

"The gate is rarely closed. There should at least be guards standing by to let us in."

"Think of what's happened. Your sister was abducted. The magi tried to overthrow the king."

"And I disappeared."

Terran squeezed her hand. "There's that."

"Hopefully, Lira will have explained the reason why."

Terran chuckled. "Otherwise, we're in for an interesting greeting."

She shot him a look as she walked to the gate and placed her hands on it. She quickly jerked away. Cold—almost angry—iron burned her hand. As she'd touched it, her connection to the distant Svanth Forest was severed.

"Iron," Terran said.

Eris frowned. "What about iron?"

"Iron does something to keepers. You'll have to ask Lira what it is."

She remembered the cage the magi held Lira in after they captured her. Eris hadn't understood at the time—and hadn't thought to question since. If iron could cut her connection to the forest, she needed to know why. It was another reason for her to return.

Why would the palace even have iron gates? Was this some remnant of the magi influence? Eris didn't think so; the gates were old—much older than her and her family, but hadn't the keepers been around longer? Why, then, would the first builders have used iron?

More questions.

Hooves thundered up behind them, pounding across the stone.

Eris turned to see a line of horses approaching, riding hard. As they neared, they turned toward her and Terran. Men wearing gleaming mail and heavy helms rode quickly. A bannerman carrying her father's sigil led the column. Eris smiled when she saw a blond-haired man near the back of the line, a long sword hanging from his waist. Blue eyes surveyed the wall as they neared. Her brother Jacen had changed since the last time she'd seen him, but she still recognized him easily.

Jacen saw her and halted his horse. "Palace is shuttered while the queen is ill," he said.

Ill? Her mother was sick? Why hadn't Lira sent word?

"Open the gates and let me in, Jacen."

He frowned at her, his brow furrowing deeply. Jacen tossed his reins to one of the other men and leapt from the saddle with a crash of mail. He glanced at Terran and then dismissed him, turning toward Eris. He kept one hand on the hilt of his sword as he approached her.

"You speak to me as if you…" He stopped and frowned, looking at her with wide eyes. "Eris?" He dropped his hand from the hilt of his sword and hurried over and framed her face between his palms, twisting in from side to side. "It *is* you! Sacred Mother! Where have you been? What happened to you?"

She shook him off. "Nothing happened to me."

Jacen took a step back. "Nothing happened..." He shook his head. "Jasi told me how you saved her. That you got her away from the magi."

She looked from the closed gate to Jacen, planting her hands on her hips. Too many questions about that day still remained unanswered. The magi had attacked them both, but how had Jacen escaped?

Terran regarded her with a careful expression and took a step to the side. "Eris..." he whispered.

She didn't take her eyes off Jacen. "About that. How is it you managed to get away from the magi?"

Jacen frowned. He looked from Eris to Terran before his gaze settled on Eris again. "What are you talking about?"

"When they took me. How did you get away?"

The image of his attack came back—struck from behind only moments before she was hit. And when she'd awakened, strapped to the side of a horse making its way toward the Svanth, she'd thought Jacen had been with her, only to learn it was Jasi.

"They didn't want me. When they attacked, they stabbed me—" he tapped his right chest with his fist "—and left me for dead. I feared they did the same to you. It wasn't until I found Jasi that I learned it was the magi."

Eris frowned, and the anger waned. Jacen had been *stabbed*? How must he have felt, lying near the trees, his life seeping from him, not knowing what would come next? How frightened must he have been?

"Jacen...I'm sorry."

He shut his eyes, as if pushing back the same memories Eris suffered. When he opened them again, they fixed Eris with a hard gaze. "But what happened to you since then? The Mistress of Flowers returned and said you were safe, but that was all. She convinced Father he didn't need to send anyone to search for you. I'm still not sure how she managed to do that, but we've been so busy with patrols that he didn't really have men to spare anyway. And she seemed confident you were well." Jacen looked at Terran, considering him as he hadn't done before. His hand drifted back to his sword, a dark expression painted across his face. "I remember you. One of Master Nel's assistants."

Terran nodded.

Jacen snorted and turned back to Eris. "So you *are* well. And with a gardener. Is this the reason you didn't return? You feared Father's reaction over your running off with a gardener?"

Terran coughed but didn't say anything. Eris shot him a look before turning back to her brother. "Is that what you think I did, Jacen? That I ran off with a gardener?"

Jacen shrugged. "You've been gone months, Eris, and now you return with him, looking different than you used to." His eyes widened briefly. "You're not..."

"Not what?"

Jacen fixed Terran with the same hard expression he'd used on Eris. His hand gripped the hilt of his sword, flexing before releasing. He looked over at Eris. "Are you with child? Is that why you ran off?"

Eris looked from Jacen to Terran. Terran's face had gone a deep shade of red that clashed with the green of his jacket, making him look like a striped dahlia. She considered letting Jacen think she *was* pregnant. At least then he'd have to help her.

"What sort of prince are you to leave your pregnant sister standing outside the gates to the palace?" Eris said it hoping maybe he'd open the gate and bring her to her parents.

Jacen's eyes widened.

Seeing the look on Terran's face, she shook her head. "No, I'm not with child."

Jacen let out a soft breath and nodded. "Good. That might be more stress than Father can bear right now. If not that, then what?"

Eris considered how to answer. Did Jacen know what she had

become? Had Lira let on that she was a keeper? Eris didn't know what they knew about Lira. Certainly her mother knew, but did her father?

"I came to see Lira."

Jacen jerked around to stare at her. "Lira? She's the only reason you returned?"

"Of course not," Eris said. "I heard Mother fell ill. I came to see her."

Jacen considered her for a moment before nodding. "Well, Father will be pleased to see you. It is time for him to have good news. And Mother…" He shook his head. "Well, maybe your return will help Mother as well."

Eris noted that he didn't sound convinced.

He pointed to two men atop their horses and made a circular motion with his finger. The men nodded, climbed from their saddles, and handed the reins to Jacen. Jacen gave them to Eris and Terran and nodded to the horses.

"We'll ride from here."

"Not through the gate?" Eris asked.

Jacen shook his head.

Eris waited, but he didn't say anything more.

Once they were saddled, Jacen started off, circling around the inner wall and away from the gate, leaving most of the men behind. Eris looked back to see the men turning the other direction, streaming around the wall toward the north.

"Where are you taking us?" she asked.

"You want to see Father?"

She nodded.

"He's kept the gate closed. We have to go through the servants' door."

"Why? What's happened while I was gone, Jacen?"

He looked over. For the first time, she noticed how tired his deep blue eyes appeared. Lines that weren't there before now worked along the corners of his eyes. His hair hung limp around his shoulders. He held his reins in his left hand. The right clenched slightly and seemed thinner than the other.

"After the magi's attack failed, I convinced Father to let me march toward Saffra." Anger filled his voice, and his face seemed to darken. "The king had to have known what the magi intended. Jasi pleaded, telling me that her Prince Petra was innocent." He snorted and shook his head. "So innocent he led the first attack on our men."

Eris blinked slowly. "What did Jasi say?"

He shook his head. Eris understood. Jasi didn't know.

"Is that where you've been? You've been battling with Saffra?" As long as Eris had been alive, Errasn had known peace. They had occasional attacks along the northern border but nothing more than minor skirmishes.

Jacen looked at her, eyes harder than they'd ever been. "We're at war, Eris."

# CHAPTER 3

*E*ris rode silently the remainder of the way to the palace. The wall circled around the palace as it weaved through the city, separating her home from the rest of Eliara. It was not as high as the wall surrounding the city itself, but guards carrying crossbows stationed atop kept anyone from attempting to climb. Those guards hadn't been there when she'd last been home. Had they been, she might never have gotten stuck on the wall. She might never have met Terran.

Terran sat atop the horse stiffly, clutching the reins. He glanced over at her from time to time but never said anything. Eris wondered if the return or her brother silenced him more.

They passed through the servants' gate. It was a small door near the Braxon section of the city, a place of tidy, neat houses tucked close together where most of the handmaidens lived. As a child, Eris had often wandered through Braxon, accompanied by her mother's maids. The homes always had a comfortable feel to them, warm and inviting.

Now she sensed none of that. The roads passing toward the wall were narrower here, and the air had a musty, aged odor that was different than other parts of the city. The door stood barely wide enough for the horse to slip through. Jacen climbed from the saddle and pushed it open before leading his horse. Eris followed, with Terran not far behind.

Once through, the palace grounds spread out before her. The contrast from the city to here was stark, more so than when entering through the main gate.

The grounds had once been mostly green space with a few towering elms. Lira's arrival changed all that. Now, rows of flowers all set in a pattern Eris still didn't understand stretched around her. The fragrances of the flowers filled the air, nearly cloying and nothing like the heavy earthen scents she'd grown accustomed to while in the Svanth Forest. The energy around her was palpable.

Terran watched her as they made their way toward the palace and looked as if he wanted to take a step toward her. She shot him a look and waved him off. When she'd last been here, the power of the garden had been a mystery. In many ways, it still was. She was a forest keeper, with skills unlike Lira, but even still she felt—could likely access—the power stored within this garden.

Jacen caught her looking. "You thought it was destroyed?" His mouth tightened, and he shook his head. "After the magi attacked, Master Nels spent much time repairing the garden. Seemed particularly important to him. To Mother, too. Father placated her by giving her a few extra men to help replant." He grunted. "A waste, if you ask me. Men needed to watch the walls were up to their elbows in dirt putting *flowers* back into place."

At least Eris had the answer to one of her questions. Jacen didn't know about Lira. Would he believe her if she told him those flowers likely kept the palace safe? Jacen believed in the force of man, and though he had seen the magi work, she doubted he would understand.

But Eris did. The power worked in the leaves, in the petals, gave Lira the energy she needed to keep Eliara safe. There was safety all around her, spreading out with a sense of warmth, radiating like the sun on a cloudless day.

That Lira hadn't come to her troubled her. In a war with Saffra, there was much Eris might have been able to do to help. Lira's power filled this garden, swelling and spilling over the walls, encapsulating the city. But there were limitations to the power. Couldn't Eris have helped?

Terran walked alongside her and touched her arm lightly. "You wouldn't have been able to do anything," he whispered.

Jacen overheard Terran, and his mouth twisted into an amused expression. "Eris? She could have yelled at Saffra. I've been on the end of her wrath before..."

Terran laughed until Eris glared at him. Correcting her brother wouldn't change anything. Doubtful he would believe what she was. Sometimes Eris still didn't believe the abilities she now had.

They reached the main path leading toward the palace, and Jacen veered off toward the stables. A pair of grooms took their horses and led them away. Jacen nodded and started back toward the palace.

Terran hesitated. "I'm going to find Nels."

Eris looked to Terran. "You don't have to. Lira might have questions for you, too."

He shook his head. "I'm sure she will, but you can answer those as well as I. Nels might have answers for me."

Eris felt a fool, realizing that Terran might feel just as uncertain about his role as she did.

He touched her hand again before disappearing into the garden. Even as he did, Eris could feel where he walked. The garden granted her a sort of reassurance, letting her sense his presence as she had within the forest. Having that awareness reassured her, regardless of how she came about it.

Jacen watched her. "You're going to have a difficult time explaining to Father how you ran off to be with a gardener."

"I already told you that wasn't what happened."

Jacen chuckled, looking at where Terran had disappeared. "And I see the two of you together. Don't deny you have feelings for him."

Eris could no more deny that than she could the awareness she had of all the plants growing around her. There was a closeness between them, forged from living beneath the trees, from sharing the experiences of the first keeper, the stories she'd woven into the roots of the trees. They'd shared touches as well, a comfort in holding hands or the simple familiarity of him resting his hand on her arm and, sometimes, her leg. As much as she might want more from him, she sensed his reluctance. As keeper and gardener, there was a bond between them. Neither knew what would happen if they violated that bond.

Maybe Lira would have answers there as well.

Eris flushed and forced the thoughts out of her mind. "What happened with Mother?"

The smile faded from Jacen's face. "I don't know. She's grown weaker. At first, she thought it was the stress of the attack on the garden. You know how much Mother loves this garden." Jacen looked around and shrugged. "Maybe that's why Father spent so much energy having Master Nels repair it. But she kept growing weaker. Once Mistress Lira returned, she really began getting sick."

"What do the healers think?"

"You know how they can be. They give her teas and medicines, but nothing has made a difference."

Jacen turned. The eyes staring back at Eris were different than she remembered. No longer twinkling with a glimmer of amusement, now they were hard and dangerous. The eyes of a stranger.

"You won't recognize her when you see her, Eris. She is... different...than she was." He sighed. "Maybe having you return will lift her spirits. Regardless of your affection for the gardener."

Eris made as if to punch him, and Jacen smiled. It didn't reach his eyes.

"There's the little sister I remember." His voice shifted, turning serious. "You've changed, too. Not so much as Mother, but you seem..." He shook his head. "I don't know how to explain it. Stronger, maybe." He snorted. "Maybe you *should* go yell at Saffra. Likely you'd be able to convince them to turn back and leave the borders."

"Well, I *am* with child," she said.

Jacen coughed, his eyes bulging, and she laughed. The coughing turned into choking.

"Serves you right," she said.

They hurried up the wide steps and into the palace. Dim lanterns hung on walls, flickering with a pale light. A faint smoke trail led up the walls, coating the stone with dark soot. The air smelled musty, giving her a sense of confinement. How was it she missed the forest after only days away from it?

"You will want to see Father first," Jacen said. "And then you should see Mother. I hope..." He trailed off as he turned and looked at her. "I hope your return can do something for her."

Eris didn't think she could do anything more than Lira had done. And her mother had never seemed overly fond of her, not like the way she fawned over Jasi or Desia. Even Ferisa, with her dedication to the Sacred Mother, pleased their mother more than Eris. Likely Eris' return would bring only memories of her disappointment.

So, rather than arguing with Jacen, she only nodded.

"Careful what you say around Father. This war with Saffra consumes him."

She looked up at her brother and frowned. The tension in his cheeks and the way his hand drifted toward his sword spoke volumes about what the war had done to him. "Only Father?"

His eyes blazed briefly. "I'm here, aren't I?"

Eris wondered why he focused on that. "For Mother?"

Jacen blinked and shook his head once. "Father needed a report from the border. And I need more men."

"He doesn't send them?"

Jacen snorted again. "He sends enough to push Saffra back, but that is not enough. We need to end this war."

The vehemence to the way he said it left no doubt in her mind how Jacen would end it.

They stopped outside the council room. A deep voice came from within, rough from yelling. Eris recognized the old general Tholen's voice.

"We do little but hold them on the edge of Errasn, my lord. And they are relentless. We don't have the men needed to battle both soldier and mage. I begin to wonder if Jacen might be right—perhaps we need to press the attack into Saffra."

Her father said something she couldn't understand.

Tholen went on. "Nothing more than a slip of water holds them back. The men wait for them to try and cross and…"

Jacen glanced at her, a grim expression knotting his brow, and stepped into the room.

Eris followed but stayed along the wall. A long table filled most of the room, a thick parchment rolled open across its gleaming surface. Stout oak chairs circled around the outside. Only a few were occupied. Her father sat at one end, atop a rivenswood chair much like his throne. A window cut into the wall overhead spilled bright light into the room to fall on a pot filled with perisals and listhanis. Lira's touch, likely, and one that never would have been allowed when Adrick served as advisor. Did her father even know the importance of the flowers?

Eris pulled from the energy of the flowers to shade herself.

"My lord," General Tholen said, nodding to Jacen. "You've returned from the border."

He nodded and strode toward the end of the table to take a seat next to their father. Eris noted the change in him clearly, then. Tholen had once worried about Jacen's abilities in the field, but now deferred to him nearly as much as he did to their father.

"I have. It's much as you describe, Tholen, except the magi

remain hidden in Saffra. We have nothing that can counteract the fire or lightning, which they continue to throw at us. The only good is that they harm their men nearly as much as ours."

Her father watched Jacen, nodding. He hadn't looked toward her yet. His face had aged in the time she'd been away, and his hair took on more grey than not, though he kept it cut short, as if trying to hide it.

"We will need a different tact, or else we'll have to retreat from the Loess River. That is all that keeps their fire at bay. If I had another company of cavalry, I would be able to—"

"Do what? Push against the Kernig Mountains?" Lashen said. The frail soldier had once served as her grandfather's advisor and was widely regarded to still have a keen mind. At least he had been before she'd left.

Anger flashed across Jacen's face as he turned and looked at Lashen. "Yes. Let me push them against Kernig and destroy them. Once we possess the mountain passes, Saffra won't be able to send any additional troops."

"It's not the troops we should fear," Lashen said.

"No, but since I can't do anything against the magi, I have to focus on what I can. Once the soldiers are gone, the magi will have to face us rather than hide."

"Yet they still hide and throw lightning. If we lose another company, the rest of Errasn is in danger." Nasally Eldan looked from Jacen to her father.

Her father sighed and leaned forward to rest his chin on his hands. "I am loath to give up even an inch to them, but what other —" His gaze darted toward the end of the room and settled on her. "What is this?" He looked to Jacen. "Who did you bring into my chambers, Jacen?"

Jacen nodded toward her. "I thought you might want to see her, Father."

Her father stood and made his way toward her. One hand

rested on the hilt of his sword as he walked. Eris noted a limp, and he stooped slightly.

When he neared, he blinked at her. His hand fell away from his sword.

"Eris?" he whispered.

She stepped away from the wall, releasing the energy of the flowers. The edges of their petals had rolled, wilting slightly as she tapped their energy.

She nodded. "Father." She bowed her head slightly, making certain to watch his face as she did.

"Where have you been? You've been gone all this time and now you return. Why now…" He glanced back at Jacen for answers. When Jacen shook his head, her father turned back to her. "No matter. You have returned. The Mistress of Flowers was right." He pulled her into a tight embrace.

Eris hugged him back. How long had it been since her father had hugged her like that? Months? Maybe a year?

He smelled of age and something else, like the edge of rot.

She pushed away. "I heard Mother is ill."

Her father's face changed, falling as if the strength left him. He nodded. "She is unwell. The healers can do nothing—"

"And Lira?" She hadn't asked Jacen whether Lira had tried healing her mother, but she suspected her father knew of Lira's power.

He shook his head.

Behind him, Jacen frowned.

"There is nothing she can do. You will go to her. Seeing you might be enough to lift her spirits," her father said.

It was the same thing Jacen had said. Eris didn't think it likely but nodded.

He sighed and smiled. "It is good you came when you did, Eris. She needs this."

"Can you take me to her?" she asked softly.

Her father looked at the men of his council and nodded to Jacen before taking Eris's hand and leading her from the council room. As they left, Jacen began the meeting again. His voice carried authority that it hadn't possessed the last time she'd seen him. Only a few months away, and already much had changed. Eris wished she knew whether any of the change was for the better.

"The Mistress tried everything she can, Eris," her father said as they made their way from his council room. "She…delays…what is happening, but does not think she can stop it. I think she even fears leaving the palace."

Rather than making their way deeper into the palace, they walked away from her parents' quarters. "Where are you taking me?"

Her father looked over at her. "You said you wanted to see your mother."

She nodded. "She's not in the palace?"

He shook his head as they reached a wide door leading out into the garden. Through the glass, swirls of color streaked together. Energy emanated from the garden. Even without a connection to it, she knew where her mother would be found.

How sick must she be for Lira to have brought her here?

"How much time does she have, Father?"

He swallowed. A tear welled in the corner of his eye, and he shook his head. "Not much, I'm afraid. I'm thankful for each day she has left, but those become fewer and fewer. At least her suffering will be over. The Sacred Mother will give her that much."

# CHAPTER 4

*E*ris followed her father into the garden, clutching her dress in her hands. She wished Terran were with her, if nothing else for his comforting presence, but Jacen had already shown how that would open her up to questions she was not quite ready to answer. Her father might believe she was a keeper, but would he understand Terran's role, or would he react much like Jacen? She didn't want to put Terran through that again.

They passed rows of flowers. Tulips. Anosems. Ulsens. Eris no longer knew how many varieties she'd learned from simply wandering the garden and how many she'd learned from her connection to the forest. Some she'd learned by spending time sorting through books in the library as Master Billiken sat watching.

She inhaled the fragrances, noting the subtle shift as they moved deeper into the garden, away from the main gate leading toward the palace and toward the tall elms near the center. The greenhouse would be there, and likely, Master Nels with Terran.

The energy coursing through the plants was a near palpable thing. Eris could almost touch it. From the arrangement in her father's council room, she already knew she could borrow energy from the flowers. She suspected she could do the same here in the garden.

Strange how she could command the power stored within the flowers yet she had to ask the trees for assistance. Had it always been there, thrumming below the surface, waiting for nothing more than a soft touch for her to draw upon it?

The power might have been here, but she had never been aware of it. Even now, her connection to it was different than what she shared with the Svanth. Within the forest, there was strength far beyond what this garden held, but a sense of age and something more. The forest garden needed her to understand her role. It was the reason the lessons were woven into the roots, plunging deep into the earth beneath the forest. This garden had nothing like that.

"She wanted to come here. I think it reminds her of when we first met."

Eris realized her father had been carrying on as they walked. She hadn't been paying much attention and now turned to listen. "She once said the elms were lovely then." Eris couldn't remember when she'd heard her mother speak of the trees, but it felt right to say.

He glanced over, and a sad smile worked across his face. Tired eyes held a hint of moisture. In spite of the arranged marriage between her mother and father—a union designed to knit the fractured north more tightly with Errasn, much like the union intended for Jasi and Petra—they had found real love. "She always loved the trees. Something about how she could sit in the shade and feel their age and wisdom."

Eris nearly stumbled. Could her mother have been a keeper?

She'd always thought she was nothing like her mother. She had none of the beautiful golden hair or the deep blue eyes—not like her sisters. Or even Jacen. Instead, she looked more like her father. Chestnut hair that seemed to grow darker with each year. Brown eyes that looked to belong to another family. But if her mother shared her gifts, Eris might finally feel connected to her.

It would only take her dying to make it happen. Sorrow pulled through her.

They reached the elms, and her father slowed. The trees grew in a circle, but everything else about the place spoke of her father's influence. A shaded pavilion had been set between the trees. A low tent blocked the sun working through the branches. A thick rug rolled beneath the pavilion. Even the pair of guards stationed between each tree, eyes vigilant for imagined threats, hands gripping the hilt of their sheathed swords, were her father's.

The air beneath the elms smelled off. Eris almost delved then, to understand.

Within the pavilion, she sensed Lira's touch. Pots of fresh flowers were set around the trees. The colors within each bed worked together in ways Eris still didn't understand but at least began to recognize. Each augmented the energy, strengthening the effect, drawing from the rest of the garden and focusing its energy here. The power building here practically buzzed.

Her father hurried forward. Under the overhang, he paused and beckoned her forward, waiting until she joined him before ducking fully underneath.

More flowers greeted her here. There were precisely placed. The colors might look beautiful, but the power drew inward, drawing from the rest of the garden and focusing it on her mother.

In the face of this much effort, how could her mother still be sick?

And then she saw her.

Her mother lay on a plush cot covered with thick blankets. Patterns woven into the blankets reminded Eris of the flowers around her. Only her mother's face was visible, and it looked different. Pale and sunken. Her once golden hair now held no luster and had taken on a greyish sheen. Her head swiveled toward them as they approached, eyes milky when they'd once been bright.

"Hanrik," she sighed. "I have visions now. I see Eris standing beside you. Were she only here..."

Her father grabbed her hand beneath the blankets. "But she *is* here, my love. Eris has returned home."

Her mother blinked and tried to sit up. Her father shook his head and made soothing sounds, keeping her from moving.

"Eris? But Lira said..."

Eris swallowed. Could it be that her mother was actually *pleased* to see her?

More than anything else, that change surprised her the most.

"Mother." Eris took a place alongside her father and looked down at her mother. The blankets made it difficult to see how thin she'd become, but Eris recognized it in the prominence to her cheeks and the way her eyes pushed forward. "I've returned."

"Have you completed your lessons?"

For a moment, Eris thought she was back months ago when Lira had sent her to the garden to find her flower. In those times, she often disappointed her mother, always having to answer that she hadn't found her flower. When she finally had, Lira refused to explain it to her, forcing her to search for answers on her own.

The lessons she had now were different, but no less urgent. Likely more so, now that she knew what she could do, what she could be.

"I...I don't know, Mother."

Honesty. With her mother dying, she owed her honesty.

"Does Lira know?" her mother asked.

Eris frowned. Could her mother's mind be slipping as well? She'd believed she had a vision when Eris appeared, what else did she experience?

"Does Lira know?" Eris repeated. She felt like a child again, standing in front of her mother, disappointing her as she had so many times before.

"That you still need to complete your lessons."

Eris blinked against the tears coming to her eyes. "I will tell her."

Her father patted her mother beneath the blanket for a moment and then turned to Eris. "She is very sick. I think it's good you came back. I..."

He trailed off, looking over Eris's shoulder. She turned and saw Jacen standing along one of the paths, watching them with worried eyes. Her father took a deep breath and nodded.

"Stay with her a while, Eris. You can comfort her." He forced a smile onto his face. "And when you leave her, find Jasi. She will want to know you're back, too. She runs the household now that your mother is...well, now that she's unwell."

Eris nodded, and her father strode off. His steps held less of the power and lithe grace than they used to, a slight hitch now to the way he swung his legs, but he still carried himself with the authority of his office. The guards standing between the trees saluted respectfully.

When her father joined Jacen and turned back toward the palace, Eris walked back to her mother. Her mother's head rested against a wide pillow, and her breathing came slowly and shallowly. Eris sighed and touched her hair, running her hand across it in a familiarity she'd never had when her mother was well.

Was there nothing Lira could do?

The power moving through the pavilion spoke of Lira's attempt, but the way her mother looked told Eris all she needed to know about how the attempt fared. How much longer did her mother have before the Sacred Mother took her home?

With all this power, was there even anything she could do?

Outside the forest, she didn't have the same access she did within the trees, but she had used that power to heal before. Terran would have lost his leg—or worse—had she not summoned the power needed to heal him, though that had been freely given by the forest, simply passing through her hands rather than guided by her.

Eris needed to know.

She pushed off her sandals. When her feet touched the bare earth, she inhaled, pressing her awareness deep beneath the surface, delving as she did in the Svanth Forest. Eris could trace through the roots, follow them toward the twining power held within the trees and flowers and grasses growing within the earth.

Awareness of the grasses came to her first, thready and weak. Faint. Like the transient grass itself. Eris gripped onto the roots tenuously and followed them until she reached the thicker roots of the towering elms. These reminded her of those growing within the Svanth, mighty and old, but different as well; they yielded before her, as if recognizing her as a keeper. Were she to push, she could track to the flowers growing in the garden and tap into their power as well. But doing so felt like a violation, so she refrained.

Filled with the power granted by the elms, she pushed it through her hand, letting it out like an exhalation so it washed over her mother. It resonated back to her, filling her with knowledge of the illness. Eris gasped.

"What do you sense?"

Eris turned and saw Lira watching her. The Mistress of Flowers stood in the center of the pavilion. Eris imagined the energy flowing through the garden centered upon her. Dressed primly as always in a flowing gown of purple and silver, her hazel eyes held Eris in a powerful gaze.

"Lira." Eris took her hand off her mother's head and turned toward her teacher. How long had she believed Lira hadn't wanted to teach her, only to learn Lira didn't know *how* to teach her?

"How did you hear of her illness?"

No welcome back. No questions about what she'd learned. No questions about her time in the Svanth. Nothing other than formality.

Eris swallowed and pulled herself up straight. "When *we* returned. I met Jacen at the palace gate."

Lira tilted her head. "Terran is with you?"

"He went to speak with Master Nels." Eris turned back to her mother. The illness working through her was a sort of wasting illness, like she'd seen in the trees. Terran had taken to striking them down. After enough time, all that remained was a hollow and lifeless core. "Is there nothing you can do?"

Lira furrowed her brow and shook her head. "A keeper should be able to feel what I do."

"I can feel it. I don't understand it, but I feel it."

"There are lessons the trees cannot teach. Had we more time, I might be able to help, but..." She looked over at the queen. "I do all I can to keep this at bay. I do not have the strength to heal her completely."

"What if she came to the Svanth?" The power stored within the forest would be enough to heal her mother, if only the forest would allow Eris to do it.

"She would never survive the journey." Lira stepped away from the center of the pavilion toward Eris's mother. "Had I recognized it in time, she might have, but I thought myself strong enough to help her." She shook her head again. "This is my folly. I was foolish. Now I do nothing more than prolong her illness."

"What is it?"

Lira looked back. "I don't know."

Eris looked at her mother, at the slow and steady breaths working through her frail body. Nothing of the regal woman remained. "So she will die."

Lira inhaled deeply. "I am sorry, Eris. There is nothing more I can do. All I can hope is to keep her comfortable in the time she has remaining."

Eris sighed. "Do you know why this happened?"

"Why does anything happen? There is no why to illness."

Eris borrowed energy from the trees for a moment as she set

her hand back onto her mother, letting the energy wash over her. The way it pushed against her felt off. Within her mother, the effects of age worked through her, the way her vision faded, the way her hair slowly turned to grey, but none of it felt the same as this illness.

"This isn't natural," she whispered.

Saying it made it feel more real.

Lira looked at her and shook her head. "Illness often feels like that, but I have seen sickness like this before. There isn't anything we can do but ease her suffering."

Eris shook her head and reached a hand toward Lira. "Feel this," she said, pulling the energy from the trees through her— through her mother—before pressing it toward Lira.

Lira flinched back and her eyes narrowed. "What did you do?"

"Nothing. I simply pushed the energy I borrowed through her."

Lira dropped her hand. "You summon so *much*. I have a fine control but cannot pull nearly as much as what you manage." She frowned. "Do you reach all the way to the Svanth in what you do?"

Eris shook her head. "The elms only. I didn't know the protocol for borrowing the energy stored within your garden," she said.

"The elms?" Lira looked up at the trees and let out a shaky breath. "So much is different between what we do. Yours is a powerful gift." She inhaled deeply, pulling the energy around her until it focused on Lira. "All of this connects me to my small garden in the Svanth, but nothing I control would give me nearly the power you manipulate."

"Can you use it?" She allowed herself a sudden surge of hope. Could her mother be helped? If Eris could borrow the power from Lira's garden, what kept Lira from using the power she commanded?

"If only it were so simple. Do you not remember when Terran was injured? My connection to the forest was tenuous, too weak to be of any good. Were it not for your ability, the way you trace the roots..." She shook her head. "The power stored within the Svanth is too foreign for me. I cannot listen to the stories of the past as you can. I hear nothing more than echoes, like voices calling from a great distance. I know they are there, but no matter how hard I try, I cannot hear them."

Except Eris didn't have the power Lira thought. The Svanth did not grant that to her.

These elms were different. Eris wondered if their connection to Lira's garden granted her the access to the energy they stored, access she didn't have within the Svanth.

She sighed. If only she had the skill needed to help her mother.

"Why did you come, if not for her?"

Eris took her hand away from her mother. Her reason seemed so insignificant now. Had she known about her mother, she would have come. Perhaps that was the reason to share with others. But not with Lira. Lira needed the truth.

"I..." she began, but didn't know how to go on. Would Lira understand how Eris traced out from the forest and followed the twisted connections beneath the earth all the way to the border with Saffra? Would she be able to explain what Eris felt there? "I felt something along the border." She shook her head, realizing how foolish it sounded. "I don't know how to explain what it is. A sense of nothingness." She'd taken to thinking about it as a desolation, but it sounded strange to say aloud. "It's painful when I press along toward it. If I push too hard, it hurts, like a burn."

Lira nodded. "You feel the Conclave. I am not surprised you do. It took me years to recognize the sense and many more before I knew to fear it. But you have a different strength. As a keeper of trees, I suspect you are more deeply connected than I am."

"What is it? Why can I feel the Conclave?"

"The Conclave has always yearned for more power. They thrive on discord. It fuels them, like the sun and rain fuel the power we control."

"I thought we would have more time." Only a few months had

passed, and already they began their attack? And forcing Saffra into battle with Errasn? How much would be lost?

"As did I."

"What can we do?" Eris asked. She had seen the horrible power of the magi far too closely. If they already managed to press the attack, it meant she and Lira had done little to slow them. And they were outnumbered. From what Terran said, there once had been many keepers, all tending to massive gardens, each larger than what Lira had within the walls of the palace. But the magi had destroyed them, scattering the keepers, leaving only Lira to fight back against the magi.

And now Eris.

Her presence made the difference the last time, but she had surprised the magi when they were near the Svanth Forest. They would not make the same mistake again.

Lira blinked and met her eyes. "I fear there is little we *can* do."

# CHAPTER 5

*E*ris found Terran along the back wall of the garden, fingers deep into earthen beds of shade plants. She watched him for a few moments before stepping into view, thinking of what Lira had said. If the magi made a concerted push into Errasn, there might be nothing they could do. All the gardens would fall, and then what would be left? What would the magi turn Errasn into?

She sighed and Terran turned, a smile crossing his face.

"Did you find Lira?" He slid to the side, focusing again on the planter where his fingers worked at the dirt, pinching through loose soil.

Eris recognized what he did, the way he picked at burrowing pests threatening to destroy the plants. This on a taranth, a shade plant she recognized from the Svanth. She touched the earth and delved into the plant. Tiny grubs chewed on the roots, damaging them. With a gentle suggestion, she instructed the taranth to focus a brief surge of energy through the bed, destroying the grubs. Doing so with flowers was much different than working with the energy stored within the trees. Less potent, but easier to direct.

Terran frowned at her. "What did you do?"

Eris shrugged. "I helped."

Terran offered her one of his lopsided smiles. "You could've helped the trees in the Svanth this way."

The pointed comment reminded her of how much she'd neglected while trying to learn from the roots. She looked away. If she didn't delve deeply into the roots, she would never learn what she needed to help the rest of the forest. "You heard about my mother?"

He grunted and moved onto the next bed of taranths. Eris considered helping him again, but after his reaction, decided against it.

"It's all Nels could talk about, at first. The queen, resting in the heart of his garden. I'm not certain he approves."

Eris swallowed, looking back toward the elms. From here, the energy that the flowers of the garden focused seemed so *small*. If only she could get her mother back to the Svanth. There she might have a chance. "But Nels knows *why* she's here, doesn't he?"

Terran nodded absently.

Eris sighed with frustration. First the magi, and now her mother. And she, a keeper, unable to help. "Lira only delays it. She can't heal her."

Terran paused and looked up. He wiped his hands across his scarred, green jacket and took a step toward her. "I'm sorry, Eris. There are limits to even a keeper's power."

Eris fought back tears that threatened to spill again. She knew of the limitations. She still didn't know enough to command the forest to help. Ask, definitely. Suggest. But not command.

It began to feel like when Lira had sentenced her to wander the garden, each day searching for her flower. Each day failing, returning to the palace only to realize she hadn't found what she sought. The forest seemed to be waiting—the ancient keeper as well—for Eris to learn *something* before it unlocked the next secret. Only, for this lesson, she had no idea what she searched for.

"Lira says the Conclave pushes Saffra toward Errasn."

Terran looked back to the pot and began working through the dirt. "You told me the same."

She shook her head. "I wasn't sure that was what I felt."

She turned to the bed next to where Terran worked—a combination of teraspal and vipeslar arranged in a pattern that resonated against her, as if creating even more energy this way than alone—and touched the dirt. As she delved, a surge of understanding washed over her, fainter than she had with larger plants. A few beetles worked their way across the leaves, chewing and leaving tiny creatures that worked inside the thin veins of the leaves. Over time, they poisoned the plant.

Eris frowned. She hadn't noticed that before.

Another surge of energy, and the miniscule creatures died. The plants surged with renewed life, noticeably more vibrant.

"Would you stop?" Terran looked up at her. "There's little else I can do to help, and if you go around the garden taking care of everything I *can* do..."

"You wouldn't have been able to do anything about this one."

Terran looked at the teraspal, his gaze immediately going to the chewed edges of the leaves. "Hesha beetles. Easy enough to deter." He looked back at her. "I think I can manage here, Eris. Besides, wasn't there another reason we came to Eliara?"

She considered saying something about what she sensed working through the teraspal plant but decided against it. Terran might take offense, and she meant none by offering to help. Out of anyone, she didn't want to anger him. And he was right. He *could* manage here without her help; this was Lira's garden, not hers.

"I...I thought I could help you," she said.

Terran glanced around the garden as he came over to her. He set his hands on her arms, unmindful of who else might be around, his calloused hands warm and familiar and achingly comforting. "I know. And I know there's something you're trying *not* to do, or something you can't do now that you've learned about your mother. You don't need to worry about me, Eris. I am your gardener. Where you go, I'll follow."

Eris couldn't help but think about the gardener from her dreams. He hadn't followed his keeper.

She wanted to ask Terran if that was all they were—just gardener and keeper—but Master Nels appeared at the end of one of the rows. He studied her with wrinkled eyes as he swept his hat off his head and crumpled it between his hands. Then he nodded, almost respectfully, before turning away.

Eris watched him disappear and then laughed lightly. "That was odd."

Terran follower her gaze. "Nels?"

Eris nodded.

"He sees you differently now."

"He knows?"

Terran nodded. "He wasn't Lira's first gardener—I don't know who he served before her, and he won't say—and he knew the reason I left. Now that we're back in Eliara, I offered to help, but he holds me under no obligation."

Who Nels might have served before Lira? He had served her father long before Lira arrived at the palace. Even before the magi appeared, she thought. But that meant he'd served before the gardens were destroyed.

She shook off the quandary. What did it matter, now? The gardens were gone. The keepers were gone. Now, only she and Lira remained.

They would be able to do nothing against the full might of the Conclave.

"Not all the keepers were lost, were they?" she asked.

Terran shook his head. "Not all. Lira might know where they've gone, but I suspect even she isn't sure where most went."

Why would the keepers simply scatter? Wouldn't they *want* to remain near their gardens and do whatever they could to keep the

Conclave in check? Unless they knew something...or those who remained went somewhere else, started a new garden as Lira had.

"What is it?" Terran asked.

He watched her, a worried expression twisting the corner of his mouth. A smudge of dirt lined his forehead, and he rubbed his hand against it, only smearing it worse. It reminded her of when she'd first met him, and she smiled.

"What if Lira knows where other keepers have gone? What if we can find them and get help?"

"Don't you think she would have contacted them if she did?"

"Would she? Do we know why she came to Errasn in the first place? Why, if all the other keepers scattered, did Lira come here while the magi had already established themselves with my father?"

Terran frowned. "Isn't that reason enough?"

Eris looked around the garden as she sighed. "You're probably right. I wish I just knew more. About being a keeper. About what happened to the other keepers. About the Svanth." She shook her head, suppressing her annoyance. "And now Lira is too busy keeping my mother alive to teach."

"I'm not sure finding another keeper would help. From what my father said, the keepers could be...picky...about who they taught."

That wasn't what Eris remembered from her dream within the heart of the Svanth, but how long ago had that been? Hundreds of years ago? Even a thousand? How useful were the lessons woven within the roots after all this time? Some were valuable, especially those that gave her the history of the Svanth Forest, but the lessons about the keepers? Eris didn't know what to make of those stories, especially since the keepers were essentially no more.

Even if she were to find another, what made her think they would help against the magi? The keepers knew what the magi intended but chose to hide rather than oppose them.

Was Lira that much different?

But what could Eris do? She couldn't go to the border with Saffra and face the Conclave on her own. The first time she'd had the might of the Svanth with her, but she'd been lucky. Luck wouldn't hold again.

She had no choice but to learn. It was why she'd come, after all. Compared to how Lira managed what she had within the garden, the way she arranged the flowers to increase the potential and power, Eris was little more than a novice. Worse, she recognized the effect of what Lira did but had no idea how she managed what she did.

Even here, surrounded by family, Eris felt isolated. It almost made her want to retreat back to the Svanth again, trace the roots until she found answers.

"Thank you for coming with me, Terran," she said.

He smiled and touched her arm. For a moment, it was like they were back within the forest, only the two of them.

Then he laughed and smiled. "As long as you don't torment me like you did with Prince Jacen, I'll say you're welcome."

"I'm going to have to tell my father."

The color drained from his face.

Eris laughed. "About who I am. What I am. He should know."

And her sisters, though Eris didn't know how she'd bring that up to them. Especially Jasi. After all the time Jasi had spent teasing her about her failings at Lira's lessons, Eris should want to show her sister what had become of her. That she wasn't a failure. But Eris didn't feel a particular need to throw that at Jasi. Jasi had been through enough. Maybe then Eris wouldn't feel so alone.

"Let me know when you do. I think I'll need to be anywhere else."

Eris smiled, swallowing back the uncertainty growing within her. As soon as she told her family, everything would be different, fully and finally. She should be happy about it—how long had she wanted to do and be anything other than what she'd been while living in Eliara?—but the anxious feeling wouldn't leave her.

Terran watched her, as if knowing her thoughts. He said nothing, instead pulling her toward him and wrapping his arms around her. She stiffened at first before finally relaxing and letting him hold her.

# CHAPTER 6

The halls of the palace were different. More than simply the seasonal change in the tapestries hanging on the walls; at least those had a certain air of familiarity about them. Perhaps the air tasted different, the flowers blooming within the garden now focusing on her mother. Or maybe the faces of the servants had changed. Or even the simple fact that Eris' prolonged absence made everything new again. She found herself pausing at each sconce and tapestry, looking at each closed door with a frown, wondering why she felt as she did.

It wasn't until she turned toward the hall leading to her room that she recognized what seemed different. The palace was no longer home to her.

She stopped at her door and nearly knocked before grabbing the handle. She swallowed as she pushed it open, more uncertain about this than the decision to return to the city.

A lantern burned in the room.

Eris nearly stepped back. Months living with the awareness the forest granted left her feeling exposed without it.

"Jacen said you'd returned."

Eris froze in place. "Jasi," she whispered.

She pushed the door open all the way and stepped into the room. It was nearly as she'd left it. A massive cabinet lined one wall. How many dresses did she have inside? Certainly more than she needed. A copper basin tucked against the opposite wall. Two plush chairs faced each other, angled toward a door along the far wall. Behind the door would be her wide bed, topped by the canopy that now seemed like so much unnecessary pomp. No flowers or other plants. That would have to change if she were to remain in Eliara.

Jasi rose from one of the chairs. "Where have you been?"

It wasn't so much a question as an accusation, and one filled with hurt.

"Lira didn't tell you where I've been?" she asked.

Jasi frowned and shook her head. "Lira hasn't said anything to me. Only to Mother. And now she's too sick to say anything." She leaned on the arms of the chair. "You left me and didn't even bother to find out what happened."

Eris turned to her cabinet and pulled it open—changing into a fresh dress might feel better, especially after traveling all day—but all she saw were clothes that no longer felt like her. And more than a change of dress, first she needed a bath. After washing in the cold Svanth streams, hot water and scented salts would be a welcome change.

She sighed and pushed the cabinet closed. "I ensured you survived. I was the one who risked death."

Jasi made a choking sound. "Survived? I made it back to the Kingsroad and came across soldiers. Had it not been for Lira finding me—"

Eris frowned at her, cutting her off. "What? You wouldn't have managed to convince them you were the princess? I find that hard to believe. The first thing you do with me is remind me how you are firstborn."

Jasi pursed her lips in a familiar expression that was strangely comforting. Eris hesitated, the question she'd wondered about since she was first abducted resurfacing.

"What happened with Jacen? Lira said you came across him?"

Jasi's face softened. "Jacen? You were with him, weren't you?"

Eris nodded.

"Then you know how he was taken—"

"We both were, Jasi."

She blinked and nodded once. "You both were taken. Only they brought you to the forest, tied to a horse, otherwise unharmed."

"What did they do to Jacen?"

Jasi shook her head. "He won't speak of it. When I found him, he was a bloodied mess. His face purple and swollen, like some grotesque darthshade. His nose was broken, and he couldn't walk…" She swallowed, as if imagining what Jacen had endured.

"I didn't know." Jacen had mentioned the stabbing but none of the rest. Eris imagined he tried to keep the horror of what he'd gone through from her, but Jasi had witnessed it firsthand.

Jasi sniffed. "Of course you didn't. Father's men saved him. Said they found him near the Varden border. Had they not been sent on patrol, there's no telling *what* might have happened to him." She took a deep breath. "He's been different since he came back, Eris. Focused. Driven."

Eris thought of the Jacen she'd once known. Happy and carefree, flirtatious with highborn and common girls alike. When she'd seen him near the palace, she almost hadn't recognized him. Mostly his eyes. They held age and anguish that had never been there before, but she saw other things that worried her. The anger he carried worried her most.

"So tell me, Eris, where have you been? Mother says you've been away on business for Lira, but I know how far you progressed in your lessons. Lira wouldn't trust you with some task and not tell me. But I can't understand why Mother would protect you. Now she's too weak to do anything. And with what Father is working against…"

"What happened with Petra?"

She still didn't know how Jasi felt about her failed betrothal.

Or weren't they married? They had gone through the ceremony before Errasn and the Sacred Mother, weren't they married now?

Jasi's face darkened. "Petra. If I ever see him again—"

"You think he knew what the Conclave had planned?" Unlike Jacen, Eris suspected Jasi knew more about Petra.

"How could he not? Shortly after the Conclave abducted us, Saffra attacked on the southern border."

Eris frowned. Jasi knew the truth of the attack, of how Petra betrayed her. As least she didn't have to keep that knowledge from Jasi. But after defeating the magi near the Svanth, the Conclave would not have wanted to push forward again so quickly, would they?

"You haven't answered me, Eris. Where did you go? Desia thinks you ran off with some boy. She said she saw you with one of the gardeners before you left, and after you'd gone, he disappeared as well. I told her you wouldn't do something so foolish as that."

"I did run off with one of the gardeners. His name is Terran, and he came back with me." Eris said it more out of spite than anything else, expecting Jasi's response after the way Jacen had responded.

Jasi's face flushed a deep red. "You what? Is *that* why you've returned? You think to get father's permission to wed a *gardener*?"

Eris sighed. She'd had enough of hiding who she was. It was time Jasi took her seriously as more than her sister. She grabbed Jasi's arm and pulled her from her room. Jasi fought for a moment, but the months working within the forest had given Eris a different kind of strength, and she managed to drag Jasi down the hall. As they proceeded, Eris summoned more strength from the arrangements staggered about the hall, barely registering how the petals curled slightly as she passed.

51

It wasn't until they stopped at the wide, sweeping steps leading out of the palace and into the garden that Jasi managed to jerk herself free. "What do you think you're doing?"

"Just come with me."

Jasi shook her head. "I think you need to go see Father. Beg him to take you back in. You *might* still be able to wed some quiet northern lord and help..."

Eris didn't wait for her to finish. She grabbed Jasi again by the sleeve and pulled her down the steps.

Jasi followed, sputtering all the way.

When they reached the garden, Eris dragged her down the main path through wide flowerbeds, noting Jasi's perisal briefly. One of the gardeners saw her storming through the garden and turned away, eyes going wide. He scurried off, likely to find Master Nels.

"Eris!"

Now that they were in the garden, Jasi finally managed to find her voice. Eris let go of her arm as they neared the start of the shade flowers underneath the wall.

"What are you doing?"

"You want to know where I've been the last few months. I'm going to show you."

"Show me? I don't understand!"

"I can see that. Now watch."

Eris slipped off her soft slippers, the same ones she'd been wearing when they'd been abducted, the only shoes she had during her time in the forest. They had served her well, keeping her feet covered but easily coming off so she could more easily connect with the earth. Jasi gasped softly as she did, almost as horrified that Eris would remove her shoes as she'd been when Eris said she'd run off with Terran.

Eris ignored her. Sinking her feet into the earth, she delved into the roots.

Life sprang up around her. Eris traced the deep roots—those of the elms at the center of the forest—the most easily. From there, she connected with fainter lines, those of twisting grasses growing throughout the garden between the paths and the beds. These touched on everything else, merging with every other flower in the garden, twisting and twirling together in a way that connected her to everything else around her.

With a command, Eris instructed the flowers to turn toward her.

Were she in sunlight, she might have had more hesitation about whether the flowers would listen and respond, but she had chosen shade flowers intentionally. Her flower—the teary star—was a shade flower, like so many others within the forest. She had a greater connection to them, rivaling only that which she shared with the trees. And flowers responded so differently than the trees. With the flowers, she could demand they obey.

The flowers all looked toward her, waiting.

Jasi gasped again. "Did you see that?"

With a ripple of energy, Eris pulled on the wind, sending a gust fluttering around Jasi's dress. The last time she'd asked that of the flowers was when she'd confronted the magi. Like then, the wind responded, spilling over with her borrowed energy, swirling as she directed. Were she to demand, the wind would spiral with more force. That was how she'd managed to defeat the magi.

"Eris..."

She turned to her sister and met her eyes.

"I think a storm is coming."

Eris looked to the crystal blue sky. No storm brewed on the horizon. "*This* is what I have been doing. I told you Lira was a flower mage. In that, I was wrong. She is a keeper of flowers, a woman who commands great energies from them."

Eris let the wind die, not wanting to borrow too much from the energy of the garden. Connected as she was, she felt the way Lira drew it toward her mother, the way it spiraled inward, slowly building, the focus holding the illness at bay. If that energy were to disappear...Eris didn't know what would happen to her mother, but she could guess.

She did not release the flowers. They still turned toward her. This took very little energy, and she wondered if they would do it even if she didn't command them. Hadn't Terran said something about how the flowers turned toward her being a sign that she was a keeper?

"She made you a flower mage?" Jasi seemed more offended than surprised.

"Made me?" Eris shook her head. "You understand little of it—"

"Little? I've been Lira's student longer than you! And while you've been gone, she continues our lessons. I can work messages into the flowers and can read those she's written."

Those were lessons Eris tried learning from reading the roots within the forest. The first keeper had written instructions for her there, a way to read the messages keepers wrote in the flowers. The lessons weren't detailed—Eris had the impression the first keeper didn't know as much about flowers as what Eris had seen from Lira—but enough to grasp the basics.

"That is but a part of it. A small part, and one that truly means little." Eris could see the utility in hiding messages others couldn't read, but how often would she need to be able to do so? And who would she communicate with? Lira? Her sisters? They were all here with her.

Jasi was shaking her head. "That's not what Lira says. She tells me the writing of words is difficult. That few can manage to master the art. I have a talent." The last carried with it the same pride Jasi always managed when speaking about her lessons.

"You asked why I had been gone from the palace. I wanted to show you..." Show her what? Demonstrate that Jasi would never be a keeper? Doing so would only anger her more. Eris sighed. "I wanted you to know what I am." Eris met Jasi's deep blue gaze and forced away the thought that Jasi was so much more like their mother than Eris would ever be. Thoughts like that were dangerous, even now that she didn't—shouldn't—care. "Mother knows. That's why she never questioned Lira when I didn't return. I think Father even begins to understand, though not in the same way as Mother. I think Mother was Lira's first student."

She hadn't considered that before, but after saying it, the idea made sense, at least more sense than the alternatives. Why wouldn't Lira teach their mother? Having the queen understand the value of the keepers would provide protection. Enough to keep the magi influence lessened as they sought to gain power in Errasn.

"But why *you?*" Jasi asked.

"Lira didn't choose me, if that's why you ask. This is something I was born into."

"We are born the same!"

Eris pulled her feet out of the dirt and slipped her shoes back on. She touched Jasi's golden hair and pointed to her own black curls. "Are we? You don't see the differences the Sacred Mother gives us? Am I so similar to you that you mistake me as a reflection?"

"No...but—"

"Then why should we not have different abilities? I will never have your gift of duty, of simply knowing and accepting what must be done for Errasn. That, I think, was why I fought against my place for so long. Now I know what I am to do. I am a keeper."

Jasi's face changed, the outrage turning into uncertainty. "And Mother knows this?"

Eris nodded.

Jasi's jaw clenched briefly as she looked around the garden, her gaze touching on the shade flowers and her mouth twisting disdainfully. Her back straightened as she turned back to look at Eris, face becoming more regal. It was an expression Eris would never obtain.

"Then can you help her?"

Eris blinked, surprised at the sudden turn. "I..." She hesitated, uncertain how to answer her sister. "I am still learning. My ability is different from Lira's. She uses flowers and this garden. My garden is different—the Svanth Forest—but I'm too far from it to use it to help her."

Jasi nodded, as if she understood. "If there's anything you can do, promise me, Eris, that you'll help her. I don't know what will happen to Father when she's gone. Already he is different than he was before she became ill. Less confident, always deferring to Tholen, where he commanded him before. Now that Jacen has more experience, he's been leading the armies."

Eris looked toward the tall elms marking the center of the garden and sighed. "I'll do what I can." Truly, she had no idea if she could even do anything to help, and anything she did manage would only delay her attacking the magi.

Jasi nodded again, as if something had been decided.

# CHAPTER 7

*E*ris stood in the hall. She'd not rested well. Dreams haunted her sleep. One dream bothered her most. In it, she surged through the forest, running from a creature with bright, golden eyes. Eris tried pulling on the power within the forest, but it failed her again. And as the beast reached her, she'd awoken, drenched in sweat.

She knew she could never be an effective keeper until she had power over the forest. Until she could command rather than request the energy stored within.

The creature frightened her. She had sensed it within the forest, but always it had been a distant thing, a presence the forest didn't seem to mind so she never bothered with it either. What did it mean that she dreamt of it chasing her?

When she'd finally managed to fall back asleep, she hadn't rested any more soundly and finally got up to begin her day. Now in the hall, she stood near a corner, a grand display of flowers filling a massive ceramic vase. Thistlebuds, thulis, dyrans, and camogines all mixed with a few vipeslars.

At first, Eris didn't know what to make of the arrangement. She frowned, wondering if it was one of her sisters' works. There was a certain power to the way the flowers were arranged, but nothing like what Lira would manage. The camogines were one of Desia's favorites, so Eris figured it was hers.

But something about the display gave her pause. Eris frowned, staring at it before realizing what she saw. There was a message within the flowers.

At first, Eris couldn't decipher it. What she'd told Jasi was the truth; working messages into the flowers wasn't a skill she'd spent much time mastering. She held only a rudimentary understanding. This was complex, much like the mastery found in Lira's arrangements.

As she puzzled through the message in the flowers, it became clear. *Keeper. Return.* And Eris suspected the vipeslars implied the forest as they only grew beneath dense canopy.

*The Keeper of the Forest has Returned.*

Not Desia then. Eris hadn't gone to her, and if even if she had, she doubted Desia would create an arrangement like this. Jasi wouldn't have done this, would she?

A young handmaiden dressed in servant white nodded to Eris as she passed. She had pale skin and reddish gold hair. "They are beautiful, aren't they, my Lady?"

Eris thought she should know the girl but couldn't think of her name. "Do you know who put them here?"

The girl's eyes widened briefly. Likely she hadn't expected Eris to speak to her.

Eris tried to force a smile onto her face and make herself less intimidating, but most of the handmaidens stepped lightly around the princesses. Desia, in particular, could be harsh with the girls. Eris had never had much use for them, so perhaps she had been equally harsh.

The girl bowed her head, keeping her eyes from looking up. Eris realized she carried a handful of linens as she worked down the hall. Toward Eris's room.

"I'm sure the Mistress placed them there. She puts many such arrangements around the palace."

Eris nodded and turned back to the arrangement. The girl waited for a moment before scurrying off down the hall, moving more quickly than she had before.

The flowers. Something about the flowers.

Eris touched one of the deep purple leaves of the dyrans. They furled together, rolling into a long, slender tube. The purple of the petals deepened the closer it got to the stem, until it practically merged with the deep green stem. She pulled on the energy stored in the flower, touching it lightly. The flower curled slightly inward.

Eris frowned.

This flower was not from the palace garden.

She pulled a little harder on the energy, tracing the faint stores of power. A brief vision of a small meadow swam through her mind. Then it vanished. The meadow had stretched before a lake, a few trees dotting its shore. The sun shone bright overhead. A patch of dyrans furled toward the sunlight along the shore, taking in deep draughts of water from the water's edge.

Eris blinked. She didn't recognize the lake.

She touched the thulis. Again she felt a faint awareness that this wasn't from Lira's garden. As she drew on it, she had another vision, this time of a rolling hill dotted with different flowers. The thulis and the camogines grew here.

Eris reached for the thistlebud. This was closer. Near the palace. She felt the draw of the palace from the vision, the strength of the nearby garden to the south.

And then the vipeslar. This she touched hesitantly. Lira kept vipeslar growing in her garden, but she did so only surrounded by taller flowers—darthshades and piksans, each with long stalks that grew like trees rimming the vipeslar. As she touched it, she knew immediately that this was nothing like the vipeslar Lira grew in her garden.

Eris had a surge of energy, stronger than the others. The leaves curled lightly before unfurling. The vision that flashed before her was one she'd seen countless times over the last few months. Massive Svanth trees grew all around, stretching high toward the sky, obscuring the sun. Thick vines swirled around the trees, the hint of the coming teary star along their stems. These vipeslars were from within the Svanth, though near the edge.

Her hand trembled as she took it away. Who had placed this arrangement here? Who could have entered the Svanth without her knowing?

Only another keeper. That meant Lira.

But why would Lira place this arrangement here?

Eris couldn't think of any reason Lira would do so. Why place a message in the flowers for her sake?

Unless it wasn't for her.

Would Lira have arranged the flowers for her sisters? Did she do so as some sort of test?

That made little sense, but no other answer made sense either. She stared at the arrangement another moment before hurrying off, a quicker step driving her forward.

When she reached the steps at the base of the western wing, she hurried up, barely pausing long enough to bunch her dress in her fists. She wore a simple green dress with hints of brown worked into the collar. One she never would have chosen before, but now the colors suited her better. She wanted to check on Terran but figured he would be happiest left alone working with Master Nels. Besides, hadn't he wanted to reach the city more than her? And he didn't want more questions about why he'd been with her during the last few months.

Atop the stairs, she turned toward Lira's quarters. It was time for the Mistress of Flowers to work with her. Eris had returned for whatever lessons Lira could offer, and waiting did nothing to get her closer to the knowledge she needed.

When she reached the thick wooden door before Lira's rooms, she hesitated. The last time she'd been here, she still hadn't learned anything about her flower. She had barely discovered her flower, then. And now? Could she really have come so far since then?

Eris knocked.

There came no answer. In spite of knowing she should wait, she tried the handle of the door and pushed, opening it slowly.

Flowers filled the room, but something about them was off. Rather than fresh-cut or planted flowers like she'd seen the only other time she'd been in this room, now the flowers had a sense of age. There was a palpable sensation about the room, prickling her skin. Colors were faded and muted, and the air held more of a musty sense than the fresh vibrancy she should feel when around the flowers.

It took only a moment for her to realize Lira hadn't been to her room in some time.

The window was shuttered, and Eris threw it open. Warm sunlight spilled into the room, burning away the shadows. A breeze scented by the flowers of the garden outside gusted inside, whipping away the sense of age and ruffling the stacks of papers around the room.

She shouldn't be here—these were Lira's rooms—but the room felt *wrong* closed up like this. Besides, for Lira to have left her quarters like this meant she was preoccupied with her healing of the queen. Likely Lira would never even know.

Eris considered Lira's quarters. The bed looked meticulously made, sheets and thick blanket pulled neatly up over the mattress. It had no canopy, not like the one stretching over Eris's, but massive plush pillows covered with colorful slips of fabric made the bed look inviting and cozy. One door to her wardrobe cracked open. Eris didn't need to peek inside to know the types and colors of Lira's dresses; she'd seen them often enough to know how Lira dressed quite properly, always in complementary colors to the flowers she preferred. Only now did Eris recognize how the clothing might have worked with her flowers. Had she selected the green dress for the same reason?

And then there were stacks of books. Hundreds of books stacked along open shelves or tabletops throughout the room. Lira was nowhere to be found.

Eris turned back toward the shutters, to close them despite the sense of wrongness they created. She could see her mother and delve the elms again and determine if there was anything more she could do. Heart heavy, she barred the light, once more.

A flash of red caught her attention as she turned for the door.

Eris spun, scanning the room to see what it might have been that caught her eye. At first, she didn't see anything other than the bright leaves, and even those hadn't been nearly vibrant enough to draw her attention.

What then?

A stack of books near the bed. The topmost one bound in a dark red leather.

Eris glanced out the door but saw no sign of Lira in the corridor. She made her way to the bed and grabbed the book from atop the stack. Immediately, she recognized the author. Feliran. She'd sought books by Feliran for weeks while struggling to learn of her flower. Master Billiken claimed he'd once had several books by Feliran, but Eris had only ever found one. That book had been full of detailed drawings, depictions so neat—so perfect—Eris had no trouble identifying plants when she saw them again. She'd searched for a book on the Svanth region written by Feliran but hadn't found what she sought, finally sneaking one from Lira without her knowing. And now here was another.

Eris flipped it open. This was different than the last. Written in the same neat hand with pictures making it easy to see what Feliran drew. Notations in the margins hadn't been in the book Eris had taken. The other book Eris had found depicted shade plants. From what she could tell, all the flowers in this book grew in bright sun.

She skimmed through the book, glancing at the pictures and noting the names of different plants. Most she knew. The connection to the Svanth Forest gave her some knowledge, but the time she'd spent searching for her flower—time she once thought wasted—had given her the opportunity to study the hundreds of varieties throughout the garden. And with Master Nels always curating more, Eris had plenty of opportunity to continue to learn about different flowers.

But it wasn't the *flowers* in the book she found fascinating. As she skimmed through the contents, she read through notes in the margins. Most were simple comments on where certain varieties could be found or their related species. Some notes remarked on proper arrangements, color combinations, even ways to utilize particular blooms for different intents.

They were Lira's notes.

Eris frowned. The writing in the margins looked so similar to Feliran's neat scrawl, but there seemed differences as well. Almost as if Lira's notes tried to mimic the tight writing Feliran preferred.

She could learn much from this book, especially if Lira chose not to teach her.

Eris glanced around the room. Would Lira even miss it? From the look of things, she'd been gone for days, possibly longer. And besides, it wasn't as if Lira needed to study these anymore. Not with as much as she clearly knew, the way she used her keeper knowledge. Wouldn't she *want* Eris to have it?

*No.*

Eris set the book back down atop the stack and turned from the room. She would have her knowledge, but not that way. Her mother's illness might have changed the focus of her return to Eliara, but not the reason for it. Eris needed to learn what it meant to be a keeper. And Lira was the only one who could teach.

As she turned back to the door, she touched one of the arrangements and borrowed some of the remaining energy stored before letting out a deep breath. Then she closed the door behind her.

Eris finally found Lira in the library. She hadn't considered looking there, but after wandering about the palace and scaring a half dozen other maids, she'd made her way into the garden. She could use the connection to the flowers to determine if Lira was there, but felt nothing. On a whim, she'd gone to the library.

The library had not changed since Eris last visited. Tall shelves filled with books stretched from one end to the other. A ladder on wheels leaned against one of the stacks. Frail Master Billiken glanced down at her through his thick spectacles as she entered, nodding as if she hadn't been gone, before returning to where he shelved a stack of books.

Near the back of the library was a long table Eris had used when trying to learn about her flower. Now, another keeper leaned over the table. Lira rested her chin on her hands, staring at a large, leather-bound book splayed open in front of her. One foot tapped against the stone with a soft regularity.

Eris cleared her throat as she approached.

Lira looked up. "Eris. Are you here for your studies?"

Eris's heart lifted. With the sickness that had taken over her mother, she'd feared Lira wouldn't be interested in teaching her, but maybe she'd been wrong.

"I tried finding you in your quarters."

Lira waved a hand and looked back to the book. She took one finger and began tracing lines of text as she read. "I haven't been able to spend much time there. I need to focus on the garden, and I can't do that from within the palace. Nels lets me stay in the greenhouse."

Eris tried imagining what it must be like staying in the green-house. The only time she'd been there, the sweltering heat and humidity nearly made her pass out. What must it be like at night, when the air cooled?

Probably no different than staying under the canopy of svanth trees at the heart of her forest. Like the Svanth for her, the flowers in the palace courtyard were Lira's garden.

"Master Billiken should be back shortly," Lira said.

Eris nodded. "I saw him as I came in." She hesitated, wondering how to broach the subject. Hadn't Lira promised to teach her when they last saw each other?

But why did Eris feel so nervous?

"What have you come to research?" Lira asked.

"Research?"

Lira nodded but didn't take her eyes off the page.

Eris frowned. "I didn't come to research." She took a steadying breath. No use putting it off, and besides, she *was* a keeper. "I came to ask if your offer to teach still stood."

Lira's hand hesitated as it slid across the page, and then she looked up. She blinked slowly, hazel eyes focusing on Eris. Then she sighed.

In that moment, Eris knew the answer.

"When I saw the power you wield when we were in the garden—"

Eris cut her off, rather than letting her finish and tell her she wouldn't—she *couldn't*—teach her. "That's just it. I can access great power, but don't know how to use it, not like you. I can delve the roots of the trees—even the elms here in the garden have stories they can share—and even delve the roots of your flowers, but *using* that energy is another matter. The Sacred Mother knows I don't even know how to set a proper arrangement, not as you do to focus the power of the garden."

The words came out in a rush. Eris noted how Lira simply watched her, palms flat on the table, the fingers of her left hand running over the edge of the pages.

"Sit, Eris Taeresin."

Eris swallowed briefly and then complied.

"Let me tell you of how I first came to Eliara."

Eris frowned. This wasn't what she expected Lira to say.

"By now, you've likely learned much about the Gardens of Elaysia."

Eris shook her head. "Terran has told me what he knows, and I've seen memories stored by the forest, but there is much I don't know."

Lira smiled. "I'm sure Terran has told you what he can, but the gardens were destroyed before he ever had a chance to see them in full bloom. And your memory would be a pale reflection of what had been."

Eris remembered the vision the forest had granted her of a sea of flowers stretching as far as she could see, swirls of colors, each growing deliberately, the pattern only hinted about in those visions. What must it have been like to see those gardens?

What must it have been like to lose them?

Eris hadn't given much thought to the pain Lira must have suffered at the loss of her garden. What grew now—both the within the palace walls and that which resided under the protection of the Svanth—paled in comparison.

How would Eris feel if the Svanth were to burn? Would she have the strength to rebuild?

She debated asking Lira about the message in the arrangement, but what would Lira say? Would she be frustrated that Eris had to ask? Lira seemed to expect something of her, almost as if she needed to have some basic knowledge before she would teach.

But did Eris know what she needed? The Svanth hadn't explained everything, and Eris didn't have access to the great Gardens of Elaysia. If she had...perhaps Lira might be a better teacher.

"I see from your face that you recognize what's been lost." Lira sighed, her shoulders sagging slightly. "The order of the keepers existed long before kingdoms ruled these lands. The keeper who instructed me claimed that once, everything around us was the domain of the keepers. Over time, the gardens shrunk, receding to what I remember. And now...now they are nothing. The keepers are gone."

"But they aren't gone. You're still here. *I'm* here."

Lira forced a smile. "I was not a keeper long when the gardens were destroyed. I had much still to learn, but in those days, I had many teachers. After the gardens were destroyed, most who survived scattered. But not me. I watched my teacher burn. I saw the destruction the magi inflicted."

Eris shivered at the darkness in Lira's voice.

"And so I came to Eliara for vengeance. A terrible reason, but it is the truth. And I would have carried it out, gone against the earliest teachings I'd learned when training to be keeper, had I not been stopped."

Eris blinked, uncertain what to say. Lira spoke of teachings as if they were things Eris should know. But without Lira to teach them, how could she? The forest didn't grant that sort of wisdom, only memories, tales of what had been. Woven in that were hints of lessons, but Eris hadn't learned how to tease them out.

"Who stopped you?"

Lira looked up. Her eyes were wet, and she wiped the tears away. "A very wise woman." She shook her head. "And so I stayed, creating a new garden here. It will never rival what once existed, but like what I see when I wander the emptiness of Elaysia, there are hints of what once had been. Echoes. That has to be enough."

Eris studied Lira as she fell silent. Lines along the corners of her eyes spoke of the strain she was under. How much effort did she exert in trying to keep the queen alive? How much did she really help keep back the Conclave?

And how much longer could she go on?

Lira sighed. "I remember when you first worked with me. How much you rebelled even searching for a flower. Your sisters took to it quickly, willingly. But you, always so stubborn."

Eris swallowed. Stubborn. Different.

And now Lira still wouldn't work with her.

She almost asked about the message in the flowers, but old hurt came out instead. "I thought you didn't want to teach me. You welcomed Jasi, Desia, and Ferisa so quickly, letting them choose their flowers so easily."

Lira nodded, her hazel eyes going distant. "And I thought you didn't want to learn. Had it not been for your mother pushing, I might have given up. Think of what we would have lost."

"I didn't know."

Lira smiled sadly. "She did not want you to know. She suspected your potential even before I did, though she thought your sisters might have some potential as well. And they have some. Weaving messages in the flowers is not an easy skill, so in that, your mother was right."

How had Eris not known that her mother suspected she would be a keeper? Why had she kept that from her? How had her mother known about the keepers?

What more did she not know about her mother?

They were questions she would never learn the answer. Her mother lay struggling against a sickness working through her, one that would eventually claim her life.

Eris would do anything to change that outcome. "How can I help?"

Lira inhaled deeply and ran her fingers along the side of her head. A strand of hair popped free and dangled in front of her face. The only other time Eris had seen her disheveled was after her capture by the magi.

"I..." She met Eris's gaze, looking uncertain for the first time. "I'm not sure. Your abilities are so different than mine. Had I learned more before the gardens failed, I might be better equipped to teach. But now?" She shook her head. "I don't know if there is anything I can even teach you."

A knot formed in her stomach. This had been her fear. And if Lira couldn't teach, then where would Eris go? How would she learn what she needed to help her mother? How would she be able to push back the Conclave?

"There is much I could learn from you," Eris suggested. "I see the way you organize your arrangements, how that focuses the energy formed by them. That's something I can't learn from the forest." All that knowledge, she needed to help her mother. But it was more than that. After what they'd done, she needed to know more about being a keeper to destroy the magi.

"Does it matter if you learn about flowers?" Lira asked. "As I've said, your abilities are different. You reach a depth I only imagine. But you work with age and time whereas the flowers grow and die in a season. As you're a keeper of trees, I'm not sure anything I know can help."

Eris swallowed. Could she have wasted her time coming here? Time that would have been better spent searching the forest for glimmers of lessons?

But no. Had she not returned to Eliara, she would never have learned of her mother. Eris would not have wanted to remain ignorant. And if there was anything she could do to help, she would.

"Is there anything you can teach?" she asked.

"I will see." She shook her head. "I make no promises, Eris Taeresin, but I will see."

Eris nodded. It would have to be enough.

# CHAPTER 8

*E*ris stood next to Terran, fidgeting. Lira's comments left her feeling uncomfortable.

She looked over the gardens. Sunlight slanted past the top of the palace, casting odd shadows. Some seemed to move, almost alive. The effect was unsettling.

The air was still, as if the wind itself waited on what would happen to her mother. It didn't help that Eris could smell the sickness, could practically taste it.

"Do you know why Lira came to Eliara?"

Terran frowned, his hand pausing above the dirt bed he worked in. "I know she came here after the gardens were destroyed."

Eris nodded. "She came to get vengeance on the magi."

Terran stood and wiped his hands on his green jacket. He glanced toward the center of the garden, as if expecting Lira to come strolling toward them and overhear the conversation. "That's not the way of the keeper."

Eris laughed bitterly. "And if I were to go after the magi?"

He studied her. "I would help. You know I would."

Eris wasn't sure. Terran did not want her to go toward Saffra,

70

as if he was afraid of what she'd do. After what the magi did to her—to Jacen and now all of Errasn—they needed to be destroyed. "You speak as if you know more about keepers than I do."

Terran turned toward her. His eyes were troubled. "I've grown up around gardeners. My grandfather served the keepers. My father would have. I have known about keepers as long as I can remember. But knowing what you can do?" He shrugged. "After what happened to the Gardens of Elaysia, I never expected to serve. And then Lira summoned me. Now I learn alongside you." He hesitated. "Something she said bothers you."

"She won't teach me."

"She won't or she can't?"

"Does it matter?"

Terran shrugged again. "Of course it matters. With Lira, it always matters." He looked back toward the bed of flowers he'd been working on. "You know that you're different, Eris."

Her heart pounded. Hearing Terran call her different hurt more than anything else. Always different. It shouldn't bother her. And it usually didn't...except this time it did.

He raised his hands and stepped toward her as he tried to soften the comment. "Listen—you don't have the same connection to flowers as Lira. You have some—choosing a teary star tells me that—but I wondered if your connection to the trees made a difference."

Eris sighed. "Lira won't even tell me that. She thinks I can access more power than her. I tried reminding her about how little I know about arrangements and the way a proper arrangement can focus the energy drawn. All she promised was that she would try."

"Give her time."

"We don't have time. Not with what I know the magi are doing. Not with what's happening to my mother."

Terran looked around the garden and then touched her arm.

71

Eris glared at him. "You're still worried about what my brother said?"

Terran shrugged and swept his hat off his head, balling it into one of his hands. Dirt stained his knuckles, and Eris reached over and wiped it off. He closed his eyes as she touched his hand and took a deep breath.

"Worried isn't quite the right word."

"Then what? You *have* been avoiding me, haven't you?"

"Eris—"

She shook her head. "You're the one who pushed me to return. I would have stayed in the Svanth and listened to the trees. There were other lessons for me." She suspected she could delve through the roots of the forest for years and still not learn everything the first keeper wove there. She would try, though. "At least there I have the chance to learn. Here, Lira won't even look at me."

"You know that's not it."

"And now you're hiding from me because you're afraid of my family."

Terran met her accusing stare. "You're still a princess. And your father…"

She shook her head. "I'm a keeper. And you are my gardener. My father will understand that." Eris would do what she needed to make him understand.

"You think it's so simple?"

"Why shouldn't it be? Once I've learned what I need from Lira, we can return to the forest."

"Just like that."

Eris took a step toward him as a surge of annoyance bloomed within her. "What are you saying? That you don't want to return to the Svanth with me? Will you make me find another gardener?"

She didn't know where his reticence came from, but the idea of returning to the Svanth Forest without Terran left her feeling empty inside, like a week of rain without the sun.

Terran glanced around the garden before shaking his head and touching her arm. "You know I won't do that. It's just..."

"Just what?"

Terran sighed. "You're not the only one with much still to learn. What you can do...the way you read stories from the roots of the trees in the forest...that's nothing like any keeper I've ever heard about. I don't know what it is you do, and I'm not entirely certain how to help you. I had hoped returning here would give you a chance to connect with Lira and I could..."

He trailed off and took her hands in his without looking around the garden, the familiar gesture something they'd done often while alone in the forest.

She understood now why Terran pushed so hard to return to Eliara. "You wanted Master Nels to teach you as well."

Terran nodded.

Eris looked at his crisp, green jacket, and began to understand. "He won't teach you?"

Terran sniffed. "As much as I've tried, he tells me there's nothing more he can teach me. Oh, he'll take all the help I'm willing to offer, he just doesn't think he can instruct me as a gardener any longer."

Since Lira felt much the same, was it any wonder Nels would, too?

Terran squeezed her hand. "Don't worry. I can be nearly as stubborn as Nels." He led her away from the greenhouse, still holding her hand.

Eris wondered if he realized that he guided her toward the elms at the heart of the garden or if it were accidental. "There's nothing I can do for her," she whispered as they approached.

Terran nodded. "You told me that already."

Eris nodded. "I was with her today. I just sat, searching for something I could do." She shook her head. "I don't know enough to help. Even were I strong enough here, I don't know enough to help my mother."

Terran pulled her to a stop and steered her toward him. She looked up into dark eyes that gazed upon her with concern. His hand held hers gently. She couldn't help but notice how he smelled of dirt, a different earthy odor than the way he'd smelled within the forest. Not unpleasant, only different.

"If what I've seen means anything, your ability as keeper isn't what makes you strong. Your ability is different than Lira's, but not so much that you can't use what she knows or share the connection with her garden."

The garden felt unlike her forest. The connection more tenuous, delicate, than what she experienced within the forest. There, the heavy undercurrent of power raged like a river. The power around her within the garden was more like a breeze. And outside the palace, surrounded by nothing but grasses, it was little more than a stale wind.

"But she's not willing to share what she knows," Eris said.

"She said she'd try."

"She did. But with everything else..."

As they continued past the elms, Eris glanced toward the trees, sensing a rising shift in the power around them. Lira would be in there. During the time Eris had sat with her mother, Lira had not come at all. Maybe she'd known Eris was there and had preferred to stay away.

They reached the door leading into the palace. Terran stepped away from her, as if unwilling to enter.

"You can come with me."

He glanced at his dirty hands and stretched them out before him. "I'm sure the king doesn't want me inside the palace like this. Besides, there are other things I can be doing for Nels, especially if I want to get him to help me."

"I can make the work go more quickly," she offered.

A smile spread across his face. "And leave nothing for me to do?"

"There are other things for you to do. I'm sure Jacen would find tasks for you if I asked."

Terran's eyes went wide, and Eris laughed.

She turned toward the door and stopped.

Next to the door was another arrangement of flowers. Neatly done, vibrant colors swirled together. Had she not seen the message earlier, she might have missed this one.

Hyanlillies and ulsens, greens and yellows with some deeper shades of red interspersed. Were those orchics?

"What is it?"

Terran stepped up alongside her. With his presence, she wished they were back in the forest, wished it would be just the two of them again. She looked over to see him frowning.

"I'm not certain. A message." But one she couldn't quite read. The message wasn't as simple as the last. That had been bold, the meaning clear. This...this was something else. Too subtle to be one of her sisters. That left Lira, but why would Lira leave messages in the flowers for her to find, especially after what she'd said in the library?

Unless...was it some kind of test?

Lira had said she would see what she could do. Did she want Eris to learn on her own, much as she had while trying to find her flower? That had been a struggle, each day spent wandering the garden, each day learning in spite of herself, until she mastered more flowers than she realized.

A sudden surge of excitement worked through her. Maybe Lira expected her to be able to puzzle out the meaning in these displays. Perhaps they were lessons, or messages meant to start her lessons. Could that be why Eris hadn't seen much of her since her return?

"Ask Lira what it says if you don't know. She can't expect you to have learned everything from your time in the Svanth."

Eris shook her head. "I don't think she wants me to ask. That's not what this message is about."

Terran shot her a quizzical look. "I thought you couldn't read what was written here."

"I can't. But like with my flower, she wouldn't simply *tell* me the answer. She wants me to work it out on my own."

The idea excited her, the first thing to do so since returning to Eliara. As much as she'd hated it at the time, she had learned much while wandering the garden and sitting in the library. Besides, if she hadn't spent so much time in the garden, she never would have met Terran. Though, perhaps she *could* have met him a different way.

She suppressed a blush, thinking of how he'd found her sitting atop the wall after she'd climbed up looking for a flower. While she'd found her teary star, she had gotten stuck and needed him to rescue her. And now...now he was her gardener.

Eris closed her eyes, wishing he would hold her as he did in the forest. There, his touch seemed to make everything better. Here, she had to figure it out on her own. If only she could figure out what she needed to do.

"You don't seem disappointed."

Eris inhaled deeply, tasting the fragrance from the garden. She had returned to Eliara to learn, hadn't she? And if this was the way Lira intended to teach, then she would follow.

Only, she had no idea where to start to learn how to read what was written in the flowers.

# CHAPTER 9

$\mathcal{T}$erran came up with idea first.

Eris sat alone along a shadowed wall of the garden atop a rough-hewn bench. She'd spent the afternoon combing through the palace looking for other messages, only to find another that she couldn't read. By evening, she went looking for Terran.

Again, he'd been difficult to find. This time, rather than getting frustrated with him, she found a quiet spot in the back of the garden where she could simply sit.

With slippers off her feet and toes dug into the earth, she listened to the sounds around her. The air practically hummed with energy, attuned to the way Lira had grown her garden. Life swirled around her. Not just flowers and trees, but the insects crawling along leaves, the squirrels jumping from tree to tree, the birds flittering through the garden, some pausing to snap up a bug or nip at nectar. So much life.

And then there was her mother. Disease worked through her, eating at her, serving as a sharp contrast to the life around her.

Only Lira's touch kept her alive, holding the illness at bay. But it advanced, slowly, ever so slowly. Eventually, it would overcome even what Lira did to delay it, and her mother would be gone.

Eris breathed slowly, knowing it was the cycle of life. The priestesses had taught her that lesson at a young age. Now, as a keeper, she'd seen the way the forest cycled, the dying becoming food and sustenance for the living. Had not the first keeper taken her final breaths beneath the trees towering at the heart of the Svanth—trees she had planted and nurtured herself—before slowly turning into nutrients for the trees themselves? A cycle, one meant to repeat again and again, no matter what anyone did.

But there was something different about what she sensed.

Eris almost knew what it was. As she tapped into the energy of the garden, its touch tingled against her senses like a faint aberration.

"You could ask for help."

Eris looked up. Terran leaned against the stone wall towering over them, shadows coursing across his face. As within the forest, the shadows didn't quite obscure the look of concern he always wore when looking at her recently.

"I don't think that's what Lira intends." She hesitated, uncertain how Terran would react to what she planned to say next. "I'm starting to wonder if maybe I need to return to the Svanth."

Terran frowned. "You need someone to teach you."

Eris shook her head. "I'm not sure Lira plans to teach me. Or if the messages in the flowers are even Lira's design."

"You asked Master Nels for help finding a flower. I remember you asking me for help learning about the teary star. The Sacred Mother knows you even harassed poor old Master Billiken until he found you books to read through."

"I didn't harass him!"

"No? Didn't you tell me you climbed the ladder in the library and pulled books from the shelves? I'm sure that didn't throw him into a fit at all. After all, Master Billiken loves it when people come into his library and start undoing all his carefully done work."

"I only did that once."

Terran laughed and sat next to her on the bench, scooting her over. She resisted at first—if he was going to tease, he could stand for all she cared—but he was persistent. Besides, she liked the way he leaned against her and the warm reassurance of his body.

He took her hand and rested his head against the wall, sighing. "You've been sitting here how long?"

"Less than an hour."

"I don't know enough about the flowers to help you. That's always been a keeper's role."

"Not always. Lira taught Jasi and Desia..." She trailed off, perking up on the bench. Maybe her sisters *could* help her some-how. They might not have Lira's knowledge, but they'd been sitting through her classes. How much had they learned in the time? Enough to puzzle through the messages she'd found? Would it be enough to craft a response?

"See? Maybe I *can* help you."

"You haven't done anything."

Terran grinned. "That's your opinion. I like to think I guided you to the right answer."

As he laughed again, she leaned away from him. It didn't matter *how* nice it felt to have him so close. "I'm not sure my sisters will know enough anyway. If I can't read the messages in the flowers, why would they be able to do so?"

"It doesn't hurt to ask. Besides, you've barely seen them since we returned."

"I saw Jasi."

Terran frowned. "Not Princess Desia or Ferisa?"

"You don't have to call them that."

"Aren't those their names?"

Eris thought about punching him. "Are you going to start calling me Princess Eris?"

His face turned mock serious. "If that's what you want, my lady."

She stepped into her slippers and stood. The disconnect from the garden left her feeling hollow.

"Where are you going?" Terran asked, grinning at her.

She put her hands on her hips as she looked back at him. "I'm going to find my sisters. And then maybe I'll send Jacen to find you."

She didn't have to look back to know the smile had slipped from Terran's face.

---

The great hall seemed particularly empty when Eris found Jasi and Desia. They sat together, leaning toward each other and whispering unintelligibly. Desia looked over when Eris entered. Jasi made a point not to.

Eris stood in front of them, hands clasped behind her back. After the conversation she'd had with Jasi, Eris wasn't certain they *would* help.

"I heard you'd returned."

Desia wore her hair down and in curls. Eyes the color of the sky fixed Eris with a hard stare, a reminder of the way their mother always looked at her. Like with their mother, Eris sensed the disappointment hiding behind her eyes.

"Has Jasi told you?"

Desia glanced at Jasi. "She told me enough. I'm not certain whether to believe what I've heard. Once I find Lira, I will ask her."

Eris suppressed a smile. Jasi had not taken her at her word either, though Jasi had also been captured by the magi with her.

"She teaches you, still?"

Desia's mouth twisted. "And why would she not? Because we weren't born to this flower magic like you? I seem to remember you not having any particular talent for it."

Eris bit back the retort that came to mind. Arguing with Desia wouldn't do anything to get them to help her. As much as she hated it, she needed their help if she was to decipher the message Lira had worked into the flowers.

"That's not what I meant."

She took a deep breath and wiped her hands along her dress. The silky fabric was much nicer than what she'd worn the last few months; the only dresses Terran had managed to acquire for her were heavy cotton. They were warm during cool nights, but not as smooth as what she'd been accustomed to wearing within the palace.

Jasi looked from Eris to Desia. "Mother would not want us to argue."

Desia shot Jasi a hard glare. "Mother is in no condition to tell us what she wants."

Jasi looked up at Eris, a question plain in her eyes. Eris breathed out a sigh and shook her head. Desia seemed angrier than she remembered, but how could Eris blame her? Everything had changed for her, and the life she wanted was now so far away.

"There is nothing I can do. I…sense…the sickness, but don't know enough to help." Eris swallowed. "That's why I returned, Desia, to learn from Lira. Only I need your help for that."

Desia looked to Jasi and frowned. "Why would you need our help?"

"Because I think Lira wants me to get your help."

"Is that what she told you?"

Eris shook her head. "I haven't spoken to Lira much since my return."

Desia shrugged. "Then I don't want to help."

"Desia!" Jasi breathed. "If it could help Mother…"

Desia looked up at Eris and considered her for a moment. "You think anything Eris can do will help Mother? After she left us for all this time? You might not have seen it, but *I* saw how hurt Mother was when Eris didn't return. Lira didn't say much about why she was gone, only that she was safe." She shook her head again. "Eris has already left Errasn."

Eris leaned forward and forced Desia to meet her gaze. They were so different, like her and Jasi, but shared the same stubborn streak. Perhaps that was why, even more than with Jasi, Eris had never really been close to Desia. "Lira knows where I've been. And *Mother* knows where I've been. If you will not help me learn what I need, then—"

Desia pushed to stand. "Then what? You'll use this flower magic on me? Maybe then I'll believe it works!"

With that, she turned and stormed from the great hall, leaving Eris and Jasi staring after her. The door closed with a solid *thud*.

Jasi took a shaky breath and looked up at Eris. "I'm sorry, Eris. Since Mother's been ill...it's been hard on us. All of us, but Desia the most. I think part of her was disappointed I returned. And then after what happened with Mother..." She sighed. "She'll come around, I'm certain."

Eris glanced back at the door and wondered. Desia had more anger than she'd remembered. And Jasi seemed to have less. So much had changed in the time she'd been away. She thought of Jacen, how different he seemed, the darkness in his eyes, the anger that matched what Desia seemed to have. Had Ferisa changed as well?

"You said you needed help?"

Eris blinked and turned back to Jasi, nodding. After all the years she'd spent antagonizing her sister, strange that it would be Jasi who would help her. But they'd shared an experience, the time spent trying to escape the magi as they raced through the Svanth forest. A bond had formed; Eris had felt it then. Thankfully, Jasi still did.

"The flowers," she began. "Lira has taught you to read messages in the flowers?"

Jasi nodded. "I thought you said you'd learned the same."

"Some. Not enough, apparently."

Jasi frowned. "What do you mean?"

Eris took a seat on the long bench across from Jasi and rested her arms on the table. Sitting here like this brought back memories of when she'd been younger, forced to sit and eat peacefully with her sisters, a task that never quite happened as well as their mother and her handmaidens wished. Even then, Eris had instigated trouble. And then she was sent back to her rooms to eat alone.

Maybe she was meant to be alone.

Eris looked over to the door again; back only a few days, already she created trouble with her sisters. Had Jacen seemed bothered by her return or was that only her imagination?

"I found an arrangement in the hall the other day," she said. "A collection of thistlebuds, thulis, dyrans, and camogines. A few vipeslars."

Jasi nodded. "Such an arrangement would be quite lovely. I imagine the dyrans and camogines complement each other quite well." Her lips curled in a frown. "I'm not sure about the vipeslars. Not much use in such an arrangement."

Eris decided not to disagree. In that arrangement, the vipeslars were the crucial piece for the message. At least, that had been what she'd thought. But what if she'd been wrong and there was a different message in the flowers?

"Can you think of a message that might be written with such flowers?"

Jasi tilted her head, her golden hair spilling onto her shoulder. Even with her lips pursed and eyes narrowed, she carried a regal air about her. What would she have thought of Eris had she seen her during her time in the forest, sweating and covered with dirt and leaves? What must Terran have thought, for that matter?

"There are a few messages that could be written with such flowers. Can you describe to me what you saw?"

"I will do better than that."

Jasi looked at her, waiting.

"Let me show you the arrangements, and you can tell me what you think."

Eris didn't know with certainty, but she thought Jasi had an almost eager gleam to her eyes.

# CHAPTER 10

They stood in front of the ceramic vase that was now empty. A few petals lay strewn about the floor, but nothing that gave any clue to the message. Eris looked up and down the hall, wondering if there might be another.

"Are you certain it was here?"

Eris nodded. She'd come from her room searching for Lira and had stopped when she came across the flowers. That had only been the day before, but more than enough time for Lira to move the flowers, especially if she knew Eris had already seen them. And maybe that was all part of a test.

But how would Lira have known Eris already saw the flowers?

The answer was obvious. Eris had used the energy of the flowers, had *touched* the flowers to sense where they'd come from. Of course Lira would know that she'd been here.

"Lira must have moved them."

Jasi shook her head. "Lira leaves any arrangement she makes for many days."

From what she'd seen of how Lira used the garden, the flowers placed about the palace helped focus her energy and create the protections around the palace. This arrangement might not have been for the same purpose.

"Maybe I saw it right before she changed it."

Jasi's expression told her that she didn't think it likely. "You said there was another?"

Eris nodded and they hurried through the palace, stepping out the door into the garden. The sun hovered on the horizon, streaks of orange and reds mixing like celias and corinths in some massive arrangement made by the Sacred Mother. Not for the first time, she wished a message were written for Eris to read, to provide guidance on what she should do.

Terran knelt in one of the beds nearby and glanced over at her. His eyes met hers, and he nodded, pushing to stand. He hesitated before shuffling over to another box to begin work. Eris frowned at him.

Eris turned when Jasi laughed softly.

Amusement pulled her mouth into a smirk. "That's your gardener?"

Eris frowned. "That's Terran. Apparently he's too busy to speak with us." She said the last loud enough for him to hear.

"I can see why you'd run off with him."

"I did *not* run off with him."

Jasi laughed again. "Finally I've found something you're sensitive about."

Eris turned away and stared at Terran. He seemed to make a point of ignoring her, working with his back to her. If he were to remain her gardener, he would have to get comfortable around her family. That wasn't the only reason, but the only one she'd let herself think about for now. Once she had a better understanding of what she needed to do as keeper—about what it meant to *be* keeper—then could she let herself consider the rest.

"Is this the other arrangement you saw?"

Eris turned. Jasi stood in front of a large vase. The flowers were the same as she'd seen before—hyanlillies and ulsens of green and yellow with the red orchids mixed within—but there seemed to be a different shape to the arrangement. Eris couldn't be certain, but had the message *changed* since she'd been here before?

Why would Lira do that?

"I think so. They're the same flowers, at least."

Jasi stood in front of it and studied the flowers. She tipped her head from one side to another, as if moving would help her see something standing still would not. Eris took a stance next to her and looked at the arrangement. It *was* different, though subtly so.

"I think...yes. There is a message here but it makes no sense."

"What do you see?"

As she asked, she recognized the message herself. *Follow the Path.*

"Follow. Path. There is something else, but I'm not exactly sure what it says." She turned to Eris. "Are you certain you can't ask Lira? She would be the best person to help decipher something like this. Especially if it's important."

"I don't think that's what she expects of me. She wants me to discover on my own."

Jasi set her hands on her hips. "Discover on your own? And how is asking me you discovering what you need to know? Do you want to get me in trouble with Lira?"

"I don't think she cares if I ask for help as long as it's not from her. When I was looking for my flower, she didn't mind Master Nels helping me. And then once I'd found it, she didn't seem to care that I asked Master Billiken for his aid searching through his books. I spent far too long reading through books trying to find *something* that would help me understand the flower I'd chosen."

And it wasn't until she'd gone to the Svanth Forest that she really understood. Even then, she hadn't learned all that she needed. There was still so much for her to understand, but no one willing to teach.

"She made you search through the library?" Jasi asked. "With old Master Billiken? That must have been horrid!"

Eris shrugged. The library hadn't been so bad, but he hadn't had anything she needed. The Feliran books were gone, likely taken by Lira. Maybe Eris should have taken the book she'd found in Lira's rooms. Then she might have been able to work through the message in the flowers on her own.

"The library wasn't—"

"Master Billiken must have *hated* having you come disrupt his day. He's always been so dour when I was forced to go to the library. Thankfully, that wasn't often. Most of the time, I just sent one of my handmaidens to fetch what I needed. Lira never made me spend time researching my flower, though much is known about the perisal..."

Eris turned away from her sister's rambling. Something she'd said triggered a thought. Master Billiken hadn't minded when she'd visited, but he *had* been preoccupied. The magi asked him to collect books for them, though with everything that had happened since then, Eris couldn't think of what those books might have been.

"Are you even listening to me?"

Jasi grabbed her sleeve and pulled her around. Eris was so startled by the sudden contact that she didn't bother resisting.

"Really, Eris, you come to me asking for help but then you can't even be bothered to *listen* to the help! I don't know why I even bothered. Maybe Desia is right."

Eris shook her head. "I'm sorry, Jasi. Something you said reminded me of the magi."

A wash of anxiety clouded Jasi's face. "What about the magi? Do you know something more than what Jacen brings back to us?"

"And what does Jacen bring back?"

"Only how the magi aid Saffra and attack from the border. They use their destructive magic, throwing lightning and fire at Father's men. We've been lucky so far—fires haven't spread too far across our lands, but I know Father fears that won't last long."

Lira's work. With her focus split between keeping their mother alive and protecting the borders, it was amazing she managed to make time to put messages into flower arrangements. When Lira failed, the border would fall, and the magi would be able to come across unimpeded.

She shook off the thought. Worrying about the borders would have to come later. When she had more skill as keeper, she would be able to help there. For now, she needed to focus on learning whatever she could from Lira. Then she could begin to explore what other ways she could help. Maybe then she could help her mother.

Only...would it be in time?

Eris sighed. Whatever the sickness consuming her mother, she couldn't help her until she knew enough to understand more of the intricacies of her abilities.

*Follow the Path.*

The message Eris could read, but not the one that had been here before. Maybe Lira knew she hadn't been able to read the first message and made it simpler. Did that make it less likely Lira would teach her? Or was there a different reason for the altered message?

"How has she taught you to read the messages in the flowers?" Eris asked.

Jasi had been saying something but Eris hadn't been listening. When interrupted, Jasi frowned at her. "What was that?"

"What does Lira use to teach? Are you learning from books, or does she work with you individually?"

"Individually? Lira doesn't have time for that. She's given us books to work through. She said they were many of the same ones she'd used when she was first learning the language of flowers."

Eris's heart hummed a little faster. Could she have books by Feliran? Hadn't Jasi implied that before? "What kind of books?"

"Not like she expected from you. We never had to go to Master Billiken, thankfully. Lira provided the books she wanted us to read. I think they're hers."

Hers. If so, then they *were* books by Feliran. "Did they have explanations for what you saw? Examples of arrangements?"

Jasi shook her head. "Nothing like that. Mostly detailed descriptions of flowers. We are to take those, along with Lira's notes, to create messages."

There was more to it, Eris was certain. Jasi hadn't learned quickly, but she seemed to know enough to understand more than simple messages. "Can I see them?"

Jasi bit her lip, looking around the garden, as if Lira would come across her and punish her for considering. "Why do you want this, Eris? What is it you hope to gain?"

It was a question much like what Terran had asked. What did she hope to gain? Understanding, certainly. But there was more to it. She wouldn't really be able to help until she knew more about her abilities and that began with working with and learning from Lira. Until she knew what she was meant to do, she would be of no use to anyone, isolated and alone.

Eris sighed. What could she say to make Jasi understand? Probably nothing. "I don't know. Enough for me to help Mother."

She didn't say how she wanted to use it against the magi. Jasi might understand, but Eris didn't know.

Jasi studied her, seeming to wait for more. When it didn't come, she nodded.

# CHAPTER 11

*E*ris sat in her room atop her plush bed, legs crossed under her and wearing only a thin shift like the one she'd worn during her time in the forest, only much cleaner. The silky green dress she'd worn for most of the day lay in a heap near the corner of the room. She should really get up to hang it in the wardrobe, or at least over one of her chairs, but couldn't pull herself away from the slender, leather-bound book splayed out on her lap. She might have to learn on her own—left again alone to figure out her role— but at least she might have a book to keep her company.

Jasi had delivered the book to her room, making her promise to return it. Eris had agreed without question. How else would she be able to pour over one of the books that had let Jasi learn to read the messages in the flowers?

As she had suspected, the book *was* a Feliran. Not the same as she'd seen in Lira's room. She was tempted to return to Lira's quarters and—not *take* the book, but borrow it—but she would work through what Jasi lent her first.

This was another book on flowers that preferred full sunlight. Eris flipped through many of the earliest pages, looking at the diagrams, again marveling at the detail Feliran managed to work into each drawing. Species name was written across the top of each page. Along the edge appeared to be characteristics associated with the flower; it took Eris a few moments to realize these characteristics had more to do with what effects keepers had used the flower for.

When she discovered this, her heart raced. Eris had suspected Feliran was a keeper—knowing as much as she did about the flowers would only come from one of the keepers—but had no way of proving it before now. Had other books noted the same? Eris wished she still had the Feliran book of shade plants to reference, but it had been lost during her abduction. Besides, she could simply delve the forest to learn about shade plants.

Eris continued flipping pages. Each page for a different flower. From her time in the garden, she knew there were thousands of different flowers, but most were variations of the same species. Each page consisted of different species. Notes along the sides referenced other colors or different patterns that might be found in the wild.

Toward the middle of the book, Eris noticed comments about how to cross the flowers. Her hand hesitated. Did Feliran describe how to breed the flowers to create new flowers? If that was the case, why hadn't she simply documented the crosses?

She turned back to the beginning. Other pages were the same. The information tucked into this slender book was dense. Each page provided more information about each flower than she would have found in any single book in Master Billiken's library, though even he had admitted Feliran had the premier reference on flowers.

Where, then, were the comments about how to mix messages?

Eris turned to the back of the book. Maybe Feliran had packed that information toward the end of the book.

But the last pages were more of the same.

She sat back, shaking her head. She should have asked Jasi how

Lira intended her to use the book to understand the messages written in the flowers, but already she asked too much of Jasi. And Desia would be no more help. She was too angry about Eris' absence to help. What did it matter that Eris had finally discovered what she wanted to do, what she was *meant* to do?

Jasi had brought her a few other books as well, and Eris turned to these and grabbed the first one off the top of the stack. The cover was made of a dense parchment rather than the supple leather used to bind the books by Feliran. A detailed diagram of a flower was etched onto the parchment, parts labeled. The title had been written in a flowing scrawl, and she couldn't read it clearly. Eris didn't expect much.

The first few pages matched what she expected from the cover. Each depicted a different type of flower with markings clearly labeling the parts. Eris flipped through quickly, wondering why Jasi would have given her this.

Near the middle of the book, she stopped.

The diagrams continued, but now several flowers were shown on each page. Eris studied the diagram. There didn't seem to be anything particularly telling about these flowers. An anosem, trishelia, and bitterspoon. She tried to think of what might make the combination special but couldn't come up with anything. A few notes had been made around the edges but most seemed to do with light requirements and how often to water to keep the flowers healthy.

The next few pages looked much the same. Eris turned the pages more slowly. They were the same, only with different flowers. As she turned each page, she began to have a sense of something more. How could the combination of yellow roses, goralds, and sureens need so much to keep them healthy?

Unless Eris interpreted the drawing wrong.

She frowned, hurrying through the book.

The last third was different. Instead of two or three flowers drawn together, now the page contained six or eight or even a dozen different blooms. The same markings were made along the margins. Eris still didn't know what they meant. Maybe if she took more time working through the book she might understand, but she was tired.

She set the book aside and moved to the next one Jasi leant her. At first glance, it seemed the same as the last. Page after page of diagrams of different flowers, showing various stages of growth. Helpful, but Terran might find it more interesting.

A few more books like that, and then she grabbed the last. This had another cover made of thick, yellowed parchment. She opened it and nearly dropped the book.

The first page looked like the other book bound in parchment. A few flowers were diagramed on the page. No notation was made around the sides of the page, only a single word.

The next page was the same. And the next.

Eris flipped with growing excitement. Some pages had phrases instead of single words. None of the flowers were labeled, but Eris didn't need the labels. This was what she'd been searching for.

She laughed and grabbed the book and the other like it and hurried out of her room.

Eris stood in the garden. Pale moonlight washed over her, providing enough light to see. Even without it, she sensed the flowers around her with something like the awareness she had while in the Svanth Forest. The undercurrent of energy diverted toward helping her mother pressed against her, focusing through the garden toward the heart. Only the elms didn't contribute to it. Eris suspected that had more to do with Lira's ability than the elm's willingness to participate in healing her mother.

She searched for the arrangement she'd shown Jasi but couldn't find it.

Eris turned, looking around and letting the sense of the garden fill her. Could she find another arrangement this way?

All she felt was the pull of the garden.

She sighed and turned back into the palace. With as late as it was, she should get to bed and search for other arrangements in the morning. Maybe she could share with Lira what she'd learned from the book and convince her she was ready to learn more about arrangements, but her mind raced and hope—for the first time in a while—filled her. Maybe she *could* learn enough to help.

The halls of the palace were empty. No lantern lit her way, and only the faint moonlight streaming through open windows gave light for her to see. Eris barely needed any. She'd grown up in the palace and made her way by feel as much as by sight, but she would have liked having a lantern with her.

As she walked, a few simple flower arrangements set throughout the halls pulled on her. She paused at each and considered the flowers. The dim light made it difficult to know with certainty, but none had any messages. Each served the distinct purpose of focusing the energy coming from the garden.

Eris continued on, pausing only where she'd seen the first arrangement. No sign of it remained. Strange that it had been here such a short time.

What if Lira hadn't been the one placing messages in the flowers?

Who else, then? The message of the first arrangement she'd discovered had been clear—*the keeper of the forest has returned.* The other was not as clear, but she'd thought the instructions to follow the path meant she needed to learn how to read the language of flowers first. With the books Jasi brought her, Eris finally thought she might be able to accomplish that.

If only she could find another arrangement, she might be able to test whether the book would help her interpret the message. Instead, she had only more questions.

Eris continued down the hall back to her room, her steps

hollow echoes along the stone. At times, other echoes seemed to follow. She paused and listened, but nothing chased her. If only she had the same awareness she had within the forest.

Maybe she should never have left the forest. What had she gained since returning to Eliara? A sense of hopelessness about her mother? Realization that she could do nothing to slow the magi? Frustration that the knowledge she thought she'd gained from the forest wasn't enough—that there had to be *more* to being a keeper than she realized?

Back in her room, she leaned against the door and thought about what she should do next. Sleep first. Exhaustion washed over her, and she wanted nothing more than to sleep, but she couldn't yet, not after what she'd seen in the books Jasi lent her.

Eris grabbed one of the books and started back to her chair. As she sat, a soft knock startled her. She closed the book and set it atop the chair.

Who would come to her room at this time of night?

No one else had even moved in the halls. No servants would knock this late.

Maybe Terran?

No, Terran wasn't willing to even come too near her in the garden.

Unless something had happened with her mother.

Eris pulled open the door, cold fear already working through her.

Ferisa stood on the other side. She wore a long yellow dress that matched the color of her hair, which was pulled into a bun atop her head. Tension pulled the corners of her eyes, rings now around them. A band of silver circled her throat, the gentle swirls the marker of the Sacred Mother. She held a long, slender book in her hands.

Another priestess, dressed in a rich golden robe of office, stood next to her. She wore a long drape from her head that covered black hair streaked with gray. Hard eyes looked at Eris.

Eris looked from her sister to the priestess.

This was it. Her mother had passed.

"Ferisa?"

She nodded with a tilt of her head, barely moving otherwise. "I heard you had returned. I hoped you would come to me…"

Come to her? What was Ferisa talking about? "Is everything all right?"

Ferisa glanced at the priestess before looking back at Eris. "Some say everything is *better* now that you've returned."

Eris couldn't help but note the hint of disdain in her voice. She should have sought her youngest sister, but had been so preoccupied trying to find Lira and then her mother that she hadn't bothered. The youngest of them all, Ferisa was born to serve the Sacred Mother and had taken to the calling as naturally a flower took to the sun.

"I'm sorry, Ferisa. I came when I heard of Mother." Telling Ferisa the same lie she'd told the others wouldn't hurt.

The priestess next to Ferisa pursed her lips. "You came for the Mistress of Flowers. Only then did you learn of your mother."

Eris blinked and looked from the priestess to Ferisa. "How—" She shook away the question. The how did not matter. "You know of what I am? Of what Lira is?"

The priestess's face turned in a sour expression. Ferisa nodded, looking at the book she pinched between her white fingers.

Eris recognized the book as the Writings, a book of prayers sacred to the priestesses that they used in worship to the Sacred Mother.

So Ferisa had begun memorizing the prayers, then? That might explain some of why she'd become so serious. The prayers were said to change the priestesses but were a sign that Ferisa advanced in her studies. Soon, the priestesses would claim her fully, and she would no longer be Princess of Eliara.

"We have known about the Mistress of Flowers for many years," the priestess said.

Ferisa looked up from the book and nodded.

A growing unease built within Eris. If the visit wasn't about her mother, then why did Ferisa come to her so late? And why would she bring one of the priestesses with her?

She held onto the edge of the door, not wanting to let them into her rooms. "It's late, and there is much for me to do. Why have you come to me, Ferisa?" Eris pointedly ignored the priestess for now.

"What did you think to accomplish by coming here?" Ferisa asked.

Eris frowned. "Accomplish?" she asked. "I don't know what I thought to accomplish. If you know about me and Lira, then you know I have much left to learn. I hoped to learn more about my ability, help Mother if I could..."

She trailed off, looking from Ferisa to the priestess. Something about the way the priestess stared at her made her nervous.

"You came to learn of flowers," the priestess said.

Eris took a deep breath as she looked back at the priestess. Her heart fluttered. She wished she'd placed a few arrangements in her room before now, anything that might lend her strength. The gardens were there at the edge of her senses, too distant to access.

"And if I did?"

"You will not be able to save her. The Sacred Mother calls her home."

"Save who? Mother?" Eris frowned and looked to the priestess. Her face hadn't changed and still had the hard edge to it, so different than the serene expression most of the priestesses wore. "What do you know of her illness?"

After looking over at the priestess and sighing, Ferisa answered. "There is much darkness in our future. I have not yet learned enough of that gift, but I do not see much light. And without light, how can the Sacred Mother shine?"

"Ferisa?" Eris stepped around the door, looking at her sister. Her face had changed, the soft lines that had once made her look beautiful—lovelier than the rest of them—had faded and become hard. "What are you talking about? What about the future?"

Eris had never paid much attention when it came to the priestesses. They served the Sacred Mother, but she knew little about how. They kept their ceremonies held tightly within, only the priestesses knowing them fully, but the Sacred Mother had been worshipped throughout Eliara and the North for centuries. But what did Ferisa mean about seeing light in the future? Did the priestesses claim to have some sort of premonitions about the future?

Ferisa offered a tight smile and pointed to the Writings. "If only the magi had ignored you, as they were instructed to do, you would never have known."

Eris's heart pounded loudly. Had Ferisa known about the magi plan? "Never have known what?"

The priestess shook her head, cutting Ferisa off. "It no longer matters. All that matters is that you are here. That the keeper has returned."

A cold flush washed over Eris. Had she been right? Were the messages *not* from Lira?

The harsh tone to the priestess's words told Eris all she needed to know about her view of keepers. She took a deep breath and turned to the priestess. "If you've come to me, then you know she has."

The priestess stared at her, eyes unblinking.

Out of the corner of her eye, Eris saw Ferisa shudder.

"That's what I feared. I'm sorry, Eris."

With that, Ferisa stepped into the room and toward Eris. She pulled a slender knife from within the Writings and stabbed it toward her, slicing into her stomach. A rune on the edge of the knife flashed as it stabbed through her skin.

Eris gasped, the pain hot.

The priestess stood over her as she bled onto the stone floor, her expression flat, her face unmoving. As Eris's vision faded, Ferisa turned and closed the door softly behind her.

# CHAPTER 12

*E*ris didn't move. Couldn't move. Bands seemed to circle her wrists and ankles, biting and painful. Nothing but blackness around her. The air even *smelled* dark, if such a thing were possible. Certainly none of the sense of flowers and life she smelled all around her in the palace.

She tried to blink, but her eyes didn't open.

Was she dead?

The last thing she remembered was seeing Ferisa and the knife in her hand, but why would her sister attack her? Sweet Ferisa. Had she really changed so much?

Pain ached dully in her stomach. She wondered if she still bled. Of course, were she dead, it wouldn't matter. Her lips were dry, and she attempted to moisten them with her tongue, but it wouldn't work as it should.

The only thing she knew was pain.

Not dead then. Were she dead, the pain would be gone. That was the lesson the priestesses of the Sacred Mother taught. In the afterlife, there was warmth as one rejoined the Sacred Mother, but no pain. Only contentment and peace.

Eris felt none of that.

Panic set in. If she wasn't dead, it meant she was trapped again.

The last time she'd been captured, the magi had taken her and Jasi, hoping to carry them into the forest, thinking one of them would be able to lower the protections built into the forest enough that the Conclave would be able to destroy the last garden standing against them. Only, they hadn't counted on Eris being a keeper.

What had she done to free herself then? She remembered begging the bindings to release her when tied to the tree, and then the tree itself seemed to take a breath, draw itself out, and give her a chance to slip free. Could she do the same thing?

If only her feet touched the floor. They hung suspended over nothingness. Eris imagined herself tied to a long board, practically spitted like the hogs Jacen liked to hunt, waiting for the roasting flames.

"Help!" Her voice barely croaked out. Even were anyone near enough to help, she doubted they would hear.

Why? Why would Ferisa do this to her?

The question kept returning. Of her sisters, she'd always felt closest to Ferisa. Partly because Ferisa always seemed at peace with who she was meant to be—the way she'd been destined to join the church from birth, accepting it without question, possessing an almost preternatural calm about her role as if she truly were meant to become a priestess. But there had been more to it. Ferisa never tormented Eris the way their older sisters did, never teased her about her failings in lessons.

Why, then, would Ferisa do this to her?

Why her and not Jasi or Desia? Lira had been teaching them longer than she'd ever taught Eris.

Unless Ferisa had something more planned for them.

She took a few steadying breaths. If she could control her thoughts, maybe she could reach the power of the gardens around her, use it to help her escape. And then she would need to find

Lira. Whatever else, Eris realized she was still woefully under trained for what she tried to accomplish.

More than Lira, she needed to find Terran. What would he think if he couldn't find her?

Could *he* come for her? He had come for her when the Magi took them. Could he come again? Did the bond of keeper and gardener work like that or would he simply not know what happened?

Eris pushed away the hope of help coming.

She was the keeper. She would have to find a way free on her own.

She swallowed. Her tongued loosened somewhat. Pain still gnawed at her stomach.

How much blood had she lost? She was no physician, but surely she couldn't survive a knife to the stomach for long, especially bleeding as much as she remembered. Would Ferisa and the priestess leave her here until she died? Was that what she intended?

Frustration surged to the surface. Her mother dying. Her father weakened. Jacen nearly so different as to be unrecognizable. Jasi and Desia.

But this…this was different. How could Ferisa do this to her?

Her fingers twitched. Pain shot through her, starting with her arms and moving up to her neck.

Eris blinked, trying to clear her vision, but failed.

The blackness returned.

---

Eris came around long enough to hear sounds near her. Voices, distant and soft, echoed toward her. A flash of yellow at the corner of her vision, like eyes staring at her.

She tried shivering but couldn't move.

The voices sounded closer. One almost sounded like Ferisa.

"She doesn't know about it yet."

"It no longer matters. She returned. That is danger enough."

"But she's my sister!"

She heard a sound like a slap followed by a grunt.

"She was once, but no longer. Now, we're your sisters."

Eris heard soft mumbling but couldn't make out the words.

"Because she's different. The Mistress of Flowers has proven harmless. Her...we see light around her. Dangerous light. This is for the best."

Eris tried swallowing, but her tongue didn't work.

"She doesn't know—"

"She would learn. And when she does, everything will fail."

The speaker paused. Soft steps shuffled toward her.

"I will do it, if you cannot."

Someone sobbed. Ferisa? "No. I will do it."

A sound like metal sliding across metal rang toward Eris's ears.

"No!" she croaked. She didn't know if the word came out.

Something struck her again, hitting her on the neck. Blackness overcame her once more.

---

Eris dreamed.

Fields of flowers flowed around her, massive spreads of colors. Most she could name, but many she could not. They spilled all along the countryside, running up and down hills in regular waves and creating an undulating pattern. If she only focused, she would understand the meaning of the pattern—it hung just at the edge of her comprehension.

Tucked between the flowers were glimmers of gold, like a pair of glowing eyes.

The image shifted.

Eris *felt* it shift, so different than a dream should be.

Colors streamed around her, swirls of orange and red and

yellow mixed with bright greens and slashes of browns and purples, all moving too fast for her to identify. She thought she should know the flowers, could almost feel them pulling against her, straining toward her, but the image sped past. As it moved, she thought she recognized the pull of the Svanth Forest, but it blurred by too quickly to know. She barely had time to wonder why she would sense the Svanth Forest in her dream before it was gone.

Colors faded into nothing but shimmering lines. Speed, faster than Eris could imagine, pulled them past her. There was motion, but she could do nothing to slow it, no more than she could control her dreams.

At least the pain was gone.

She knew nothing other than the sense of motion and hint of colors, now translucent, a glowing streaming around her, like thousands of shooting stars, slowly building, growing brighter and brighter and brighter...

Finally, it slowed.

Barren earth stretched around her. There was no movement. Even the air was still and stifling.

Eris blinked, letting her eyes open and take in the life around her, but nothing lived. Where grass should be instead was only char. Rocks heaved from the broken ground.

In the dream, she took a step. The ground crunched beneath her bare feet. Hot earth threatened to burn her before crumbling to nothingness. She glanced to the sky, looking for anything with color, but saw only blackness.

Eris shivered.

What was this image?

She turned, hoping for something else, but all around her stretched a vast emptiness.

Eris ran.

The ground hurt her feet, the rock tearing through her flesh before it crumbled away, but she refused to stop. She could see nothing of where she ran. Nothing surrounded her. Perhaps she *was* nothing.

A charred, misshapen body lay unmoving. Eris didn't dare slow long enough to look at it.

Finally, she stumbled. A towering rock grabbed at her feet, and she fell forward. She threw her arms up to stop the fall, knowing the rock would rip through her hands, and braced for the impact.

No impact came.

Eris fell an impossibly long time. She felt the motion around her but could see nothing. Not even the rocks around her any longer. There was nothing.

Instead, the blackness faded as she fell.

Speed picked up, the sense of motion dizzying. There was no sense of wind, no colors. It was as if her senses failed her.

A nauseating fear rolled through her, building on the increasing speed.

And then Eris knew no more.

When her eyes opened again, she found herself with nothing but white surrounding her. There was the sense of something more, almost at the edge of what she could perceive. Warmth flowed through her, and her pain was gone. A flash of color blinked and disappeared.

Her breath caught in her throat. Was she dead?

What had happened at the end? Why had her hand twitched?

She didn't know, and so closed her eyes, falling back into darkness.

A gnawing ache built in her chest. She frowned. If she were dead, she should not feel pain. This was different than before, slow but building with an agonizing sense, pressure squeezing around her chest, pushing down on her breasts, stabbing through her neck.

Eris realized then that she had forgotten to breathe.

She took a deep breath, and the pain faded.

Her eyes flickered open. She saw only bright light. This looked so different than the darkness—the nothingness—that had surrounded her before. She no longer moved

But no bindings held her, either.

Eris moved her arms but still did not see them. She moved her legs, kicking them, but could not see where they were. Only the surrounding whiteness.

She took a step.

No pain worked through her feet from the rocks. The only pain came from deep within her chest.

Eris forced another breath and took another step.

Slowly, she moved. Each step sliding forward, carefully feeling her way. She had the sense that if she could reach whatever it was she felt, she might finally escape this...whatever it was. Dream? Nightmare?

Or was it real?

That scared her more than anything.

Another step. And another. Each moved her across the unseen ground.

As she moved, she slowly felt a power drawing upon her. It started slowly, more a nagging sense at the back of her mind, but each step took her closer and closer to what it was she sensed.

Eris kept her hands in front of her. Her mind was blank, like the whiteness around her. Were she to stop, she would have to wonder about her sister, about the slender knife with the strange rune marked on its edge, and about the way Ferisa slipped the knife so easily into her stomach. Eris wanted none of that.

So, she let the light surround her.

As she moved, she imagined the beautiful garden she'd seen earlier in her dream. The massive swells of flowers running over the hillside. Had that been Elaysia? Could she have dreamt of the ancient garden? Or was her vision something else? Only a dream.

She continued forward, but the walk seemed endless, nothing but whiteness around her, never changing. Eris stopped. Had she gone too far? Had the sense of something else changed, shifted away from her? She no longer knew if she traveled in the right direction. But what *was* the right direction anymore?

Eris took a deep breath and sat.

This was all a dream, some vision she had as she lay dying. If she waited, she would eventually find the Sacred Mother waiting for her, welcoming her toward warmth.

As she sat, she took deep breaths, needing to remind herself to breathe. The image of the flowers she'd seen in the other vision kept returning, mixing with the strange, soft glowing eyes. She hadn't had long to see them, but flowers—especially patterns to the flowers—stayed with her. In her mind, she built the image back up, putting the flowers around her as if she stood in the wide, sweeping meadow. Color began to seep around her, the yellow of the corinths, the blue of listhanis, a field of red and orange roses, all stretching as far as she could see, and then farther, beyond her field of vision.

The fragrance of the flowers almost touched the air, a hint, nothing more, of what could be with this garden. Eris smiled. She might be surrounded by whiteness, but she could *imagine* a garden.

But not this garden.

Eris blinked, pushing the garden from her thoughts. This was not the garden of her dreams. The whiteness returned, leaving her feeling the emptiness—the sheer vastness—all around her.

Taking a deep breath, she focused her thoughts, pulling together the image she wanted.

She built massive trees around her, stretching high overhead until they blocked the pale surrounding light. Vines trickled down from some of the branches, and she wove others around the bases of the massive Svanth trees, recreating the heart of the forest, *her* forest. As she did, the air seemed to change, a trick of her mind, becoming more earthen and damp.

She smiled.

This was her garden.

Eris relaxed, letting the garden surround her. It might not be real, a vision or some trick of her mind, but she no longer cared. If she could be surrounded by the familiarity of the Svanth Forest, could feel the magnitude of the trees rising around her, the heaviness of the air, the sense of calm and quiet she felt while moving beneath the massive canopy, then she would welcome the Sacred Mother.

Imagining her feet, she pressed them into the dirt, pushing past the leaves and detritus her mind created for her, a record of the last time she'd been in the forest. As she did, there was a familiarity of the forest, the energy humming around her. Then she knew she was dreaming.

Sighing, Eris delved, pressing into the roots.

And everything changed.

# CHAPTER 13

The forest tore from her mind, ripping away as it changed around her. The massive Svanth trees receded, twisting and turning into stunted elms and pale-barked birch. Pine trees with thick needles interspersed amidst the others, their aroma rising over everything else. Light diffused through the upper branches, reaching the floor of the forest in a way it never did while in the Svanth. Wind rustled quietly through the trees.

Eris frowned, wondering why her vision had changed.

She stood and took a step. Not just the vision had changed, but her perception of it. Now, her feet touched the ground, different than when touching the stone as it powdered away in front of her. With each step, she sunk softly, toes touching brown, fallen pine needles and decaying leaves from the elms. A few scrub trees rose nearby, attempting to climb toward the light. Thorns twisted around some.

What was this vision?

Letting herself reach into the depths of the forest, she delved.

Power hummed around her. And awareness.

The forest—the *garden*—was nearly as alive as the Svanth. This felt different than what she experienced in the Svanth Forest. Younger, perhaps, with less a sense of overwhelming age. The roots carried with them a story, different than what she'd learned from her garden. If she traced along them, she could get a sense of where she was...

But something repelled her.

Eris blinked. Always before, she'd been able to access the gardens she'd found. First within the Svanth when she'd learned she was a keeper and then within the Verilain Plains, when she'd used the power of the needlegrass, pulling on it to help dispel the magi. Even within the palace, she managed to access the energy and power stored within Lira's garden. Why not now?

Could this be real?

How? Eris remembered clearly lying on the table, pain aching through her stomach, and then...blackness. Nothing. Had she died? Was *this* the afterlife?

But if so, why did it feel so real?

She looked down, taking in the thin shift she wore, so similar to when she'd been abducted by the magi and nearly died. Blood stained the cloth where she'd been stabbed. Eris touched the silky fabric, carefully placing a finger through the hole. When it touched her stomach, she felt no pain.

Tearing away the fabric, she looked and saw her flesh unharmed. How? She had been stabbed—that much was real—but how had she been healed?

Or was she? Could this still be a dream?

Eris looked around the forest. Everything was different than it had been within the visions. The air pressed in around her with its cool, humid touch, smelling distinctly of pine and life and everything she loved about the Svanth. That much seemed real enough. Birds chirped distantly, their songs fading into the trees. And the wind. The wind hadn't blown against her skin while under the influence of her visions.

She took a step. Dried branches crunched painfully beneath her feet. She touched the nearby branches, and thorns pricked her finger.

Real then, and not a dream.

But how had she come here?

This was not the Svanth Forest. It was no forest she knew, too cool to be within Eliara. In spite of the chill on the wind, she did not shiver. The pine trees told her she was someplace in the north, but even Varden was too far south and too flat for these pines. Some grew along the mountains in the west of Eliara, but not forested like this.

Where was she?

And why couldn't she delve the forest?

Eris tried again. This time, she delved slowly, cycling down within the forest, twisting along the roots as she went, searching for understanding. She listened, letting the forest guide her as she slid along the roots, carefully moving as she searched the patterns she recognized written within the twisting growth. A story, so much like the one written in the Svanth, but different in a way that she barely recognized it. Pressed within the story was the edge of a barrier meant to keep others out, as if the keeper of this forest knew others would come and she meant to prevent them from learning the secrets.

As much as she tried, Eris couldn't get past the barrier.

"What is this?"

Her voice startled her; she hadn't meant to ask aloud.

The wind sighed in answer, drawing along her arms and flickering through her hair.

Eris withdrew from delving the roots, but not before she realized something—someone—approached. Somehow, she had been discovered.

If the forest was a garden, it might have a keeper.

Eris waited. If there was a keeper, she could ask for assistance. The first question she'd ask would be how she got here in the first place. And then she needed to return. She could seek out Lira, ask for her assistance, and do whatever she could to help heal her mother.

The keeper came with another sigh of the wind.

Eris felt her arrive, distantly as though a memory of the sense she had within the Svanth, nothing like the awareness her garden granted. It was almost as if the forest tried to shroud the arrival of the keeper. Eris still knew she came.

And as she did, she knew with certainty this was no dream.

"I know you're there."

She spoke to the trees, looking past a clump of pines rising from a gentle slope. Shadows swirled around the pines that the sun piercing the overhead canopy couldn't penetrate. Eris shivered.

"Who are you?"

The voice sounded small and frail. In her mind, Eris had an image of a tiny woman wearing a shawl covered with dried needles, greying hair falling around her shoulders.

"I am the Keeper of the Svanth Forest."

Eris used the formal title as she knew it. Likely there had once been more to the title, but that wasn't something she could pull from the trees and Terran didn't know it.

Thinking of him made her heart flutter.

What must he be thinking? Did he even know what happened? If it was still night, he might not know anything yet. Only when she failed to go to the garden would he wonder.

"A keeper. There are no more keepers of the trees. Only those of the flowers remain, and they have scattered."

"You are this place's keeper."

Now that the woman was near, she recognized the connection, and it was strong. The trees pulled around her, shielding her, but nothing like what the svanth trees would do for Eris.

The woman laughed lightly. "You mistake me, girl. I am nothing but an old woman."

Eris frowned. Could she be mistaken?

She let herself delve into the roots of the forest. The barrier kept her near the surface, as if the deeper and more ancient roots of this place were forbidden to her, but she could trail along the shallow roots, winding along the grasses and scrub trees, letting herself reach toward the woman.

Power echoed back to her when she reached the woman.

"You hide behind the pines, but you are a keeper."

Eris waited, wondering if the woman would step forward or not. This was her forest. Were she to want to, she could banish Eris with a request of the trees. Or a command, had she power over them.

Slowly, the branches twisted, relaxing away from the woman. Sunlight streamed down, glowing gently in a circle around her. Eris's breath caught.

Dark hair, not grey, hung down along her shoulders and back. Deep brown eyes stared at her. Skin peeking from the ends of a simple grey dress nearly glowed as it caught the flickering sunlight. There seemed something familiar about her.

The woman took a step forward, almost gliding across the forest floor, as if the fallen leaves carried her, sliding her toward Eris. The trees twisted back away when she passed. A rustling around them caused Eris to look.

All around, the trees moved, writhing and shifting as they hemmed them in. Eris stood, unmoving, *afraid* to move.

She would go nowhere until the trees released her.

"Who are you to recognize a keeper in my forest?" The woman stopped just out of arm's reach and looked up at Eris, eyes and face hard. This was not the gentle compassion she saw from Lira or the elderly wisdom she recognized from the keeper in her visions in the Svanth. This was a hardened woman, almost angry.

"I told you. I am the keeper of the Svanth Forest."

"Bah! The Svanth has no keeper. None will bond there—none *can* bond there. There hasn't been a keeper in the Svanth for hundreds of years."

Hundreds? Eris hadn't known how long. "How do you know this?"

The woman's eyes narrowed as she frowned at Eris. "If you are truly its keeper, how is it you don't?"

The woman turned her back to her and started away. She flicked a hand, and the trees began moving again, sliding in between her and the woman, separating them.

"You will leave now."

The woman kept walking.

"Wait!" Eris yelled after her, afraid to let her get too far away. If she left, Eris might lose the opportunity to learn from a keeper of trees—a keeper like her, rather than like Lira.

The woman hesitated but did not turn back toward her. "You have some skill, girl. You would not have noticed me coming if you did not. Perhaps you could learn to be a keeper of flowers. It's easier to master. The flowers don't argue back. But a keeper of trees? And of the Svanth?" She shook her head. "None can master that forest. Not any longer."

The woman started away, and the trees thickened between them. Eris knew that if the woman got too far from her, she would lose her chance to learn. More than anything, Eris needed to learn how to do what this keeper did. How to convince the trees to listen when she commanded. If Eris could manage that, she might be able to help her mother. She might be able to slow the magi.

But what could she say that would get the woman to return? How could she prove she really *was* the keeper of the Svanth? What secret did she know that could convince her?

And if she couldn't convince her, would Eris ever find another keeper of trees? Would she be doomed to learn everything on her own, isolated and alone?

The keeper had nearly faded into the foliage when Eris realized the answer. "The teary star!" she yelled.

The forest seemed to hold its breath. The wind paused, and the rustling of leaves fell silent. The thick barrier of trees between her and the woman thinned to little more than a line. The woman stood on the other side, now turned toward her, looking in and past the thick trunks, waiting on Eris.

"I bonded a teary star. That is my flower."

The woman seemed to frown. Eris sensed it through the connection she still held beneath her. "A teary star is a flower, and a shade flower at that. As I said, you may have some talent with flowers, but trees are a different matter."

The woman turned, and the trees began separating them again. Amazing how they moved. Or did she move?

"It's a flower, but the vine wraps around the svanth trees, supporting them as they grow. Without the vine, the trees fail. With it, they both thrive." This was the earliest lesson the trees had taught her.

The woman paused again. This time, the trees slid completely away, showing Eris the woman again.

"A vine?" She asked it thoughtfully, a finger coming to her lips. "Could it be we've missed the secret all these years?" She looked over at Eris, her face softening. "Can you prove this?"

Eris blinked. Other than taking the woman to the Svanth Forest, how would she prove the teary star vine supported the svanth trees? Would the woman have vines available for her to work with? Sapling svanth trees? Even within her forest, she hadn't attempted growing the trees, choosing instead to focus on what she could do, attempting to help the trees grow stronger. Even that she hadn't fully committed to. Most of her effort had gone into learning about the forest.

But if she didn't convince this keeper, Eris would be sent away.

"I can," she said with more confidence than she felt.

The woman nodded and motioned for Eris to follow, disappearing into the forest.

# CHAPTER 14

The forest opened up in front of her. The pine trees grew taller, needles thickening as boughs bent toward the ground, sweeping away as the keeper strode through. Eris struggled to keep up. With each step, vines and exposed roots grabbed at her feet, threatening to trip her and send her sprawling to the ground. She wondered if this was how Jasi felt making her way through the Svanth.

"Who are you?" Eris asked as she finally reached the woman.

She glanced over, seeming to notice how Eris struggled, and slowed her pace slightly. Only enough that Eris didn't have to gasp for breath as she hurried along.

"As you said, I am the keeper of this forest."

That much was obvious from the way the forest moved around her, in some ways more alive than the Svanth. None of her trees would bend before her, practically kneeling as she passed. None of her trees would sidle between a perceived threat, creating a wall.

Or would they? If she understood more of what it meant to be keeper, could she do as this woman did? Would her trees respond to her commands as these seemed to?

"Where are we?"

The woman frowned. "How is it you don't know? Did you not travel here yourself?"

Eris didn't know what had happened. First she'd been attacked by Ferisa and then experienced her strange visions. How *had* she come to this place? The air was so different than that of Eliara. Cooler and more damp. What strange power brought her here?

"I don't know what happened," she admitted.

The woman grunted. "Honest. Good."

They continued through the forest, Eris racing to keep up. The woman was not any taller than her, but each step seemed to be double what Eris could take. No different than when Eris moved through the Svanth; she seemed to move more quickly beneath the forest, but also had moved easily along the plains leading back to Eliara.

Less light leaked through the treetops as they went, nearing the heart of the forest. The air was stiller here and heavy with a familiar earthen odor she recognized from the Svanth. Here, it mixed with the cloying scent of pine, filling her nostrils.

And then a clearing opened before them.

Eris blinked, uncertain at first what she saw.

A small hut *grew* from the forest floor. Each corner was made from the trunk of a different species of tree; one of pine, one of elm, one of birch, and one—she thought—a young svanth tree. Branches mingled together to form the roof of the hut and hung down, creating the walls. A grey wolf sat on its haunches outside, watching with gleaming yellow eyes.

Eris hesitated at the edge of the clearing, unable to take her eyes off the wolf. It watched her with a deep intelligence, something resembling a smile coming to its lips.

"Well, come on then, if you must. Don't stand over there," the woman said.

Eris looked over to the woman. She stopped in front of the wolf and patted its head, whispering softly. Its ears perked as she spoke, but it didn't take its eyes off Eris. Then the wolf loped off, disappearing into the trees.

She shivered, thinking about the intelligence behind its eyes. The wolf obviously obeyed this woman, trained as well as any hound of her father's. What would have happened had she wandered deeper into the forest? Would the wolf have come after her if she'd managed to avoid whatever traps the trees had for her? With the barrier in place, keeping her from delving too deeply into this forest, she might never have known before it was too late.

The woman disappeared into the hut. Eris looked into the forest. She had the sense that the wolf sat at the edge of the clearing, watching her. She shivered again and followed the woman inside.

The interior of the hut was nothing like she would have expected. Walls were mostly smooth, as if the trees deformed for their keeper. The space seemed larger on the inside than it should. A doorway on the far wall separated another section of the hut. A short table, seemingly grown from a scrub tree blossoming, held a steaming pot and cups atop it. Stools made of carved wood rested around it. At the far end of the room was a wide hearth, a crackling fire providing warmth.

Eris frowned at the fire until she realized that it must only *seem* like a fire burned in the hearth. From her experience in the Svanth, the trees would not allow flames. She had other ways of keeping warm, and when they had failed, she'd huddled with Terran, sharing each other's warmth.

The woman tapped one of the stools and sat. She nodded for Eris to follow. As she did, she poured a cup of steaming tea. "Drink now, questions next."

She sat. The stool cupped her comfortably—far more comfortably that she'd expect for a wooden stool. Eris took the mug in her hands and inhaled. The tea smelled of pine and lilac and another odor she didn't recognize. She took a slow sip.

Warmth washed through her, easing away the tension knotting

her shoulders since first arriving in the forest. Really, the tension she'd been feeling since returning to Eliara. With the tea, she remembered who she was—not just a keeper, but the Keeper of the Svanth Forest. She might be inexperienced, but it didn't change who she was. She sighed and took another drink.

The woman sat across from her, studying her. She nodded. "So you are a keeper, then."

Eris took another drink. The tea tasted familiar to her, as if she'd had it before. "I told you that already."

"You also claimed to bond to the Svanth. As I've told you, none have done so for hundreds of years."

The warmth continued to wash through her, and she shrugged. "And you are the keeper of..."

The woman shook her head. "My questions first."

Eris shrugged again.

As she did, she realized something was wrong. She felt... relaxed...too at peace for what was happening around her. Saffra attacked the borders of her homeland, her mother lay dying, and her sister had stabbed her. She shouldn't be able to relax.

She looked down into the mug and blinked, trying to understand what she felt. Was this woman—this keeper—poisoning her in some way? Was that why she felt such relaxation?

"What is this?" Eris set the mug down on the table. Her mind remained clear.

Not drugged then.

The woman sniffed. "So many questions. Did I not say I would go first?"

Eris nodded. The relaxation effect already began to fade, and she looked at the mug, wishing she could take it and enjoy the effects again. But if there was anything to the tea that drugged her, she didn't want to be at risk, especially so far from her garden.

"Can you at least tell me your name?" Eris said, sighing deeply.

The woman considered Eris for a long moment. "For now, you can call me Imryll. Now. It is my turn for questions. You asked where you are but not where you're from. You mentioned the Svanth, which leads me to believe you are from Errasn." She watched Eris until she nodded. "You come dressed...strangely."

Eris glanced at her slip. Blood stains covered her stomach. The ripped fabric exposed her skin. "I was in my room when this happened."

Imryll frowned. "Tell me."

"I was stabbed. I thought I died." The visions—so *real*—had left her thinking the Sacred Mother called her to her. With what had happened, Eris had only one question: why? Why had Ferisa done this to her?

"You know who stabbed you."

Eris nodded.

Imryll sniffed again. "Of course you do, dressed as you are. Probably some lover, with your looks."

Eris blinked as the words set in. She looked at Imryll, with her hair almost the same color as Eris's and eyes that were only a shade or two lighter. And then she laughed. "My looks?"

Imryll pursed her lips. "Dressed as you are and looking as you do?"

Eris laughed softly. Her looks didn't appeal to any lover. Even Terran wanted only to serve as her gardener. "It was my sister."

Imryll frowned. "What kind of sister bloodies another?"

"Apparently she's not who I thought she was." Eris looked around the hut, trying to come up with some answer to how she'd ended up here. "How did I not die?"

Imryll grunted and stood and walked to the fire. Eris was surprised when she pulled another pot from the fire. It actually burned. How did it not damage the trees? How did the trees allow Imryll to have fire?

Imryll returned and tipped the pot toward her mug, filling it with steaming tea. The aroma smelled less of pine with a hint of sweetness, like that of honey or a sappy syrup. She nodded toward Eris's mug before filling it.

Setting the pot back onto the scrub tree table, Imryll settled herself onto her stool and fixed Eris with a cloudy expression. "You should have died. That you didn't should have told me you are more than a keeper of flowers. I didn't see this," she said, waving at Eris's bloody slip, "until you arrived. Too concerned about the trees." She shook her head. "Always too concerned."

"How did I get here, then?"

Imryll frowned. "The Guardian. He should know better than to interfere."

Eris had the impression she should understand what the woman meant. "What guardian?"

She tilted her head. "You said you were a keeper of trees."

Eris nodded.

Imryll studied her a moment. "You do not know yet, do you?"

Eris let out a frustrated sigh. "Know what?"

"How did you learn you were a keeper?"

Eris took a deep breath, pushing back the frustration rising within her. If she couldn't learn what she needed about being a keeper, her mother would suffer. All of Errasn would suffer. If this woman would teach, Eris might be able to learn enough to save her mother.

She took the mug of tea and sipped. Relaxation washed over her again like a gentle rain. "I had a dream while resting at the heart of the Svanth. After that, I was able to delve the forest."

Imryll nodded. "Only the forest?"

Eris shook her head. "The Verilain Plains. And another garden as well." She thought about how she had commanded the plains and how the flowers of Lira's garden responded to her. So different than the way the trees responded. "How did you know?"

Imryll smiled, the first time she'd done so. Her eyes seemed lighter, lines fading away, making her appear younger as she did. "Trees are hardest. They must choose to let you in. The others are not so permanent. Grasses can run deep, but not so deep as the trees. And flowers? Bah, flowers are shallow. They will let anyone reach through them."

Anyone? Was that how Jasi and Desia managed to learn the message in the flowers, or did she mean anyone could learn to be a keeper like Lira? "I didn't know."

Imryll sniffed. "But you know of keepers. How is that?"

"A keeper recognized my ability," she began.

Imryll frowned. "A keeper of flowers would not recognize a keeper of trees."

Eris shrugged. Lira made it clear she recognized her ability. That was the reason she'd come to Eliara. "I don't know about that."

"How did she identify you?"

Imryll had leaned forward, resting her elbows on the scrub tree table. The bark seemed to smooth for her, giving her a gentle place to rest. Eris marveled at the level of control this woman had over the trees, control she had never even imagined. Did it extend elsewhere, or did she only have such ability here, in the heart of her forest?

There was just so much she didn't know.

"She had me select a flower—"

"Select?" Imryll interrupted. "You do not *select* a flower. If you bond to a flower, it chooses you."

Eris remembered searching for the flower. She'd spent *months* looking, each day seemingly wasted wandering the garden for the flower. Only, it hadn't been wasted. That time had taught her more than she realized about the flowers throughout the garden. When she finally did select the teary star, she had been ready for what came next, even if she didn't really know it at the time.

"Maybe it's different for keepers of flowers," Eris suggested.

Imryll frowned but said nothing.

"This keeper instructed me to search for a flower, letting me bring it to her when I chose one I thought I was mine...that I could bond to." She understood the bond Imryll mentioned, though hadn't referred to it that way in the past. Once she'd discovered the teary star, she'd mimicked the way Lira inspected the flower, going so far as to taste it. When she'd done that, she'd felt...something. Had that been the bonding?

"And you claim a bond to a teary star?"

Eris nodded.

"How is it you had such a flower? It is my understanding they aren't in bloom for another year, unless you mean you found one six years ago."

Eris had never really considered how Lira had the teary star blooming. They did bloom only every seven years and the flowers at the heart of the Svanth weren't quite ready to bloom. She felt them—the energy simmering under the surface, waiting for its time—but had not seen another flower except in her dreams.

"I don't know how it bloomed in that garden. Maybe she'd influenced it somehow..."

"A garden? You found a teary star outside of the Svanth?"

Eris nodded.

"They do not survive. No gardener has ever understood why, but teary stars cannot survive outside the Svanth."

"They brought soil from the forest," Eris offered.

"That isn't enough. It has never been enough. You think your gardener was the first to attempt such a transfer? Others have even carted in rainwater along with the soil. None have managed to grow a teary star outside the Svanth." She leaned forward, a puzzled expression on her face. "Are you certain it was a teary star?"

Eris sniffed. What she'd learned from the forest had been clear. She had no doubt about her flower. Of all that she'd learned, that was the one part she'd never questioned.

But after seeing the control Imryll exerted, maybe she should have. Shouldn't she know more about her flower, especially if she'd bonded with it?

"I would prove it to you if I could," Eris said.

Imryll's frown slowly peeled away, replaced by lips pursed in a shadowed smile. "Proof? There is little you could do to prove it, short of..." She trailed off and blinked. "Yes. Proof might be necessary. I think..."

She hopped to her feet and hurried from the hut.

Eris sat watching after her, waiting for her to return. When she didn't, she finally got to her feet and followed after, wondering what kind of proof this keeper would need.

Without returning to the Svanth, there wasn't anything Eris could do to prove what she knew of the teary star.

# CHAPTER 15

*J*mryll crouched outside the hut near the spindly svanth tree. Not as towering or impressive as the trees found in the forest, the tree shared little more than a passing resemblance. Had Eris not had the visions of the earliest svanth trees growing the forest, she might not know what it was.

"How do you have a svanth tree?" she asked as she approached.

She knelt over the ground, her hands cupped and her eyes flickering. With the question, she glanced over her shoulder at Eris. "You recognize it. Perhaps you speak the truth. Hmm. We will know soon enough, I think."

Imryll remained where she was as Eris touched the top of the soil with her foot, delving lightly. A soft growl echoed behind her. The wolf. She made a point of ignoring it, focusing on what the forest would share.

She didn't delve deeply into the forest. Doing so would only push her against the barrier the woman had constructed over the deepest roots. Instead, she focused on the shallow roots of the grasses. Life blossomed around her, constrained somewhat, enough that she couldn't command great power, but she recognized what the woman was doing.

And gasped.

"You have seeds."

Imryll looked back at her and nodded. "Proof. You said you could offer proof."

"Like this? What do you expect me to do?"

Imryll blinked. "You said you know how the vines support the trees. That is proof. Demonstrate this."

"And then what?"

"You will have answers."

Answers. This woman—this *keeper*—might teach her. The knowledge she possessed was greater than anything Lira possessed. Possibly even enough to let Eris save her mother. For answers like that, couldn't Eris demonstrate what she knew of the svanth trees?

But *should* she? The secret of the svanth trees—the secret of the teary star vines—might not be hers to share. Svanth trees grew only in the heart of the forest and nowhere else. There had to be a reason. Would Eris be sharing knowledge she should not?

She watched Imryll. A finger of deep green vine peaked up from the soil. It slowly uncoiled, swirling toward the tree.

How did Imryll get the teary star vine to grow so quickly?

So many questions. And there was little doubt Imryll *was* a keeper. Once she would have believed keepers could be trusted, but once she'd believed the priestesses could be trusted.

Yet, if she didn't give Imryll the proof she needed, she would never learn from a keeper of trees.

The vine started up the tree, touching the trunk and trailing upward. The trunk was one corner of the house, but not as large or imposing as the pine and elms. The svanth branches dangled more weakly than they should. The tree was nearly as tall as it would ever get alone. Probably taller than it should be, supported by the surrounding trees.

The vine continued to snake its way up the tree. It wouldn't provide any support growing this way, certainly not enough to help pull moisture toward the svanth and let it reach its full potential.

"Not like that."

Without thinking more about what she did—ignoring her concerns about Imryll, this *keeper*—Eris leaned forward and touched the vine. The barbs growing along the stalk pulled away from her as she knew they would. She ran her hand along the vine, demanding its attention. As she did, she *felt* what Imryll did, how she stimulated the teary star vine to stretch out of the soil. Could Eris do the same?

Imryll stepped back, letting Eris interrupt, and watched.

Eris instructed the vine to shift, to twist around the trunk, winding in a particular pattern. Not fully encircling the tree—doing so risked strangulating it—but weaving it up the side of the trunk and around, mirroring the patterns she'd seen growing around the svanth trees of her garden, remembering from her visions how the first keeper had guided the vines. Eris made subtle changes, recognizing a difference to the soil and the air, shifting the way the vine embedded itself along the trunk.

It grew and grew. Eris pulled from the energy of the forest, borrowing from the life around her. The svanth tree gave freely, lending its strength, as if the tree itself recognized what she did for it. Branches no longer drooped, slowly stiffening with moisture and opening gaps in the woman's hut as they did. Leaves filled with water the vine helped pull from the soil, drawing it toward the topmost branches. With more time, the svanth would send deeper roots, drawing even more water and letting the teary star vine grow ever higher. But for now, this was enough.

She sighed, running her hand along the barbs of the vine, the vine *letting* her touch it, pet it as her father petted his hounds. The work left her feeling drained—had she used her own energy in the growing of the vine?—but otherwise satisfied. A piece of familiarity returned.

Eris stepped back and looked up. Already the svanth tree reached higher. With enough time, it would take over this part of the forest, stretching higher than the other trees, rising like a tower in this forest. Standing where she was, hand atop the vine, Eris sensed the soil would welcome other svanth trees, but doing so would change the composition of this forest, altering it in such a way that this woman would no longer be able to serve as its keeper.

"That was dangerous what you did," Imryll breathed. "But impressive. Even unskilled as you are, you manage great power." The remark sounded nothing like an insult, merely an observation.

"Dangerous?"

Imryll nodded. "You draw too much, pull from yourself as you do. The trees have much to lend. You can use it instead."

Eris had sensed the svanth tree lending its strength as she'd gone. She hadn't meant to draw on herself. She didn't even know how to do that. "I don't know how."

Imryll sniffed and nodded. "Keeper of flowers. They cannot teach this. They draw differently than us. It is cooperation with the trees, not a demand. You will see."

"I haven't really been taught anything."

Imryll frowned. "You pull from yourself only? Very dangerous, then."

Eris shook her head. "I think I borrowed from the trees, but I don't know what I'm doing. I returned to Eliara hoping to learn, but I couldn't get her to teach me. I don't know how I ended up here. Only that my sister stabbed me, and then I had visions and ended up in your forest..."

She rambled and trailed off, shaking her head. "There is much I need to know. I would like to help my people. Saffra—the Conclave—attacks. Can you teach me what I need to know to help them?"

Imryll stiffened as Eris mentioned the Conclave and shook her head. "The Conclave," she said the word disdainfully, "cannot harm us here. You are a keeper of the trees, not flowers. You serve the trees, and they serve you. That is how it has been. How it will always be."

"I don't understand."

Imryll nodded. "That is obvious."

"Will you help me to learn?"

Imryll glanced at the forest, cocking her head as if listening. Her brow furrowed, clouding her face like a storm washing over her. Then she nodded. "We can help, but you must help us."

Eris sighed. Did she have the time to work with Imryll? While she was here, her family suffered. Her mother lay dying. How much time did she have remaining? Enough for Eris to learn something—anything—that might help? And her brother fought a losing war against Saffra and the Conclave. And Ferisa...could Ferisa be a traitor? Eris still couldn't believe her sister had stabbed her. More than anything else, that surprised her.

More than whether she had time, did she *trust* Imryll to teach her?

After seeing the way the keeper moved through the forest, the way the trees obeyed her, could she dare not trust her?

If only Terran were here. There wasn't anything he could do, but at least she felt better with him nearby. Without him, she felt... as if she missed a part of herself. She pushed away the sentiment. She didn't know if he shared the same feelings or if he saw her as only his keeper.

"Where is your gardener?" Eris asked.

Imryll stiffened again and blinked strangely. "Gardener? So many years since he's been gone. Too many. Without his aid, I am weakened."

"I'm sorry—"

She shook her head. "No. You didn't know—how could you?—

such things are still hard to think about. The trees are so empty without him."

"He was…more…than your gardener?"

Imryll frowned. "So much to learn."

"I don't understand."

"They are always more than just a gardener. That is how the bond works."

"There is a bond." Did Terran know?

Imryll nodded. "You bond to tree—or flower—and the gardener bonds to you. That is how it has always been."

Eris thought about how Terran was brought from his home, summoned by Lira to work with a keeper—with her—without knowing anything about the keeper. Had he known that was how the bond worked? "Is it the same with a keeper of flowers?"

Imryll shrugged. "Much is different with keepers of flowers. As I said, their roots do not run as deep. They do not live long. Sometimes only a season, though others will bloom each year. But with trees, you much have depth to your connection. They are not just a gardener."

Eris thought of the dream she'd had at the heart of the Svanth, of the way the first keeper had felt about her gardener. Was that what was destined to happen with her and Terran? Did he know? Did he even *want* that?

Did she?

Eris pushed away the thought. She didn't have time to think about what she wanted. She needed to learn what she could from Imryll and use it to help her mother. Maybe even help push the Conclave back from Eliara. Help peace return.

"Where is yours?" Imryll asked.

Eris swallowed. "Terran."

The woman frowned, shaking her head.

"His name. Terran."

The woman blinked and glanced around the trees, one hand touching the teary star vine. Eris noted the barbs didn't recede as they did for her. Did they do that because she'd bonded the flower or was there a different reason?

"Where is this Terran? Did he leave you? A gardener should not do that, you know."

"He didn't leave me. He's probably worried about what happened to me." Especially if he found a pool of blood in her room. How would that be explained?

Then there was Ferisa. Eris needed to know *why* she'd stabbed her.

"Not so worried to reach for you."

Eris didn't even know if he would be able to find her. At least when he'd found her in the Svanth, he'd known, generally, where she was going. Now, he might not have any idea.

She ignored the worry. Trapped as she was within this forest, she finally had an opportunity to learn from a keeper of trees. Eris would take advantage of that opportunity.

"Do you have your proof?" she asked.

Imryll looked back at her, thin eyes narrowing to nearly slits. "I am convinced."

"Then will you teach me?"

In answer, Imryll whistled. The wolf came bounding toward her.

Eris tensed.

The wolf stopped across from the woman and watched Eris with an uncanny intelligence. Its tongue lolled out, and an ear twitched as it looked at her. Eris's heart raced.

Imryll walked over to the wolf and patted his head. She whispered something softly, and a low whine escaped the wolf's mouth. Then she stood and turned to Eris.

"We will teach you what we can."

# CHAPTER 16

he moon filtered through the overhead trees more than
Eris was accustomed to seeing. In the Svanth, the thick
canopy prevented any moonlight from reaching the forest floor
and left the forest covered in a cozy darkness. Here, at the heart of
Imryll's forest, where the trees created a small clearing, the moon
sent slivers of pale silver light streaming down the trunks of the
trees. The newly strengthened svanth tree seemed energized by it.
Already it had grown nearly a foot. Eris wondered how much of
that was in response to what she'd done.

She sat along the trunk of the tree, feet pressed into the dirt.
The svanth tree was the only one in the forest that let her delve
deeply into its roots, the barrier preventing her from reaching into
the rest of the forest not present within this svanth.

Eris savored the connection to the tree.

As she delved, she recognized something woven into the roots,
and she traced it.

It took a moment, but she found a story woven there. As she
followed it—the young age of this svanth making it relatively easy
for her to do—she almost gasped.

The story woven into the roots was about her.

Eris delved carefully, wondering how such a thing was possible. She had only touched the teary star, had only coaxed it rather than the tree itself, as the vine grew alongside the tree. That shouldn't have influenced the roots of the tree. But it had. More than that, the roots of the svanth mingled tightly with tendrils reaching down from the teary star vine. They twisted together, becoming one.

Farther from the tree, she felt around the barrier formed by the elm and pine and birch. In time, she suspected the svanth would mingle its roots with those others. Did that mean she would eventually be able to access the power stored within this forest? Would what she'd done destroy this forest or strengthen it?

The keeper stood on the far side of the clearing, her back turned to Eris. A deep green cloak covered her, similar to the one she'd given Eris to ward off the growing chill of the night. Eris hadn't seen any sign of the wolf since the woman agreed to teach.

Really, Imryll hadn't said much else since then. She'd offered Eris a collection of berries and edible stalks, which she'd gladly accepted, and left her alone as night drew long. Eris wondered when the lessons would start. How long could she spare?

Thoughts of Terran back in Eliara, likely worried about where she'd gone, troubled her. Would he think she'd run off without him, or did the connection—the bond— Imryll claimed formed between keeper and gardener let him know she was well?

Eris reached through the shallow plants of the forest, touching on the grasses and shrubs, pushing through those roots. She didn't know if she could press all the way to Eliara, so instead she tried sending a message, an impulse really, nothing more than a lightning bolt in a storm cloud, speeding along the roots as they raced south. Even if Terran didn't understand, perhaps Lira would.

"You are noisy."

Eris looked up. Imryll stood above her, the hood of the cloak pushed down around her shoulders, and her hair pulled back. In the light of the moon, her eyes seemed to glow.

"Noisy?"

Imryll nodded. "I heard the message you sent. I think all keepers would hear it, even those of flowers." She said the last with a sense of derision.

Eris frowned. "That was sort of my intent. I wanted Terran to know where I was." She shook her head. "I'm not even sure it will reach him."

Imryll laughed. "With as much strength as you fed it? Likely it reaches the ocean!" She took another step toward Eris and knelt next to her. "You think your gardener will understand the message? Even as noisy as you were, such things aren't the realm of gardeners. At least, they weren't in my day."

Eris shook her head. "I don't know if he'll recognize it or not, but after what happened to me, I needed to send something so he didn't worry about me."

"I thought you said you knew nothing about the bond."

"I don't. It's just…"

A knowing look came across Imryll's face.

Eris pushed away the thought and stood, wiping her hands across the cloak as she did. "You still haven't asked my name."

Imryll glanced at Eris. "I haven't the need."

"I'm Eris," she said, sticking out her hand.

Imryll ignored the gesture and laughed. "Does it matter what we call ourselves? All that matters is how the trees respond. They know me as keeper."

"I'm not a tree."

Imryll's laughed trailed off. "No. Perhaps that is your problem."

"Problem?"

She nodded. "You seek instruction, but you do not think like a keeper of trees."

Eris frowned. "How am I supposed to think?"

Imryll snorted. "You are to discover that on your own."

She stood and turned toward her hut and nodded. With the svanth tree now growing sturdier, the hut seemed to have grown larger than it had been earlier in the day. And then Imryll disappeared inside, leaving Eris wondering if Imryll would be like Lira —another keeper who wouldn't teach.

They sat again at the table. The hearth crackled behind them, giving light and a strange warmth. Eris still didn't fully understand how it was possible without injuring the trees. Had she known how to manage a fire, the cool nights she'd spent in the forest would have passed with more comfort.

"How do you make the fire?" she asked.

The woman glanced at her. In answer, power surged through the trees, as if the forest itself pushed back the effect of the flames.

Could she do the same? Would the trees answer her, or would they ignore as they always had before?

As Eris looked around the hut, she marveled at the way the trees wove together. Branches from high overhead bent toward them, creating a cozy roof and trapping the warmth from the hearth. Small windows crafted out of curved branches opened along each wall. The hut was another trick Eris wished she had learned. With something like this, she would have been able to stay out of the rain, though the high canopy of the svanth trees kept them mostly dry.

Imryll sat across from her, another mug of tea cupped in her hands. She'd slipped her cloak off and hung it along a knobby branch. Eris preferred to keep hers on, pushing back the growing chill of the night. At least Imryll had a long-sleeved blouse made of stout wool and thick breeches to keep her warmth. Other than the cloak, Eris had only the thin slip she wore when Ferisa attacked her.

"You seem troubled."

Eris nodded to Imryll and took a sip of her tea. "I see what you manage, how the forest bends before you, and wish I could manage such control."

Imryll snorted. "I have sensed how you work. You think to force it. You cannot force the trees to bend any more than the wind can force them. You might rustle the leaves or even sway the branches, but more than that?" She shook her head. "None are strong enough to force the trees to bend unless they wish it themselves."

Eris didn't fully understand what Imryll said. Eris already knew she couldn't force the trees to do what she wanted, but that was just the problem. Asking didn't work either. But how did Imryll manage to coax from the trees what she wanted done? What was her secret?

"I don't try to force anything," she said. "But when I ask, most of the time nothing happens either."

Imryll slapped the table with her palm. "Ask? You think asking is how you get the trees to listen!" She laughed, the sound throaty and coming out as a cackle. "Trees don't respect you when you ask. They know who's the stoutest, who reaches for the most sunlight. You have to be that one for the trees to listen."

Eris frowned. "You're saying I have to prove to the trees I'm the stoutest?" She had no idea what that even meant. Even less how she would accomplish it.

Imryll nodded. "Only yours is harder than what I have. Pines don't grow nearly so tall as a svanth tree, especially like the ones you're used to seeing."

"How do you do it?"

Imryll shook her head. "I can't explain what it is. A sense the trees must have from the keeper. One of trust and respect. Then they'll work with you as long as you keep their trust."

Had Eris lost their trust?

She didn't think so. More than likely, she'd never had it, not completely. She remembered the summoning she'd gotten from the trees after she'd battled the magi, but it had been the energy stored in the Verilain Plains that let her do that. There was a difference to the power of the plains and that stored in the Svanth. It was the same difference she noted with flowers from Lira's garden.

"Why is it easier to use flowers?" she asked. "I didn't have to gain their trust."

Imryll frowned, her lower lip curling in until she bit it. She leaned forward, hands gripping the wooden edge of the table, and studied Eris. "We're talking about trees, not flowers. A keeper of trees can't use the energy from flowers, at least not well."

Eris shook her head. "I can use the energy stored in the garden near my home. I don't have to prove anything with flowers. They simply do what I want." It was the same with the needlegrass across the Verilain Plains.

Imryll looked troubled. "That shouldn't be. The calling is different. Keeper of flowers, she touches little more than the surface, her work more one of colors and patterns. A keeper of trees, it is something else. We listen to a deeper secret, a *part* of it, rather than controlling it." She shook her head as she studied Eris. Then she let out a breath. "Could it be you're *not* a keeper of trees?" She spoke mostly to herself. "She said she bonded a teary star. A flower not a tree. Different, isn't it? And the other...there is no other bond there, is there?"

Imryll blinked and looked over at Eris. "That is why you struggle with the trees. I should have seen it sooner, but who bonds to a teary star? Such a different flower, but a flower, not a tree." She frowned. "Not many keepers of flowers can walk the roots, but there were some." Imryll nodded, as if decided. "Yes, there were some." She sniffed and pushed away from the table. "To use the flowers, you must *be* a keeper of flowers. There is no other answer. And if that's the case, I can't help you."

Eris shook her head. "But I'm not a keeper of flowers..."

Imryll stood. "You can't argue. You say you can touch the

energy stored in flowers. There have been no keepers of trees capable of using the flowers. A different ability, similar but not the same." She pointed to Eris, waving a hand at her. "Go back to your home and seek out the keeper you say is there. She must be the one to teach you."

"I can't. I don't even know where I am, and I have so much to learn if I want to help my family."

"It's as I say. You need to find your keeper. She must teach you."

Imryll turned and walked away from the hut.

Eris sat unmoving. She'd found another keeper, but even she wasn't willing to work with her.

How then would she learn what she needed?

And had Lira been wrong? Could she be a keeper of flowers just like Lira?

If that was the case, why would Lira hide that from her?

# CHAPTER 17

The trees began to close around her. Imryll let her stay until morning, but hadn't reappeared. Eris woke to sunlight streaming through one of the small windows and the sense of the hut trying to push her out, squeezing her from it. She had stumbled into the light of the clearing, only to find the clearing gone and no sign of the hut. The deep green cloak she now wore, the only sign that Imryll had been real.

As she walked, she began to wonder if Imryll was right. Had she been wrong all this time? Could she really be a keeper of flowers? If so, what did it mean that she'd chosen—bonded, as Imryll said—to a shade flower? The teary star wasn't like any other flower. It bloomed rarely and grew from a thick, woody vine. Even the vine did not do nearly so well without the svanth trees.

But if she were a keeper of trees, wouldn't she have some inkling of that? Imryll seemed to think so. She should have learned how to gain the trees trust. And other than tracing the roots, what other evidence did she have that the trees even listened to her? She'd never really even used the energy of the Svanth again.

More than anything, that likely meant Eris was not a keeper of trees. She might be a keeper of flowers—a keeper like Lira—but the Svanth was not hers.

And if she wasn't a keeper of trees, then she had no garden.

Without a garden, she had no way of helping her mother and no way of keeping Saffra from pressing forward.

The thought left her with a hollow feeling. How could she have been so wrong?

Why hadn't Lira told her?

Why hadn't the trees?

But maybe they had. Maybe that was why she could do little more than touch the energy stored within them.

She stopped at a narrow stream. The water burbling alongside reminded her of a stream running through the Svanth. Eris still felt the pressure of the forest around her, the sense that it wanted her gone. All but the svanth tree—or rather, the teary star vine—she'd coaxed. If she stopped long enough and took the time, she could delve through the shallow roots of the forest and sense the svanth growing, gaining strength as it drew from the teary star climbing up its trunk.

And Eris thought she'd helped the svanth. Maybe all she'd done was help the teary star.

After taking a long drink, she stood and continued moving. She had no way of knowing whether she traveled in the right direction. The forest pushed her, sweeping her slowly forward. Unlike when she walked through the Svanth Forest, she moved slowly, pulled down by roots and brush that never plagued her when in her forest.

She snorted at the thought. The Svanth wasn't her forest. It never had been.

She wished Terran were with her. Even if he didn't know what to do, she missed his company.

Eris had never minded being different. She'd known she wasn't like her sisters, but it had never bothered her. And then when she learned she was a keeper, she *liked* how she was different. But now—with no keeper willing to teach her—being different hurt.

Eris *wanted* to become a keeper. She wanted to tap the energy stored within the plants, to learn what she could from the stories woven into the roots. But it seemed there was no one able or willing to teach her. Somehow she would have to do it on her own.

Eris reached the edge of the forest. As the day progressed, it seemed the trees ushered her away with increasing speed. When she finally left the edge of the forest, a sigh escaped, like a breath of wind, behind her.

Rolling hills stretched out around her. She had no idea where she was. Someplace in the north, if the pines in the forest were any indication, but where?

And could she return home?

Her mother was dying—possibly had already died—and Errasn was under attack by the magi. Eris could borrow power stored in the garden in Eliara, but that would only serve to weaken Lira, a keeper who knew how to wield the power she could access. Nothing Eris did would help.

She sat, pulling her knees to her chest as she stared at the falling sun. Sweeps of orange and red spread across the sky, the colors less like ulsens and celias than simple sprays of color. A hint of a pattern stretched across the sky, but Eris didn't care enough to try and understand it. After everything she'd been through, now she learned she wasn't who she thought?

Or maybe, she'd been what others thought all along. Different.

Eris watched as the sun sunk toward the horizon. The air cooled, and she was thankful for the cloak Imryll had given her. Eris hadn't offered to return it after learning she wasn't a keeper of trees; Imryll had been most interested in seeing her away from the forest.

She should return to Eliara. Not to find Lira—she'd already shown she had no interest in teaching—but for Terran. He should know Eris was a keeper of flowers. Maybe then Master Nels would have something to teach, some way of helping Terran with his responsibility.

Only, a part of her didn't want to return. Doing so meant admitting failure after finally thinking she'd succeeded.

Instead, she would sit and watch the sun fall from the sky, marvel at the way the colors filled the horizon, and in spite of what Ferisa had done to her, pray the Sacred Mother would help her find peace. Whatever that might be.

More than anything, the ground woke Eris.

She rolled over and saw the moon glowing brightly against the sky, hanging full and yellow as it hovered above the highest hill. Eris stretched and let out her breath. The air carried a heavy chill, and she suppressed a shiver.

How had she fallen asleep?

The rest left her feeling better and helped clear away some of the doubts that had started tainting her thoughts. She might not be the keeper she'd thought, but she was still a keeper. When she managed to return to Eliara, she would force Lira to teach her.

Somehow.

First, she had to determine which way to go.

Eris slipped off her thin slippers and touched her feet to the ground, dreading the chill she knew would come. Dry grasses crunched beneath her feet and pressed uncomfortably against her. Sucking in a deep breath, she delved into the roots.

The connection felt tenuous at first. The grasses were nearly dormant, and she struggled to gain anything meaningful from them, but all she needed was the connection.

Pressing out with the connection, she felt the forest behind her.

It rebuffed her attempt to follow the roots, the barrier formed by Imryll stout enough she couldn't follow it. There came a glimmer of something more before it faded as well. Could that be the svanth tree?

She pushed outward, following the shallow roots of the nearly dormant grassy plain, stretching for something familiar. Copses of trees dotted the landscape. Wild flowers, some with massive fields like those she'd seen in visions, covered hills.

Finally, she came to the familiar presence of the Svanth. Eris swallowed as she did but didn't break the connection. The forest seemed to welcome her, though she wasn't a keeper of the forest as she'd thought. Instead, she must be a keeper of flowers, like Lira. Perhaps that was the only reason the forest welcomed her.

At least now she knew the direction she needed to travel.

She picked up her shoes and started south, not breaking the connection. As she walked, her bare feet crunching against the dry grass, she continued to press outward, reaching Eliara and Lira's garden and pushing further, reaching toward the border with Saffra...

She stumbled and broke the connection.

The border failed.

Eris recognized it as a change in the life as she pushed outward, a flash of a vision.

Grasses and flowers burned as the magi pushed north into Errasn, reaching the Loess River. But even that border began to fail. The fringes were singed. And beyond the fringes there was nothing. No sense of life. Nothing. Simply desolation.

What had changed?

Something must have changed, else why would the border fail? The only answer Eris had was Lira. But if Lira failed, what did that mean for Eris' mother?

Eris ran, afraid to consider what would happen were Lira to fall. More than her mother dying, the magi would continue to press north, twisting the land with their destructive magic. Eris

144

felt the effect even here. Once they reached Eliara, how much longer before they reached the Svanth?

And then beyond the Svanth, into Imryll's forest.

She considered turning back, going to Imryll with what she sensed, but Imryll was a keeper of trees. She would know how to follow the roots. She would know what was coming were the magi to succeed. And if she did, it meant she chose to do nothing.

Eris couldn't stand by and do nothing. Even untrained, she had to try. The magi couldn't be allowed to succeed.

Wind whipped past her as she ran, the landscape blurring. She drew energy from somewhere—probably the grasses—but didn't think about what she did or how. In that, it felt much like when she'd first used her ability to battle the Conclave. Then, she'd simply acted, pulling on power because she had the need. At least the needlegrass of the Verilain Plains had responded, even if the forest had hesitated.

The connection through the roots gave her glimpses of what the border with Saffra must look like. Visions of bleak desolation flashed through her mind.

How could Imryll hide and do nothing?

How could Lira have let it happen?

And other keepers? Surely there were others aware of what the magi had done.

But none pressed the magi back. None stood between the magi and desolation.

Anger filled her. Anger that her mother lay dying—that she might have died before Eris could reach her again—and anger that her *sister* had nearly killed her. It didn't matter that she'd somehow survived, Ferisa and the priestess viewed Eris as a threat to eliminate.

She might have to do it on her own, but Eris would learn why.

The night passed in a blur as she ran. Energy pulled from the surrounding grasses and trees buoyed her, filling her with energy so that she nearly glowed. Eris didn't question what or how it happened, simply letting it fill her.

The sun began to rise, spreading like a smear of grey across the distance. The Svanth Forest.

Her forest.

She might not be the keeper of the forest, but the teary star was hers. Whatever else, she knew she'd bonded with the flower. She would learn how to be the keeper needed.

Eris would give Lira no choice. She *would* teach what she needed. And Lira needed to know about Ferisa and the priestesses. More than any other, that was reason enough for her to return.

And then Terran was still in the city. Did he worry about her?

So she had to return to Eliara. This time, she knew the risk to her.

And once she reached Eliara, she would get Lira to teach her enough to push back the magi.

If only she made it in time.

# CHAPTER 18

*A*s soon as she entered the Svanth Forest, Eris knew something was wrong.

Along the northern fringe, the trees spruces and maples grew. The massive svanths only grew toward the center, not along the periphery. She passed between a pair of maple saplings that she sensed had mites crawling all over them, burrowing into the leaves. She shivered.

The air was different. Bitter and almost warm, nothing like the soft earthy scent she had grown accustomed to during her months in the forest. Eris didn't know what had changed, but *something* had.

She paused long enough to send a surge of energy through the trees to push back the mites. When the trees were older, they would naturally resist infection like that, but they were still young and susceptible to rot. It was something she should have done long ago, when she felt the hint of this at the edge of the forest, but she'd been too busy trying to delve the roots and learn what she could from the forest to do anything to help these trees.

With the surge of energy, the trees pushed back the mites.

Energy flowed through them, filling their leaves. The trees seemed to sigh and then stretch.

Eris nodded, pleased with the response. But if she wasn't a keeper of trees, should she even be attempting to heal the them? Did the forest resent the intrusion?

More questions for Lira, if she would ever answer.

Being within the trees, the awareness of everything around her returned, filling her. She knew where the squirrels jumped from branch to branch, carrying nuts and burying them for the coming winter. Birds perched on trees, gently bending the small branches before they took off. A herd of hogs crashed through brush too far from her to hear, though she sensed their location easily. A tree lion prowled over the hogs, waiting and watching.

But the sense of the other creature was missing.

Eris had grown so accustomed to feeling its strange presence prowling the woods that she practically ignored it. As much as it bothered Terran, she recognized from her connection to the forest that it wouldn't harm her so long as she stayed out of its hunting path. Only now she no longer sensed it.

What did it mean that it was gone? Did it have anything to do with the change in the way the forest felt?

She hurried through the forest. She needed to return to Eliara, but before she did, she needed to reach the heart of the forest. If she could delve the roots—at least reach along the path of the teary star vine—maybe she could learn something that might help.

Fatigue washed over her. She'd borrowed from the grasses as she'd made her way south, but now that she reached the forest, she had little energy remaining. And the forest wouldn't lend her any. Eris stumbled through the trees making more noise than usual and scaring away the life that had been nearby. At least the trees didn't work to keep her from the heart.

Eventually, she recognized trees around her, though didn't really need to. The forest granted her enough recognition so that she knew where she was.

When she reached the heart, she collapsed, falling forward with exhaustion.

She lay looking up at the svanth trees, at the teary star vines curling around them, and struggled to keep her eyes open. She needed time to delve into the forest, to learn what she needed. To discover what she was to do. Instead, she drifted to sleep.

---

Eris blinked against the bright light overhead. It took a moment to register that something was off. She had been in the heart of the Svanth, but light never reached the floor there. Now, shafts of sunlight pierced the canopy. A small breeze blew through the upper branches, bending them slightly. Birds chirped deeper in the forest.

She sat up, fearing she'd somehow traveled again.

The trees were familiar svanth trees, but not the ones she expected in the Svanth Forest. These were younger, tall, and still impressive, but not the towering old growth she was accustomed to seeing.

The sense of the forest still filled her.

Eris frowned and looked around. The trees *felt* the same. Only to her eyes did they appear different.

Something moved across the forest, drawing her attention.

Eris turned. A tall man of a muscular build approached. He had a familiar face, rugged and handsome. Black hair was cut close. He wore a thick shirt of green wool and simple black trousers. A long-bladed knife hung at his side. He smiled when he saw her.

"Mistress," he said in greeting.

Eris nodded. "You have returned earlier than expected, Heath."

The words were not her own.

A part of Eris suddenly understood. A vision, much like the one she'd experienced her first night in the forest. She had no control over it then, either.

"And you have been busy. I see new growth around the fringes, and the trees here reach even higher than before."

She sighed. "If only I could grow trees such as these, but that is not my gift."

Heath frowned. "You are the keeper."

She smiled sadly. "But not the *Keeper*. There is a difference, I think."

"I don't understand. Did the trees not call you to serve? Did you not bond to this place?"

Eris nodded. "The bond is there. It grants me awareness, but it is incomplete, I think." She shrugged. "I still haven't learned the secrets of the first keeper."

Heath nodded. "All say she was skilled."

"More skilled than I, I'm afraid."

Heath's eyes widened. "But you are the greatest keeper of our generation!"

"And yet, only a generation. Think of what my life means to the forest. The trees were here when I was born, and they will be here when I am gone. To the trees, I am but one generation of many." She smiled and sighed as she looked around the forest. "I am only here to serve, to offer what I may, and grow my garden as best as I can." She took a step toward the svanth tree and touched the bark. Barbs pierced her hand as they did each time she touched. So different than any other svanth she knew, if only she learned the secret, she might be able to see the saplings along the edge grow. Instead, she planted elms and maples, feeding their life force as they took root, mingling their lives with the life of the forest.

"Many wish you would come out of the forest, Mistress. You could lead the keepers, teach what you have learned—"

She shook her head. "I haven't learned enough yet to share. There are secrets hidden here; I sense that clearly. Only when I learn the secrets of the first keeper will I leave my garden. Until then, there is simply too much to learn."

If only she knew how. The forest granted awareness to her, a great sense of the life surging around her, but nothing more. She had but to close her eyes and she recognized where even the smallest insect crawled along the trunks. And the forest itself—other than the towering svanth trees—listened to her, trusted her with its safety, bending to her willingly. Gaining that trust had taken time, but she'd been diligent in her plantings, careful to help grow the forest. The saplings grew quickly, fed by the strength the rest of the forest lent, and she guided. All but the svanth.

She would learn the secret.

More than that secret, she sensed a deep well of power hidden beneath the trees. That power fed these trees, but she couldn't understand how or for what purpose. The first keeper would have known—that must be the reason she planted here in the first place—and weaved an explanation into the roots, but one she hadn't managed to read.

"Mistress...you know I will do as you instruct."

She smiled. "Heath, you have been everything I hoped for in a gardener."

"Only a gardener?"

He took a step toward her, and she was aware of his scent, the earthiness of the gardeners. Heath slipped his arms around her, and she ached, missing his touch since he'd left her weeks ago. His mouth cupped hers, and she welcomed it, kissing him back with all the strength she possessed.

When he pulled back, she smiled. "Never only a gardener," she whispered.

Heath touched her hair, smoothing it back, as he laid her onto the ground.

Eris shifted, uncomfortable in the dream, and then slipped back into sleep.

The trees were taller. Not as tall as they would become, but impressive nonetheless. She sighed, inhaling the fragrance of the forest, a mixture of the sweet and bitter of the teary star, finally blooming again, as it mingled with the woody odor of the bark and the crispness of fallen leaves. The sun pierced the upper leaves, and light reflected off the surface, twisting toward the forest floor, streaming through motes of dust and hovering insects.

"Mistress."

Heath spoke with a hint of sadness, and she turned.

"Would you come from the forest, Mistress? I cannot continue like this."

She shook her head. "I still haven't learned what I came here to learn."

He sighed and nodded. Silver streaked at his temples, and his eyes wore the years as tension twisting at the corners, leaving weathered lines. Once muscular and hale, he no longer strained against the jacket he wore. His back carried an arch to it, as if he'd been straining against some great weight.

"Will more time change what you can learn?"

"I can sense it, Heath. It is there...almost as if I can touch it. I can't go before I know."

"The others need you. With the war to the south..."

She shook her head. "The others have never needed me. And the war is a temporary thing. Nothing they cannot handle."

He took a step toward her, touching her lightly on the arm. His hand was still strong, and her skin tingled beneath his touch. How long had it been since she'd let him touch her like that? How long had it been since she'd devoted every waking moment trying to learn the secrets she knew were hidden in the depths of the forest, the secret to that hidden store of power?

"I need you," he breathed. "I have always needed you."

She tried to turn away, but he wouldn't let her. He pulled her into him, crushing her against his chest, and she rested her head there, breathing in his familiar scent.

"You are the only one who's ever said that," she whispered against him.

He shook his head. "The others need you, too. They need your guidance, your wisdom, and your strength. They know they must prepare, but do not understand why."

"And you think I know why they must prepare?"

He pushed away from her and looked down at her face, his hands gripping her shoulders. "I have seen your face as you reach through the roots. There is something there that bothers you. Why won't you share, let me take some of the burden off you?"

She did turn away then, hiding her face from him as tears streamed from her eyes. How to explain what she'd seen written in the roots like a prophecy? How to tell him that she'd seen the destruction of the keepers? Or that there was nothing she could do?

How to tell him the forest itself might be to blame?

"It is my burden, Heath. I am the keeper."

His hands remained on her shoulders for a moment before falling away. He loomed at her back, as if waiting for her to say more. When she didn't, he started away.

"Will it take another generation for you to realize you need help?" he asked.

She turned. He stood at the edge of the towering svanth trees, keeping a respectful distance from the barbs that tore at his clothes when he went too near. She'd learned to weave carefully around the trees, moving so she didn't bump against them. In time, she hoped to learn to caress the tree as she'd seen in the visions stored in the roots, but that was a lesson she spent little time on, not when there were other more important lessons stored here.

"Perhaps in another generation they will no longer ask," she said.

Heath looked at her, his mouth frozen in a tight expression. She saw through it, read the disappointment touching his eyes, and hated what she needed to do. If only he understood. If only he could see what she saw, then he might understand why she stayed here. The story would come to her in time. Now more than ever she felt certain of that.

His head bowed slightly. "Is there time for that?"

She sighed. Heath understood the stakes and pressured her anyway. "It's there, Heath. The answer is there. I only have to reach for it..."

He turned away and left her standing alone in the forest.

Eris shifted again, rising out of her sleep momentarily before drifting deeply again.

The forest hummed around her, a steady rise and fall, the chorus of insects chirping and birds singing mixing into the steady sounds of the forest. Trees rose overhead. For a moment, the shadows felt wrong, but then she remembered she'd moved away from the heart of the forest years ago. The svanth trees were not hers to grow; she understood that now. Any of the others would grow, nurtured by her touch, but not the svanth. They strained against her until she finally had to concede she was not meant to be their keeper.

What did that mean for her otherwise?

She still had not learned what she'd come to learn. The forest held secrets, some so complex she couldn't imagine anyone ever knowing what the first keeper had known, the way she had fore-told the future, predicting even her presence. When she'd seen that, she knew to move away from the heart. The trees had toler-ated her, but she did not belong, not like the first keeper.

And she would not be the last. She had known for years her time was growing short. Heath stopped visiting until even he passed, now buried outside the forest. Without him, she'd lost touch with the other keepers, but they did not need her, not really. What did she know about flowers and arrangements? She under-stood the way the sun draped over the trees, the tallest straining for more light. She understood how the rains dripped through the leaves, coating the forest with blankets of moisture. She under-stood the relentless march of seasons, spring growth turning to the steadiness of summer and on to fall with all its bright colors. Even the quibbles of man were nothing against the pressures of time.

How many seasons had she been here now?

Too many to count.

How many without Heath? Without his steadying touch and words of wisdom?

She sighed, her breath coming out in a shudder. She might not survive this fall, but perhaps that was for the best. The forest demanded a new keeper, youth and strength that could push the boundaries in ways she could not. Perhaps the new keeper would better understand the stories held within the roots. Perhaps the new keeper would be able to change the future she finally glimpsed in the roots.

She paused, looking at a tiny shoot straining from the soil and glanced up. The light coming through overhead had been just enough for the sapling to take root. Any other place, and it would have failed. She smiled. Seeing such growth—such *life*—gave her hope.

Had only Heath managed to live long enough, he might have seen this, too.

Near the edge of the forest, a hint of disease crept toward the trees. With a surge of energy, she healed the trees. The forest sighed in response. She might not have mastered the svanth trees, but she still served the forest. Another keeper would come, greater than she, but not for many years. Until then, she would serve as best as she could.

The svanth trees didn't need her anyway. Tapped into some greater strength, they pushed out with an energy she didn't fully understand. And after all the years she'd lived beneath the trees, she no longer needed to understand. That wasn't her role.

Her role was as a place mark. A keeper to tend this garden until the next keeper would come. One who would understand the deeper secrets hidden deep beneath the earth. A keeper who might be able to halt the darkness she glimpsed along the roots.

And, after all this time, perhaps that was all the answer she needed.

She sighed and turned back toward the heart of the forest, away from the edges, missing Heath as she did so many days since his passing. Soon enough they would be joined together again. Until then, she would serve as the forest needed.

She paused at another tree and diverted a flow of energy through it, strengthening it, pushing out the blight pressing up through the roots. This was her struggle. Without her, blight and disease might take over the forest, destroying the work of the first keeper.

The trees sighed again in response, pleased with her work.

She nodded and moved on.

# CHAPTER 19

*E*ris awoke slowly, blinking against the tendrils of light shimmering through the leaves overhead. She stared at the trees, wondering if this was another dream—a vision like the others—before realizing that it was not. Cold air pressed against her skin. She pulled the green cloak borrowed from Imryll tight around her, but it was not enough. If only she had as much control as Imryll, she might be able to have the warmth of a fire as company.

Tucking her knees beneath her, she sat motionless. The forest moved around her, a gentle current of life. She didn't have to close her eyes to understand, simply breathed it in, savoring the taste damp earth and leaves, and listened to the steady susurrus of insects in the trees.

Another vision. This had been much like the other, but different as well. The first vision she had seen the creation of the Svanth Forest, had *lived* it as the first keeper planted the trees, guided the roots into patterns, weaving the story of the forest and the keepers into the deepest depths of the earth and watched as it grew to become something more than what she'd ever intended.

This...this had been another keeper, but one with less skill. She could read the story hidden in the roots and recognized there was something more she needed to know, but had not discovered anything more. A keeper of the forest, but not *the* Keeper.

A keeper uncertain of her role at first, but who had learned it over time.

Perhaps Eris had this vision for a reason. Had the forest gifted it to her to teach her that she could still serve much as that keeper had? She didn't need to possess the same skill as the first keeper to serve the needs of the forest. Maybe bonding to the teary star flower would allow her to still serve the forest.

Or could there have been a different reason for the forest to grant her the vision?

That keeper sensed a deep power beneath the forest, and Eris remembered the first keeper making some comment, though she couldn't remember now what she'd said. But could that power be the reason she'd been granted the visions?

And then there was the way the keeper had obsessed over the secrets hidden within the roots, the same way Eris had obsessed over what she could learn from the forest. Terran shared many of the same fears Heath had described.

More than that, she'd felt peace as that keeper. Peace that came from accepting what she could do, the help she could offer the trees as she worked to keep them healthy.

More than anything that made Eris feel the fool. She wasn't a keeper to attack the magi. She was a keeper to help and heal. Even if the forest wasn't her garden, the teary star *was* her flower. She would do what she needed to protect it.

She sighed and pushed to her feet. And though there *were* secrets the first keeper knew, secrets she'd somehow woven into the growth of the forest, maybe Eris wasn't the person to understand.

Turning to the nearest svanth tree, she ran her hand across the surface. The barbs worked along the teary star vine twisted away, turning so as not to pierce her skin. They hadn't done the same for the other keeper, but she had been a keeper of trees whereas Eris was a keeper of flowers. And the teary star *was* her flower.

A small shoot worked off the vine as it twisted along the branch. Eris coaxed it a bit until it reached the right length for a clipping. Working carefully, she separated the small shoot and stuffed it into the pocket of her cloak. Seeds from the svanth littered the floor of the forest around their base, hard and thick, and nearly impossible to crack. Some meat could be found within, but not enough to make the work of opening them worth it. She took a dozen and placed them into her pocket as well.

She stepped out of her slippers and touched the ground with bare feet. The earth was cool and reminded her of the coming autumn. Leaves would change in the trees. Eris had never lived near the Svanth during fall but had seen the changing colors often enough in her visions that she knew what to expect. Svanth trees would turn a brilliant shade of red, blazing through the forest. Maples scattered throughout would add their own touch of auburn and red. Elms and birch would add swirls of yellow, striping through the forest. The way they were positioned would create a swooping pattern...

Eris stumbled.

How had she missed that before?

But she'd never lived here during fall; of course she would miss it. The colors couldn't be accidental, not the way they focused, swirling inward in much the same pattern as Lira created at the heart of her garden, focusing the energy so that it pierced the heart. Was that the hidden message the keeper had missed—the source of power she glimpsed? Could that power be nothing more than a pattern to the trees?

She delved, tracing along the roots. As she did, she felt one of the trees near the heart—a tall, broad oak with massive branches spreading around it—afflicted with the same rot she'd sensed along the outer edge of the forest.

If it spread, the svanth trees could be affected. Her teary stars would fail.

Though she might not be the keeper here, she had the sudden urge to protect the vines.

Eris sighed out, reaching for a connection to the teary star. It was tenuous, as if even her flower didn't want to respond to her command. She focused on the rotting tree, the sense of danger to the rest of the forest, and drew on the energy.

It came to her fitfully at first, but then flowed easily.

Eris pressed it into the oak, filling it with the energy she drew, washing over it like a heavy rain. The rot receded, almost as if it were something she could touch if she only knew how, pressed away by the energy she drew until it disappeared from the tree.

Once satisfied the oak was restored, Eris held onto the tendril of energy she drew from the teary star and delved.

This time, she focused outward. Always before, she had listened at the heart of the forest, delving through the svanth trees. The lessons were there, beckoning her, demanding she come and learn more, calling as they had after she'd defeated the magi so long ago. It was this sense that drew her attention, always pulling her deeper, always tantalizing her with hints of what she might learn but never did.

Eris ignored it.

Pushing out, she reached past the heart of the forest. Other trees lived there, not only svanth trees. There, she traced along the roots of massive elms and birch and oaks, each giving a different flavor to the forest. Now that she recognized the pattern, she saw it develop within her mind, flowering out from the center of the forest like petals. Eris trailed along each, recognizing how the different trees created a distinct trail. In her mind, she could almost recognize the pattern. There was a familiarity to it that she knew she should be able to recognize, but could not. With more time, she thought she could identify it...

And then what? She was not the keeper of the forest. Lira had been mistaken in that. The teary star was a flower, not a tree. Her bond to it meant she was destined to be a keeper of flowers, much like Lira.

At the edge of the forest, she felt Lira's garden. It filled the spaces between trees, a mixture of vipeslars and loras and sick-lethorns, dozens of other shade flowers, all growing in another pattern. The garden focused the energy it drew, storing it. Lira could draw upon it from Eliara, use its power to augment what she grew in the city.

But something about the garden felt off. The pattern faltered. Eris could not say what she sensed—did the forest attempt to reclaim the borrowed land?—but she suspected that in time, the focus Lira worked into the flowers—the pattern itself—would fail. And then Lira would be left with only the palace garden.

What did that mean for her mother?

Eris sighed and pushed out with her senses.

Several moments passed as she struggled to understand what she felt, and then she realized what seemed different. The forest creature had returned. She sensed it distantly, near the northern border, prowling around the edge.

If it had returned, then it was time for her to leave.

Eris released her connection to the trees, hating to do so as she did. She might be a keeper of flowers, but that didn't mean she didn't feel a connection to the trees. They had protected her when the magi tried to harm her and her sister. They had saved Terran when she could not. How could she resent them?

But she was not their keeper.

It ached to admit that to herself.

Eris started through the woods. It was time for her to return to Eliara and learn what she could from Lira. And if there was time, perhaps she could help her mother.

When she reached the edge of the forest, she paused. The air tingled as she passed, leaving her feeling exposed once again. There was a certain comfort being beneath the heavy canopy that she couldn't put words to, but the creature trailed through the forest and neared the heart. Eris was happy to leave it behind.

An overcast sky greeted her. Thick clouds threatening rain moved from the north, riding on the heavy, gusty wind. Eris pulled her cloak tighter around her, inhaling deeply before leaving the comfort of the forest for good.

Near her, the Verilain Plains stretched to the south. Eris started through, not fearing the needlegrass as she once would have. The long grasses pulled away from her, bending as if she spoke to them, kneeling as she moved. Eris moved carefully but quickly. Much of the damage done by the magi had regrown, but there was a bare patch near the center of the plains.

She had seen it when she and Terran made their way to Eliara before but hadn't put much thought to it. This time, she paused. The ground was singed all around her, creating a rim where the grasses refused to grow. The air held the remnant of char, as if what the magi had burned months ago still held.

And, considering what she sensed at the border with Saffra, maybe it did.

Eris touched the earth and delved.

Immediately, she wished she had not. The ground was dark and lifeless, nothing like the rest of the plains around her. There was a void where the grasses once had grown—where they should be growing now. She understood why the grasses refused to regrow. Was this what the magi did elsewhere? Was this the desolation along the border between Errasn and Saffra, the reason it felt *wrong*?

Eris stepped away from the center of the burned area. The sense of the needlegrass returned. She sent an encouragement for the grasses to move toward the center, feeling a need for life to return where the magi had decimated it. But the grasses would not, as if afraid to cross a border. Worse, it seemed as if the grasses began to pull away from the clearing, receding from the effects of the magi. Already it seemed much larger than it had when she and Terran crossed through the first time.

The grasses were not hardy enough.

How much longer before this clearing doubled? Tripled? Given enough time, Eris wondered if the grasses would pull away altogether.

As a keeper, she couldn't let that happen.

Out of curiosity, she took one of the svanth seeds and brought it to the center of the clearing before thinking otherwise. Eris hurried to the edge of the clearing and grabbed a few handfuls of dirt, piling them atop the seed. She took the small cutting of the teary star as well and held it in her hand.

Bracing herself, she delved into the grasses. The awareness of the grasses filled her. Eris swayed with them, filling her senses with the power this garden possessed. She followed her awareness of the grasses all the way from the Svanth Forest to Eliara. Then she summoned the energy stored within the plains.

She did not do so as a request.

The energy responded, filling Eris.

Carefully—tentatively—she pushed that energy out into the svanth seed.

Eris had no idea whether it would work. She'd never attempted anything like it, and she didn't know if being a keeper of flowers would allow her to exert any influence over the trees, but she'd done *something* in Imryll's forest. The teary star had grown at her command; the svanth tree had seemed strengthened by what she'd done. If Eris could only manage to coax it to bloom...

And then she felt it.

The seed cracked. Life rippled out from it, fed by the energy of the Verilain Plains that she commanded. Eris forced more and more of this energy into the fledgling svanth, feeding it with raw energy. As it poked from the ground, she set the teary star cutting alongside, splitting the power so that it fed them both.

At first, they were separate. The svanth grew, rising slowly from the ground until it reached her waist. The teary star worked downward, sending its roots deep into the earth. And then, the roots of the teary star touched those of the svanth, and the vine began twisting toward the sapling.

The energy she fed them merged, joining back together, as if vine and tree were one. It grew more slowly, rising to her chest. The teary star vine wove around the trunk, and Eris guided it, using a sense of the tree's needs as she did so. Leaves bloomed from branches, unfurling like a cat stretching after a long nap.

The energy she pulled from the plains began to wane. Before it did, she sent a command to the teary star, asking it to swirl its roots around the clearing and wall it off. There was a twinge of response, and Eris was startled to realize both the svanth and the teary star vine answered her request.

Then Eris sank to her knees.

The tree was not large, but given enough time, it should grow into something more impressive. She had given it a start, and hopefully, that would be enough.

Through her connection to the plains, she had a sense of appreciation over what she'd done. The grasses growing nearest the tree grew heartier, as if strengthened by its presence.

Eris knelt for a few moments, gathering herself. Weakness washed over her, and she pulled on the energy from the plains around her, straining for additional strength. When she managed to stand, she walked around the edge of the circle. Something had changed.

The grasses no longer crowded away from the clearing, but it was more than that. Life hadn't returned to the area the magi destroyed, but from the way the roots of the teary star and the svanth tree worked around the edges, there seemed a chance that life *might* return.

Eris delved the earth at the center of the clearing. The ground was barren and empty, but no longer did she feel the cold and harsh sense when she'd first delved.

She ran her hand along the trunk of the tree. The teary star vine twisted, writhing like an animal wishing to be petted, the smallish barbs of the thin vine bending away from her. Eris breathed a little more energy into the vine, and a shoot curled off. She pinched it off and stuck it into her pocket.

Then she turned and continued through the plains toward Eliara.

# CHAPTER 20

*A*s Eris stepped from the needlegrass, the long blades bent back together, sliding as if she'd never been there. Eris couldn't help but note how different the grasses treated her than the trees. Always before she'd felt it had to do with her knowledge. Now, she understood she wasn't the right keeper, but how did she command the grasses?

Rolling hills spread before her. A copse of trees, a mix of oak and maple, grew nearby. A figure lounged on the ground, watching the plains. It rose when she stepped away from the grasses and then didn't move.

Eris recognized Terran by the shape of his build. She hurried toward him hesitantly. What would he say about her absence? Had he even missed her as she'd missed him?

Without saying a word, Terran took her in a long embrace.

"You didn't leave without me, did you?" he asked.

She shook her head. "I—" she started, but how to explain what happened with her sister when she didn't even understand? "I'm sorry I was gone. I don't really know what happened." That much was the truth. Eris still didn't know how she had gone from the palace in Eliara to the northern forest. Imryll hadn't given her any insight either.

"Where were you?"

She shook her head. So much she wanted to tell him, but where to start? Did she begin by telling him about how she nearly died? Or had he learned? Had he seen blood in her rooms and come searching for her? But if he had, how had he known where to find her?

"North. Learning about my abilities."

His mouth tightened slightly, and disappointment crossed his eyes, but he only nodded. "Did you find what you needed?"

She snorted. "I don't know what I need anymore."

Terran tipped his head, waiting for her to say more. "You return to Eliara?"

"I need Lira to teach what she can about flowers." Eris didn't want to tell Terran that she had been wrong about being a keeper of trees. That the Svanth was not her place. How would he react?

"About her..."

"What?"

He rubbed the back of his neck and met her eyes. "Lira held together as long as she could, but Eris..."

She pushed away from him, dreading what he would say next.

"It's your mother. Something's different. Lira doesn't know what it is, but the disease is spreading beyond what she can manage. And there's more."

She didn't need him to tell her what else happened. She felt it, the same way she could trace the roots of the trees or grasses. It felt so much like what the magi had done to the ground in the Verilain Plains, only on a larger scale. Saffra pushed forward. As it did, Errasn died.

"The magi."

Terran nodded.

"Can she do anything?"

"She says she's not strong enough." He watched her, a frown furrowing his brow. "Something changed for you."

Eris inhaled deeply, uncertain how to answer him. He'd been there from the beginning, supporting her, and deserved the truth, only she wasn't certain what the truth really was.

"I…" She didn't know how to finish.

Terran pulled her against him. "What happened to you? When I came looking for you, I found nothing. Your room was empty, as if scrubbed clean. Where did you go?" His voice held the accusation he'd withheld from it, the disappointment and anger and relief.

"It was Ferisa," she started.

Terran waited, watching her.

"She attacked me. Stabbed me," she said, pointing to her stomach. "I should be dead." She still didn't understand why she wasn't.

Terran's eyes widened, and his jaw clenched. "Your *sister*? But why?"

"I don't know. She's with the priestesses now. And there was something…" She trailed off. What had the priestesses said? In the time before her visions, before she'd been taken to Imryll's forest, she overheard a conversation. The priestesses didn't fear Lira, but they did Eris.

But why?

All she remembered was something about seeing dangerous light around her, but what did that mean?

Terran held onto her, stroking her hair, her back. She leaned against him, appreciating his strength, the earthy scent that was so much his. They stood like that for a moment.

"We don't have to return," he whispered.

She sniffed and smiled up at him. "But I do. I can't simply wait for the Conclave to attack. Not if there's anything I can do."

Terran blinked slowly as he inhaled. Then he nodded. "You were gone a long time." The accusation was gone from his voice. "So much has happened."

She looked up at him. "More than with Lira?"

He nodded. "Princess Ferisa has disappeared. Your father is distraught. Had Jacen not returned to the frontline at the same time..."

Jacen fighting at the border worried her. If she couldn't do anything to slow the Conclave, there wasn't anything Jacen fighting there would do. Saffra might lose soldiers, but the magi were the real threat. Jacen knew that, but he could be so stubborn sometimes, unwilling to see what was right beneath is nose.

Sort of how she had overlooked Ferisa.

And how she hadn't learned what type of keeper she was meant to be.

"When I was gone, I met another keeper. A keeper of trees." Eris swallowed, thinking of how the trees *moved* for Imryll and how they never would for her. Even knowing she could serve as a keeper of flowers didn't make her feel better. After spending as much time as she had in the Svanth, she had a connection to the trees—just not the connection needed for her to serve as their keeper. She swallowed, trying to figure out how to tell Terran what he needed to hear. "I don't think I'm the keeper I thought I was."

He gave her a squeeze. "Keeper? Of course you're the keeper. What else would you be?"

She smiled at him. "I'm a keeper, but I'm not the keeper of the forest. I don't think I'm even a keeper of trees. My bond...my bond is to the teary star. A flower, just like Lira." She swallowed again, thinking of how much time she'd spent trying to learn the secrets of the forest. How much of that time had been wasted, struggling to learn whether she could be the keeper the Svanth needed, but the keeper she never could be. "I wonder if Lira always knew but didn't know how to tell me, you know?"

He shook his head. "Lira wouldn't hide that from you if she knew."

She sighed. "I've been wondering for a while why I can't command the trees the way I can command the grasses and flowers and why the secrets I know are hidden in the Svanth won't reveal themselves to me, but it wasn't until I met the other forest keeper that I really understood. The things she could do...the way the trees *bend* for her...that's something I never had. Now I know why."

Terran smoothed her hair. "But the trees listen to you. I've seen the way they respond to your presence."

Eris shook her head. "I know what I saw."

"How did you find another keeper?"

Eris still didn't fully understand. "Lira said the remaining keepers went north after their gardens were destroyed. After my sister—" She cut off and shook her head. "After Ferisa tried to kill me, I was taken somewhere." She shivered. Even the memory of it felt strange. "I found her in a forest to the north full of pines and elms and oaks."

"And she convinced you that you're not a keeper of trees?"

"She didn't have to convince me. I think I already knew. She simply helped me to see." She pulled her hand away. "You know the teary star is a flower, right?"

"Of course I do."

"Doesn't it make sense that I would be a keeper of flowers? If I was really meant to be a keeper of trees, wouldn't I have bonded to one of the trees? Something like an elm or pine or—"

"But you're bonded to the entire forest! You *are* the keeper of the forest."

She shook her head. "I'm pretty sure I'm not. And maybe it's better that I'm not. This way, Lira can teach me what she knows. Once my mother..." She swallowed, struggling to think about her mother passing. "Once she goes, Lira will need to focus her energy on the Conclave. They've pushed past the border with Errasn, you know."

Terran nodded. "Nels told me. He can...feel it, somehow."

"And you? What did *you* think happened to me?"

"I didn't know. I know how much you wanted to know what

the forest could teach. I know how hard it was to get you to leave, to even *consider* stepping out of the forest. I feared what I might find, but I wasn't going to let you do it alone."

Eris shivered, thinking how much that sounded like what Heath had said to his Mistress. Would she have been on the same path had Terran not convinced her to leave the forest? Would she have spent her days isolated in the forest, trying to learn a deeper secret, neglecting everything else going on around her?

Terran had come for her, determined to stand by her side, even though he disagreed with what he thought she was doing.

Eris pulled him toward her, holding tightly to his hand. Standing on her toes, she leaned forward and kissed him on the mouth.

Terran stiffened and didn't kiss back at first, but then he melted into her, his mouth working over hers, gentle at first but growing hungrier. His arms wrapped around her, pulling her toward him, and she did not fight, enjoying the strength of his hands, in the earthy way he smelled, in the simple fact of his physical presence.

When he pulled his mouth away, there was a pang of loss. They had been close many times, holding each other during the cool nights under the forest canopy, but this was the first time she dared show him more emotion. Had he not kissed her back...

But he had.

What did it mean for them as keeper and gardener now? Would she lose him like so many of the keepers in her vision had lost their gardeners, or could they be different?

Eris smiled at him, and he smiled back.

"Now, I need to speak to my father."

A horrified look crossed his face.

"Don't worry; he knows I'm a keeper." She started forward, pulling Terran along with her.

He resisted at first but then let her drag him forward. "What do you plan on telling him?"

She looked up and smiled at him. "That you're my gardener."

His face didn't change. "Just your gardener?"

She sniffed. "Do I have to show you again?"

"Yes."

They stopped near the copse of trees, and she did.

---

As they neared Eliara, Eris's heart quickened. Terran had said Ferisa was gone, but what of the other priestesses? Who else might be working with them? Even her father hadn't seen the threat under his nose—how Adrick worked against him the entire time he pretended to serve. How many others remained within Eliara who might want to harm her?

How many others knew she was a keeper?

Eris had lived within the palace for years not knowing about Lira. Now she served openly, using the garden to try and heal her mother, but did others know about Eris? About how she was a keeper? But even those who did thought she was a keeper of trees. Now she knew she was not.

Since learning she was a keeper, she had felt different. Part of it was how Lira had let her feel, how Lira had practically *made* her feel, but part of it had to do with how the teary star was her flower.

"What are you thinking?"

She looked over at Terran. They sat along the edge of Uldens Stream, a narrow slip of water that wound through the country-side on the outskirts of Eliara. They could follow the stream all the way to the city, but it would be a meandering route. With her connection through the grasses, Eris didn't really need the stream to guide her any longer.

"The teary star. It's a different flower, isn't it?"

Terran smiled as he cupped his hands into the stream, taking a long drink of water. "It suites you. Rare and unique."

She smiled and twisted her fingers through her dark hair, trying to work through what troubled her. "I keep coming back to why Lira couldn't teach me. At first, I thought it was because I was a keeper of trees—"

"I still believe that's the reason."

Eris shook her head. "If you would see the things Imryll could do, the way the trees *moved* for her, you'd understand. The svanth trees have never so much as twitched for me, let alone bow like these seemed to. No, this is different. Could Lira not want to teach me for a different reason? Is it *because* I bonded to the teary star?"

Terran frowned and plopped onto the ground next to her. "Why would that matter?"

Eris shook her head. She'd been trying to puzzle through it since meeting up with Terran but hadn't come up with an answer that seemed to fit. "Maybe because it's a shade flower?"

He shook his head. "Shade flowers don't matter. Maybe they would to other keepers, but Lira started a shade *garden* after hers was destroyed. I still think you've got it wrong."

"Nice of you to say."

He shrugged. "That's my role as gardener, isn't it? I have to share my thoughts?"

"I thought your role was to do as I said."

She said it jokingly, but Terran's face turned serious.

"What kind of partnership is that? No, we work together. That's how a keeper and a gardener should work."

Eris thought about the pairs she'd seen in her dreams and compared that to what she'd seen between Lira and Nels. They seemed more similar than different, but in each, the keeper was the one leading them. But what Terran suggested *felt* more like what it should be.

"I've seen other gardeners in my visions," she said.

Terran waited, his hand touching her leg.

"They serve their mistress, but they don't always work with her."

Terran nodded. "Too many are like that. I think Nels even views himself that way."

"But you don't."

He shook his head. "That's not what I want out of this."

He stared at her with eyes a deep brown. If she stared long enough, she wondered if she could delve even Terran. Eris swallowed at the thought.

"What do you want out of this?" she asked.

"I will try and support what you decide, but I can't do so blindly. You can't keep thinking you can exclude me from what you plan, especially if your own *sister* attacks you. There are limitations to a keeper's power and things I can do to help you, but I have to know what we're doing. We'll never be as strong as we can be if you do that."

Eris thought of the way the teary star strengthened the svanth tree, but the svanth also strengthened the teary star vine. Together, both climbed higher than either would alone.

She sighed. "You will be my svanth."

His lips curled in an amused smile. "You get to be the vine, choking me as you grow?"

"That's not how they work. If you could only see…"

Terran placed his arms around her, pulling her toward him. "I know how they work. Do you think I wasn't listening?"

She smiled and leaned her head against his chest.

As they sat for a moment, listening to the stream burbling nearby, Eris wished they didn't have to move. If they had more time together, maybe they could grow together, become something as great as the svanth trees at the heart of the forest, vine and tree together, rising toward the sun.

She sighed. As she did, her senses drifted out, slipping across the grasses until brushing against the darkness of the magi, and she knew their time to grow together would have to wait.

---

They neared the city early the next day. They walked swiftly, moving quickly across the rolling hills. Eris stopped them near a wide field of flowers, mostly thulis and camogines turning toward the rising sun. She sniffed the air, enjoying the scent of the flowers. The energy stored within this wild field recharged her, leaving her feeling refreshed after the long walk.

"I've seen this," she whispered.

Terran turned to her. "These flowers? Of course you have. Master Nels has several varieties of thulis, mostly yellow and gold. And the camogines are larger than what he keeps but, otherwise, not much different."

"It's not that." She leaned toward the flowers and placed her face close to a golden thulis, inhaling its sweet fragrance. "There was an arrangement in the palace with flowers from this field."

Terran frowned at her. "You can't know what field flowers came from once they're cut."

She shrugged. "There's a residual energy stored by the flowers that I…" She wasn't certain how to finish. She'd borrowed the energy of the flower and used it to help her see the field. "I saw this field, though I've never been here."

"There's still so much we need to learn about what you can do." Eris smiled.

They made their way through the field, stopping long enough for Eris to clip a handful of flowers that she pulled into an arrangement. She let the flowers guide her, sending a request for the best arrangement to store energy. The flowers guided her as she made her way through the garden.

When she finished, they continued toward Eliara. Each step increased the anxiety working through her until she shook with it. Eris pulled on the energy of the cut flowers to hold back her nervousness.

"What is it?"

She shook her head. "Coming back here, after what happened…"

Terran took her hand, and Eris was thankful for his presence.

"You don't have to do this alone," he said.

She inhaled deeply and nodded.

Something triggered her anxiety, more than simply returning. When they reached the outer wall of the city, she understood what she felt.

Lira's energy had shifted. It no longer focused toward the center of the garden, but instead, now pushed outward and south. Toward Saffra.

But if that was the case, it meant she no longer focused on the queen.

It meant Eris's mother was gone.

# CHAPTER 21

$\mathcal{T}$he palace courtyard was quiet.

Gardeners made their way through the rows of bright flowers, but they wore somber expressions. Eris frowned at each one, trying to make eye contact, but none did.

She took her slippers off as soon as she reached the garden. With each step, she delved, sending a request to the garden for understanding. All she could tell was that her mother still rested in the center, but not whether she lived.

She didn't see Master Nels or Lira. For some reason, that troubled her.

"You can go find Master Nels," she whispered.

Terran shook his head. He held onto her hand, squeezing tightly. "I stay with you."

Had they not been in the garden, Eris would have kissed him deeply again. As it was, she leaned toward him and gave him a soft kiss on the cheek. "Thank you."

They continued toward the heart. As they made their way, Eris began to fear what she would find. Had her mother already died and she'd missed it, spending too long away from the palace, wandering through Imryll's forest and then the Svanth?

Maybe that was what the priestess wanted. Had there been something Eris could have done to help her mother? Was that what they'd seen?

As they neared the circle of elms marking the center, Eris paused. She took a deep breath and borrowed little more than a touch of energy from the flowers around her. Starting forward again, she delved the elms, establishing a connection with each step.

Before she reached the pavilion, she knew her mother still lived, but only barely.

Lira no longer worked to keep her alive. For a moment, Eris wondered why, but then recognized that Lira's shift in focus meant she pressed against the Conclave. How much longer would she be able to keep up? The energy of the garden here wasn't limitless, and though Lira had access to a larger garden growing within the Svanth, she still didn't have enough strength to fight the entirety of the Conclave on her own.

Had Eris really thought *she* could?

They reached the edge of the trees, and Eris stepped inside. The air changed, cooler and hinted with the edge of sickness. It was like a living thing as it crawled through her mother, pulsing through her. Eris could almost touch it and cringed back, afraid to let it too near.

She approached her mother and looked down. The skin around her eyes had sunken more than it had the last time Eris was here, now leaving her mother's eyes looking like twin full moons in an expanse of shadows. Sickly yellow hair hung in clumps about her head. Her mouth lolled open, and a thick, dry tongue pressed against the top. Breaths came out raggedly, wheezing in and out. Her chest barely rose with each. The thick blanket covering her had been thrown back and lay crumpled along the edge of the mattress, revealing how gaunt and wasted she'd become.

"I'm so sorry, Eris," Terran said.

She nodded and swallowed, almost afraid to step too close to her mother. She had been sick before, but the illness had been held at bay, pressed back by the force of Lira's work. Then her mother had managed wakefulness. Now, even that had been taken from her.

She remembered how unusual the illness felt when she'd delved her mother, like it was an unnatural thing. After what the priestess had done to her—what *Ferisa* had done—she wondered if her mother had been poisoned.

Eris had to know.

She released Terran's hand as she walked to her mother. This close, the heat rising off her body was like a furnace. How did she still live through this?

As she reached toward her, Terran grabbed her arm. "Are you certain it's a good idea to touch her?"

Eris nodded. "If this were contagious, I would have already been ill."

She touched her on the shoulder. Bones pressed against Eris's hand, very little flesh actually covering them anymore. Her skin was hot, as Eris expected, but also waxy and practically lifeless. Eris shivered.

Then she delved.

First, she reached toward the grasses beneath her feet, but they didn't store enough energy. She turned to the elms, seeking to borrow from them as well. Once connected, a sense of sorrow worked through the branches. The trees recognized what was happening to her mother. Eris pushed the energy toward her mother and let it wash over her. Again, she felt the connection, the unnatural illness working through her mother's veins. Sickness eroding what she had been. Eris could almost sense the source...

She pushed against it, taking the strength she needed from the trees. The trees gave it to her freely. Eris borrowed more, taking from the garden, the grasses, from the fields surrounding the palace, and used all it all to push against the illness.

For a moment, she thought she might succeed.

Her mother's breathing quickened with a soft gasp, but then it faded.

Eris opened her eyes. Tears fell, running down her cheeks and dripping onto her mother's skin, absorbing quickly there.

If only Eris had more strength. Or even her flower.

But she had a cutting. Would that make a difference?

Without considering whether it was a good idea, Eris moved to the center of the elms and dug a small hole.

"Eris?"

She ignored Terran, burrowing enough dirt to set the small svanth seed deep within. She wanted this to start deep, to establish strong roots. Let the svanth tree rise from the center of the garden. Maybe if the teary star grew here, Eris would be able to summon enough energy to help.

And if not, then the tree would rise as a memory of her mother.

"What are you doing?"

The voice didn't sound like Terran's, but she heard the question distantly and ignored it.

Heaping the dirt back atop the svanth seed, she pulled the energy from the elms and sent it toward the seed. It was the same as she'd done while on the Verilain Plains, but there, she'd used the energy of the plains to feed the seed. This time, she drew from everything. The elms, the garden, the grasses. Even life outside the palace. She pulled as much as she could, sending it through the svanth seed.

The svanth seed exploded from its shell.

The sapling pressed from the soil. As it did, Eris pulled the teary star vine from her pocket. She focused energy through the teary star and the svanth sapling, not splitting it as she had before. She pushed as much energy as she could draw, not caring that she took from Lira and not mindful of how it might take from the elms. The energy came easily, as if freely given.

The svanth rose quickly, drawn out of the ground by the life lent to it. The teary star vine twisted around its trunk, twining its way along. Deep within the earth, the roots of the two plants mingled as they grew and dove deeper. Eris continued to draw energy, feeding herself and the svanth, until the tree rose above her head, and then higher still, first to the peak of the palace and then higher, reaching the same height as the elms.

And then Eris shifted.

She pulled energy from the svanth and the teary star, pressed through the new connection in the roots, toward a distant thrumming of power. She drew on this, not knowing what it was, and funneled this toward her mother.

The energy washed over her, practically spilling from her pores.

Her mother gasped.

In that moment, Eris touched the sickness.

Like the miniscule organisms climbing through the trees along the border of the forest, much like the mites crawling along the leaves, the sickness worked through her mother.

This was not a natural illness.

Oily and dark, it reminded her of what the magi had done on the border with Saffra. Eris could no more leave her mother poisoned this way then she could have left the burned clearing in the Verilain Plains.

Eris pressed the energy she drew against the darkness in her mother.

With that much power, the sickness receded and then faded. For a moment, it fought back, trying to push against her, but Eris drew more, she *demanded* more from the svanth she had planted, and the tree listened and lent her what she needed.

Then the sickness disappeared completely, burned from her mother.

As it did, Eris fell to her knees, collapsing at the base of the massive tree she had planted. She sent one last cleansing surge of energy out, washing over Eliara.

She looked over at Terran. He stood watching, his eyes wide. Next to him were her sisters, Jasi and Desia. They looked from Eris to their mother.

Lira stood behind them.

She shook her head slightly as she watched Eris, lips pursed together in a thin line. Her hair was pulled behind her head in a tight bun, but strands fell loose around her face, as if she'd been caught in the middle of fixing it. She wore a long-sleeved dress of shimmery purple fabric worked with streaks of black through it.

Lira stepped forward. "What have you done?" Her voice came out in a whisper.

Eris blinked and pushed off the trunk of the svanth tree to stand. She kept one hand along the trunk, the barbs pulled back so as not to puncture her skin. A heavy sigh escaped her lips. "I did what I could," she said. "I think it might be enough. You'll have to check and see. Maybe get the healers; I think she'll need nourishment." Even where she stood, Eris could tell her mother still faded like a flower in a drought.

Lira looked over at Eris's mother, her eyes narrowing for a moment as she did. There was a surge of energy, subtle and slight, and then Lira turned her attention back to her.

"She is healed."

Eris nodded.

"But you have spent all the energy of this garden to do it. Now nothing stands between the Conclave and Errasn."

# CHAPTER 22

*E*ris sat on a wooden bench along the edge of the elms. The svanth tree she'd planted and fed rose high overhead, already stretching higher than the elms. Eris wondered if it would overwhelm the other trees or if they would manage to exist together. It hadn't been her intent to crowd out the elms; they had stood for decades, the last remnant of a once peaceful glen of trees that had grown within the palace yard.

How had she managed to grow the svanth so tall? She didn't fully understand what she'd done, remembering only how she'd borrowed the energy around her to feed the svanth. Much like what she'd done in the Verilain Plains. With the tree growing—with the teary star climbing along its trunk—a deep connection bloomed around her, different than she'd felt from Lira's garden.

The garden.

She sighed as she looked around. The flowers nearest her wilted slightly, as if they'd been kept too long in the dark. All around her, the flowers were the same. In time, she suspected they would rebound, surging with renewed energy, but it would take time.

As it was, little energy remained stored in the garden.

Eris turned toward the sun and closed her eyes. Had she made a mistake in healing her mother? When she'd seen her again, languishing without Lira's healing, she'd thought of nothing else than saving her. It was the same as she'd felt while in the forest, the same sense of urgency to cleanse the dying tree of the rot working through it. This time, she wondered if she'd been mistaken.

But how could she have done nothing for her mother?

A hand brushed her shoulder. Eris looked up, expecting to see Terran, but he'd left her to her silence. Through her connection to the garden, she felt him looming nearby, watching her from the shadows.

Jasi looked at her. Desia stood next to her.

"Thank you for what you did for Mother."

Surprisingly, it was Desia who spoke.

Eris shifted where she sat to better see her sisters. "I did what I had to. I didn't mean to put Errasn at risk."

Jasi nodded.

Desia squeezed her shoulder. "Mother will live?"

Eris looked over to where she rested. Lira moved around her, hurrying from one place to another, directing the healers as she did. Their mother hadn't woken yet, but her breathing came easier, steadier, and the waxy quality to her skin had faded.

"She needs to eat. And drink. But she will live."

Desia looked as if she wanted to say something more before she nodded once and turned away, hurrying back to their mother.

Jasi breathed out a sigh and settled onto the bench. For a moment, she simply sat, staring with her eyes fixed straight ahead. Soft sobs came from her, and Eris looked over, touching her sister on her hand.

Jasi looked at her, tears staining her face. Her golden hair flowed around her shoulders and redlined her otherwise blue eyes. She looked much like their mother. "How is it you can do this?"

Eris shook her head. "Do what?"

Jasi nodded toward the tree. "That. I've seen Lira's arrangements, and Mother told me what she could do, but that?" She
turned and fixed Eris with an unreadable expression. "That isn't
anything like what Mother described. Even Lira couldn't do
anything to save her. But here you plant and force a tree to *grow*
and then heal her."

"Not a tree," Eris countered. "Mostly the vine. The teary star is
my flower. That's the one I chose after my months wandering the
garden."

As she said it, Eris realized it wasn't quite right. She *had* forced
the tree to grow, merging the teary star vine with the growing
svanth tree. But if she wasn't a keeper of trees, how had she
managed it?

Jasi took her hand and smiled at her. "Thank you for being
different, Eris."

Eris swallowed back the lump forming in her throat. "Different. Always so different." She said it mostly to herself, but Jasi
squeezed her hand harder, pulling Eris's attention to her.

"Yes, different. And if you hadn't been different, Mother would
have died."

Eris took a deep breath, letting it out slowly. "And now that I've
helped Mother, we're all in danger. I used too much. Now Lira
can't hold off the Conclave."

Jasi chewed her lip as she considered. "Could you?"

"I thought I could." That had been when she thought herself a
keeper of trees, a keeper with a garden to draw from.

"What changed?"

Eris shrugged. "I don't know that anything changed. Well,
maybe my understanding about all this changed."

Jasi laughed until it turned into a cough as she squeezed Eris'
hand. Her fingers were cold and slightly rough. "It doesn't seem
like there are too many limitations from what I can see."

Jasi squeezed again and stood. She wiped her hands along her pale yellow dress and made her way over to their mother. Eris watched as she joined Desia. Both of her sisters leaned over their mother, speaking softly to one another as they did. Eris wished she could share the same connection to her sisters.

"You were reckless."

She looked up to see Lira standing next to her. Her face was flat, though her pursed lips spoke of the disappointment she had with what Eris had done.

"I...I'm sorry, Lira."

Lira opened her mouth as if to say something before sighing and closing it again. She took a seat next to Eris. "I have never seen a keeper wield so much power. That...was impressive. Do you know what you did?"

Eris shook her head. Caught up in the moment, she'd pulled on the energy stored in the trees, drawing as much as she could from everything around her. It wasn't until she sensed the distant source of energy that she'd been able to make any difference for her mother.

"I don't really know. I planted the tree, but what I did after that..." She shook her head. "I wish I understood all this better. I wish I knew how to make arrangements of power. Even reading the messages in the flowers would be a start." She looked up at Lira. "I'm willing to learn, Lira. I *need* to learn. Can you teach me?" She asked the question tentatively, afraid of how Lira might answer.

"Eris—"

Her heart sunk as Lira said her name.

"There are many things I can teach you," she continued.

Eris's heart quickened.

"Things like learning how to appreciate certain arrangements or how to create messages. But you are a keeper of trees. If nothing else, this has proven it."

She took a steadying breath. "But I'm not. I met a keeper of trees."

Lira arched a brow.

"My abilities are nothing like hers. The trees bow to her, moving at her will. What I do..." She looked over at Lira. "I bonded a teary star," she explained. "A *flower*. I'm a keeper of flowers, not of trees. That's why the trees don't listen to me.'

Lira surprised her. She laughed.

"You think the trees don't listen? And that's why you aren't a keeper of trees?" She shook her head. "I know little about how your ability compares to what I can do. Keepers like you were rare even when the Gardens existed. But the control over your ability *is* different." She smiled and turned to Eris. 'Perhaps I should have explained that to you, but I thought you worked it out on your own. Flowers are transient. Some sprout every year and so set down roots, but many do not. They leave seeds, little more than memories of themselves, to grow and bloom the next season. It is different with trees. Trees reach deep into the earth, spreading their roots. You have already told me how you can read those roots. That is not a gift I possess. Few ever have. It is a trait of keepers like you. With something permanent, you must earn its trust before you can command it, if you ever can command the trees."

Eris shook her head, thinking to what Imryll had said. "But my flower..."

Lira smiled. "I do not see a flower. I see a beautiful tree growing at the heart of my garden. A tree you placed there and grew."

Eris looked at the svanth tree growing. Of all the plants throughout the garden, it was the only one pulsing with life. The others waited, wilted, needing sun and rain before they would be strong again. Even the elms were weakened, though not as much as the flowers. Eris sensed none of the plants resented what she had done.

But how could she be a keeper of trees? Imryll was right; she *had* chosen a flower to bond. "How is it that I can use the energy of your garden?" Eris asked.

Lira shook her head. "That troubles me as well. As far as I know, you shouldn't be able to. The keepers of trees had a different set of skills than keepers of flowers. They could command great power, but they did not work with subtle strokes. That was the domain of keepers of flowers." She nodded toward where Eris's mother lay. "But I have seen—and felt—you manage both. The power you pulled was unlike anything I could imagine, even when Elaysia existed. But you worked it with fine skill. A keeper of trees would have destroyed your mother wielding such power. Or so I thought."

"Has there ever been a keeper of both?"

Eris turned at Terran's voice. He stood behind her and rested a hand on her shoulder. She took his hand.

Lira looked from Eris to Terran. One brow arched slightly, and a hint of a smile pulled at her lips. "Only the Sacred Mother knows what is possible, Terran."

Eris looked up at him. "Why do you ask?"

"You're the one who gave me the idea. You've talked about the teary star. I think Mistress Lira assumed you would be a keeper of flowers when you chose that flower."

He looked at Lira, and she nodded.

"But then you reached the Svanth. I don't know exactly what happened, but something was awakened in you while you were there. When I found you, I knew you were a keeper, but something was off. You didn't act as I expected either. And then you spoke of your connection to the forest."

Lira nodded again. "Only a keeper of trees would bind to a forest. The Council of Keepers would know more, but they have scattered, destroyed along with the Gardens."

"I didn't bind to the forest," Eris said. Imryll had made that clear when she'd met with her and tried teaching her. "I bonded to the teary star. A flower."

Terran nodded. "But it's more than that, isn't it? You learned the secret of the teary star. You told me how the vine grows with the svanth tree, strengthening them both." He winked at her as he said it, his lips tightening as he clearly fought against a grin. "And now that I've seen it in person—seen how the vine and tree grow together—I think your gift is different than even Mistress Lira knew."

Lira looked from Eris to the svanth tree. "It *would* make sense. But I don't know that there has ever been a keeper of both flowers and trees."

"Not only flowers and trees, though, is it?" Terran asked.

Eris shook her head. "I can use the energy of the Verilain Plains as well."

Lira nodded. "You said that, but have you done so recently? Since staying within the forest?"

"When I was making my way back to Eliara, I found a patch of ground the magi had burned when they last attacked. Nothing grew there. The grasses seemed as if they pulled away. It was like the area would continue to grow, becoming barren." Eris shivered just thinking about it.

"What did you do?"

She looked over at the svanth tree. "There is now a svanth tree growing there. I coaxed the roots to circle the entire area, as if to wall it off. Maybe in time life will return."

Lira's eyes looked blank, as if she stared at nothing. Suddenly, she blinked, clarity returning to them. "Did it work?"

"I don't know. I think it might with enough time. I didn't pull as much energy as I did growing this."

Eris had a flash of understanding. She'd had to pull more with the tree here. Without the tree growing as tall as it was, she never would have been able to heal her mother. She'd needed it to connect to the distant source of power—likely the Svanth she realized—and only then could she help her mother.

Something about the way Lira looked gave Eris pause. "What is it?"

Lira shook her head and stood from the bench.

Eris followed her. Lira hurried to the svanth tree and studied it. One hand lightly touched the thick trunk where the brownish-green teary star vine worked around the smooth bark of the svanth. She winced when the barbs caught her hand. A small bud on one of the tendrils caught her attention and she looked over at Eris.

"Can you make it bloom?"

"I don't know. I've never tried."

Lira nodded toward the tree. "Would you?"

Eris glanced at Terran, who only shrugged. Then she turned back to the tree and laid her hand on it. Barbs twisted away, flattening so as not to catch her hand. She ran her palm along the vine, delving into the teary star and the svanth. Once she had a connection, she sent a request for it to bloom.

Thin streamers of vine quickly responded, flowing away from the vine and curling together. Within moments, a thick bud formed and then bloomed into a multi-colored teary star flower.

Eris smiled. Other than in her dreams, she hadn't seen one since finding it in the garden all those months ago. The last time she'd seen the teary star on a vine, she'd been forced to scale the palace wall. Terran had fetched a ladder for her to help her down.

She leaned toward the flower and inhaled deeply. The scent was as she remembered.

"What do you smell?"

Eris looked over to see Lira watching her with her hazel eyes. The question was the same one she'd asked when Eris first brought her the flower.

"It is complex," Eris said. She noted the bitter overtones that reminded her of the thick vine of the flower itself, but it mixed with the softer texture of the bark of the svanth. "There are notes of the svanth seed. Thick and oily, but sweet as well. Much like I would expect the meat of the seed to taste." She inhaled again, letting it fill her nostrils. "I smell hints of the elm and a mixture of other floral scents, too faint to make out. And then the crispness of a summer rain." Eris breathed out. Inhaling the scent of the flower energized her. Had she been able to coax the teary stars to bloom all this time?

Lira leaned toward the flower and smelled. Her nose crinkled, and her brow furrowed. Thin lips pursed into a line. "I cannot appreciate all that complexity. I appreciate the earthy tones layered with a smoky texture. Perhaps an element of bay." Lira closed her eyes and breathed in the scent from the flower again. "Your description of the seed is accurate, but without having you comment on it, I doubt I would have noted." She smiled. "Much different than the last time you reported to me."

"Maybe my nose has gotten better," Eris suggested.

"I like to think you've gained experience."

Eris touched the flower and pinched it off. She handed it to Lira. Lira took it gently, almost reverently. "What do you want with the teary star?"

Lira turned to her and took a deep breath, pushing the flower toward Eris. "I want to push back the Conclave."

Eris held the flower, the power surging through it as she touched it, and wondered if the teary star was the key to her connection. Could she use the energy to halt the steady march of the Conclave?

Lira looked at her, her hazel eyes full of hope. It was then Eris realized Lira didn't know how to stop the Conclave either.

Eris closed her eyes and pulled on the energy of the flower, letting it flow over her and fill her. For the first time, she thought she knew the secret to accessing some of the power stored within the Svanth forest.

Could Terran be right? Could she be a keeper of both flowers and trees?

It would explain why she could use the energy of Lira's garden, but why had the svanth not responded when she tried drawing power? Except, as she thought about it, the Svanth *had* responded. Hadn't that been the distant source of energy when healing her mother?

If the teary star was the secret, Eris would use it, draw energy through the flower, and do what she could to stop the magi.

# CHAPTER 23

The svanth tree seemed to glow in the waning sunlight. Thick clouds swirled distantly and thunder rumbled. The garden waited expectantly, thirsty for rain after what Eris had done.

Her mother lay quietly, breathing steadily. Her skin no longer held the pale, waxy appearance. Now it looked nearly transparent, threaded with thin, blue veins. A sheen of moisture clung to her exposed arms and her brow. She had not yet opened her eyes.

Eris held onto a sliver of energy from the svanth, enough to send a delving into her mother to know she remained healed. She did not want to move until her mother awoke.

Her father sat next to her.

The sickness had taken its toll on him as well. His eyes were sunken, but more from lack of sleep. Wrinkles deepened along his cheeks and at the corners of his eyes. "Jasi tells me you did this."

Eris looked over. He wore a navy jacket with heavy green embroidery. In spite of the regal dress, he looked ragged. A slender rivenswood cane rested next to him. He hadn't used the cane the last time Eris saw him.

"I did what I could."

"She will…" He swallowed and turned to face Eris. His eyes had a film upon them she hadn't seen before. It cleared briefly as he blinked. "She will live?"

His voice sounded as if he didn't believe it possible.

"What do the healers tell you?"

He took a deep breath. "They tell me she is stable. That her breathing has regulated. Something about her skin and the taste of her blood." He shook his head. "None of it tells me what I want to know."

"If she awakens, she can live."

Eris thought it should have happened by now. Lira seemed troubled that she still hadn't awoken but did not have the energy needed to learn why. Eris had taken too much.

Her father patted her hand. "Thank you."

She swallowed. "I put Errasn in danger, Father. Doing this—" she pointed to the svanth tree "—took all that Lira used to keep us safe."

He shook his head. "You don't know that. For all we know, you saved us. Without your mother…" He didn't finish and took a deep breath to steady himself. A moment passed, and he nodded slightly. He turned toward her, looking more like the father she remembered. "Jacen tells me there is someone I need to meet."

Eris sniffed. "I will not ask permission for him."

Her father laughed. "No? And if I forbid you?"

She shot him a look. "I might turn you into a tree."

His laugh deepened. "Then I should give my blessing when I meet with him on the morrow?"

"Meet with him?"

Her father nodded. "He requested to meet. Jacen offered to take the appointment but thought I might find it entertaining."

Eris closed her eyes and snorted. Terran had requested to meet with her father. She realized she wasn't surprised.

"Is he good to you?"

The gentle way he asked the question took her aback. She nodded. "Very good."

"And he knows what you are? What you can do?"

Eris nodded. "He is my gardener."

He frowned. "Like Master Nels?"

Eris laughed nervously. "Like Master Nels. But not."

Her father took a deep breath and sighed. "A gardener. My daughter wishes to be with a gardener." He turned to her and smiled. "I admit that you have always vexed me, Eris. Your mother and I wanted nothing but happiness for all of you, but I worried most about you. I thank the Sacred Mother you found something that brings you joy."

As he stood, Eris grabbed his hand. "Thank you, Father."

He leaned and kissed her on the forehead. "Let me have time with her alone. Get some rest. I can see you need it. You have done more than enough for her today."

Eris stood and started away but paused at the edge of the elms ringing the heart of the garden. She looked back at her father, now holding her mother's hand. He sobbed quietly.

"Father?"

He stood taller but didn't turn.

"I will do what I can to stop the Conclave."

"I know you will, Eris. I know you will."

---

Eris stood outside Lira's room, hand raised to knock, when the door opened. Lira wore a thin, silky dress of pale green. Her hair fell about her shoulders. She clutched a glass of wine in her hand, and red stained her lips.

"You should be resting," Lira said.

Eris nodded. "There is something I need to speak with you about."

She waited, wondering if Lira would invite her in or send her away. When she'd been Lira's student, Eris had rarely been allowed into Lira's room.

Lira stepped to the side and nodded. "Come in, keeper."

Eris took a deep breath and stepped into Lira's room.

It looked different than the last time she'd been here. Then Lira had been so consumed with keeping her mother alive and doing what she could to slow the Conclave that she'd practically abandoned her quarters. Now, the dust had been cleared, and the window hung open. A soft evening breeze gusted in, rustling papers on the desk. Arrangements of cut flowers looked bold and bright, nothing like the wilted and fading flowers in the garden. Eris hadn't borrowed their energy as she'd healed her mother.

Lira motioned to a pair of chairs angled toward the window. Eris didn't remember seeing them the last time she'd been here. Had Lira brought them to her room, expecting Eris to come with questions?

After Eris settled into the chair, she took a deep breath, trying to organize her thoughts. She needed to explain to Lira what had happened to her, but needed to do it in a way where Lira would offer her opinion. "You haven't asked why I left Eliara."

Lira turned from staring at one of her arrangements and met Eris's gaze. "I did not think it mattered. You are a keeper. Even if there is anything I can teach you, you may go as you please."

"Or what happened while I was gone."

Lira watched her, waiting.

"I met a keeper of trees."

"There have never been many keepers of trees."

"She called herself Imryll. She tends a forest to the north. After I met her, I did not think I could be a keeper of trees."

"Imryll?" Lira said the name and a puzzled look came across her face. She shook her head, shaking away another question. "I think Terran is right, by the way. You are different than either."

Different. Always so different. But if she hadn't been different, would she have saved her mother?

"How did you find her?"

Eris shook her head. "I don't know. I nearly died. When I awoke, I was in her forest."

Lira sat up straighter in her chair.

"Ferisa came to me with one of the priestesses. I didn't understand what she wanted at first. Ferisa said that she knew I was a keeper. She told me of visions she had. And then..." She took a deep breath. "And then stabbed me." Eris patted her stomach where the knife had plunged through. She still didn't know what had happened or how she'd survived. Imryll had only said the Guardian intervened, whatever that meant. She hadn't offered anything more before forcing Eris from the forest. Eris didn't know if Lira would know anything either.

"Ferisa?" Lira asked. She turned to the arrangements set out on the tables.

There was a subtle drawing of energy. The flowers faded slightly, the leaves curling at the ends as Lira drew from the cut flowers. She did nothing to interrupt what Lira did.

"She is gone," Lira whispered.

Eris nodded. She suspected the same. When she'd been in the garden, part of the energy she'd used had gone into sending out the final surge. With it, she'd noted that Ferisa had gone. Other priestesses remained, but not the one with Ferisa when she'd attacked her.

"Why would she attack me?"

Lira took a deep breath and looked around the room, her eyes lingering on a shelf near the back wall. "I hadn't considered that as a possibility until you said the infection felt unnatural. And even then I didn't think it likely." She looked over at Eris and shook her head. "I was too close to see it before. Could that be why we struggled to cure her?"

"What possibility?"

Lira sighed. "There is a sect of priestesses within the church who claim they foretell the future. Few outside the church know of it, and even within, it is considered a dark path to follow."

Eris tensed, thinking of the first keeper. The first keeper of the Svanth had seen glimpses of the future. It was why she had worked the story of the keepers into the roots of the svanth trees. It was the reason she had worked so hard to grow the svanth trees in the first place. "How is it you know of it?"

"Because keepers once shared the same gift."

She leaned forward, meeting Lira's eyes. "What does that have to do with me? Why would Ferisa stab me?"

Lira studied her for a moment before shaking her head. "I don't know. It depends on what they saw. If what they saw of you clashed with the direction they wanted the church to take, they would take whatever measure needed."

*Whatever measure needed.* The words seemed to hum in her head. "Including poisoning Mother?" The idea frightened her. The priestesses had full access throughout the palace. They would have no difficulty reaching her mother, especially if Ferisa were with them.

But why her mother? Why Eris and not Lira?

What vision did they have about her mother and Eris but not Lira?

Lira started to stand. "We need to find your father...your sisters..."

Eris reached over and touched her on the arm. "The last thing I did after healing my mother was send a healing wave throughout the city."

Lira hesitated. "That's what I felt, then."

Eris nodded. "I had to know others weren't infected. We need to check that others weren't poisoned as well, but none were as sick as Mother or we would have known." She turned to Lira, coming to a decision. "We need to learn why Ferisa and the church would do this."

Lira nodded. "I never thought to consider the church. The magi and the Conclave certainly, but I paid no mind to the church."

"That's why I must be the one to stop the Conclave."

Lira shook her head. "You aren't strong enough. Even with both of us, I don't think we're strong enough."

Eris nodded. "Not to destroy the Conclave. I don't have the strength for that." Not yet, though Eris was beginning to wonder if there might be a way. "But to slow them? To push them back from our borders and bring peace? I might be strong enough for that." She held Lira's gaze. "But I can't go thinking Eliara—my *family*—might be in danger. Will you stay, learn what you can of why the church would poison my mother? Why Ferisa would try to kill me?"

Lira considered the question before breaking the gaze and turning to look out the window. "You surprise me, Eris Taeresin. You have always been stubborn and independent, but now you seem to have learned how to ask for help."

"Someone made it clear to me that I can't do it on my own."

A smile crept across Lira's face. "He will come with you?"

"I don't think he will stay behind, were I to ask."

"You walk into danger, you know this?"

Eris nodded.

"It will be different than when the magi attacked near the Svanth. They had not prepared for you, and there were but a few magi. Now the entire focus of the Conclave is upon Errasn. Once they sense what you do, you will be targeted."

"I know."

And she would be all alone, other than Terran, no one else to aid her.

Eris swallowed and pushed back the fear threatening to rise within her.

Lira turned toward her and reached one hand over the edge of her chair toward Eris. Eris took it as a surge of energy washed through her.

"Then go. Know I will do all I can to keep Eliara safe while you're gone."

# CHAPTER 24

*E*ris awoke early the next morning. Dreams plagued her as she slept, keeping her from sleeping soundly. In some, she awoke after a blast of fire struck her, burning away her connection to the trees. In others, she awoke after watching Terran burn. Those were harder for her. The last dream had been the worst. In that dream, Ferisa had come to her, at first apologizing for what she'd done before stabbing her again.

She dressed in a plain green gown—the same as when she first returned to Eliara—and pulled on the heavy cloak given to her by Imryll. For some reason, it felt right to wear that cloak. The pockets held two small svanth seeds each, but nothing else.

After stopping in the kitchen for a small loaf of fresh bread, she made her way back to the garden.

The svanth tree glistened in the morning light from rain overnight. The garden around her surged with renewed life and energy. Not as much as it would in another few days, but no longer did the leaves curl and the petals look faded. Within a week, the traces of what Eris had done would be gone.

But Errasn wouldn't have that much time.

The pair of guards near the rim of trees nodded to her.

Eris stopped at the edge of the elms and slipped out of the shoes she wore. These were heavier than the slippers she'd worn during her time in the Svanth, but she chose them intentionally. She didn't know what she might encounter between here and the border. If there was anything like the singed and burned landscape like within the Verilain Plains, she wanted a thicker barrier between her and what the magi had done. But they still came off quickly and easily.

Once inside the rim of trees, she paused and delved, chasing the roots as they wound beneath the palace. Eris used this connection to trace the grasses, following the connection as far she could, pressing south, through rolling hills that opened into flatlands, the grasses there so different than the Verilain Plains. Flowers and trees covered the ground, but none were plentiful.

And then everything ended.

Eris winced, pulling back from her connection. The magi pushed farther forward than she had expected, pressing deep into Errasn, destroying everything as they came.

How could she hope to push the magi back? What did she think she could do?

All she had to do was hold the magi back, keep them from pressing deeper into Errasn. If she could manage that much...then what? She didn't have the strength to stop the magi altogether.

She shivered. She had to try. If she didn't, the magi would continue to press forward until they reached Eliara and beyond, eventually marching through the Verilain Plains and onward to the Svanth. Where would their destruction end?

She sighed, turned to the svanth tree, and ran her hand along the bark. She sent a surge of a request through the tree, and a handful of seeds dropped from above. She pocketed these. Another request, this to the teary star vine, and she pulled cuttings from the vine. If her plan were to work, she would need some of them.

Then she turned to her mother. The healers hadn't moved her.

She looked comfortable, her breathing easier and her color returning, but still she slept. Eris touched her arm and leaned down to
kiss her. What she wouldn't give to speak to her before she left,
especially now that she knew her mother had not given up on her
—had pushed Lira to work with her.

And then she turned away. She had work to do.

Terran found her in the garden not much later. A smile split his
lips, the same lopsided smile he'd always used to wear when they'd
first met. He wore his heavy green jacket, now replaced with one
without all the stitching and repairs. A wide-bladed knife hung
from his waist, and a bow slung over his shoulder along with a
quiver of arrows.

"You know what I plan?"

He laughed. "Not until I saw what you did yesterday."

"You spoke to my father?"

His smile faltered. "I did. How did you know?"

"He told me."

Terran nodded.

"What did you talk about?"

He shrugged. "The kingdom. His responsibility. How much it
meant to him that you healed your mother."

Eris frowned. "That is all?"

Terran winked at her. "There might have been something else."

Part of her wanted to punch him, but she refrained. "Aren't you
the one who made a point of telling me how we're partners in this?
Would partners keep things from each other?"

"If it bothers you, he might," he said, teasing her more.

Terran turned and started through the garden. Eris hurried
after him and grabbed his hand when she caught up to him.

"Are we walking or riding?" he asked.

Eris shook her head. "We can walk faster."

It no longer seemed strange to say that, but part of her gift as keeper meant that she could walk with great speed if she fed off the life around her. She would have to do so carefully, not wanting to waste any more energy than necessary before they reached the border, but they could travel more quickly that way. Terran moved just as easily as she, though she hadn't learned the trick of it yet.

"I suspect you would ride faster if you tried," Terran said.

Eris thought about where they were going and what they might encounter. "I think it's best if we walk."

Terran nodded.

They made their way through the city, bypassing the huge iron gates by going through the servants' door again. Eris shivered as they passed near the heavy bars, wondering why she should fear iron. It was a question she'd forgotten to ask Lira. They hurried from the city and quickly moved south, not bothering to follow any particular road.

Neither spoke much.

Eris had rarely gone south of the city. If not for the delving, she wouldn't have known what to expect. The landscape shifted quickly from the steady rolling hills found around Eliara as it gradually flattened. Tall, dry grasses grew here, nothing like needlegrass, though this was said to all be part of the Verilain Plains. Eris recognized the difference, sensing the break between the dense needlegrass and these softer grasses. They bent away from her the same, springing back as they passed, masking her and Terran's progress.

They stopped for lunch near a small stream. Terran drank from a water skin he'd brought before passing it over to her. When they drank enough, he refilled it. She bit off some of the bread she'd taken and passed it to him.

"How long will we be here?" he asked.

She shook her head. "I don't know. As long as it takes."

"Does Lira know?" He wiped an arm across his brow and looked back toward Eliara.

"She knows."

"She didn't want to come with us?" He seemed surprised.

"There is something else she needed to do."

He frowned for a moment and then nodded. "Your sister?"

"Lira thinks she might know something about a sect of the church responsible. She promised she would keep my family safe."

"While you work to keep the kingdom safe?"

Eris nodded.

Terran chewed thoughtfully on the bread. "You think to use the svanth trees to connect to the forest?"

It still surprised her how intuitive he was. "I think that's how I healed my mother. If I have any hope of pushing back the Conclave, I will need the power stored within the forest."

He laughed softly. "I think there's supposed to be an easier way than planting a tree."

"I don't think I'll be able to plant a tree this far south," she admitted. She pulled one of the teary star clippings from her pocket. A small flower bloomed on it. Eris inhaled, smelling its fragrance. "Lira gave me the idea. The flower is my connection to the forest, I think, much like her garden in Eliara connects her to her larger garden in the Svanth."

Terran considered the flower and nodded. "What are you planning to do?"

She shook her head. "I...I haven't worked it out fully."

Terran laughed. "Good thing you'll have help."

"Help?"

He nodded behind them, and she turned. A long column of soldiers on horseback streamed across the nearest hillock, following the road they had crossed. The banner waving at the front carried the king's crest. With her mother still weak, she didn't expect her father to ride south.

That meant Jacen.

They met the soldiers shortly afterward.

Eris counted at least a thousand troops. Seeing them in careful lines, led by her brother, filled her with hope. And also fear. There was little the soldiers would be able to do against the magi. Sending another company of men south risked the safety of Eliara and the rest of Errasn, leaving them vulnerable to attack from the north.

Jacen looked down from his saddle, seemingly unsurprised to see her. He wore full armor with his helm strapped to the seat behind him. A longsword hung off his saddle and, like Terran, he carried a bow.

"Father said I would find you moving south," he said. "I did not expect you to have come so far."

Eris wouldn't explain to Jacen how her abilities worked. He was too practical minded to understand. "I had not known you'd returned."

"Briefly. I came for reinforcements."

Eris frowned. "You needed to come yourself?"

He shrugged. "I needed to speak to Father to convince him to release the men. This is all he would commit. Not enough to destroy Saffra and their damn magi. Not nearly enough."

His tone told her what he thought of the men. Disappointment touched with anger.

"So now you return to the border."

He nodded. "We had to fall back from Saffra. The magi keep blasting at us, destroying as many of their men as ours. I don't know how far we've retreated." His voice rose as he spoke of the magi, and a hot flush washed across his cheeks. "Now my little sister travels south as well. What do you think to do?"

She looked up and down his line of soldiers. Could she save them? Could she save Errasn? Eris—princess of Errasn—could not, but that wasn't who she was, not any longer. Eris, keeper of the Svanth Forest, might be able to protect them.

Except Eris didn't belong to only Errasn. Perhaps that was the reason she felt so strongly about pushing back the magi. If the Conclave wasn't stopped now, they would continue forward, marching north through Eliara and into Varden, moving until everything was destroyed. She could practically see the destruction in her mind.

"I intend to stop the magi," she said. She would destroy the Conclave if she could, but doing so might require more energy than she could access.

Jacen studied her for a long moment. "Father told me about you. About your ability. I didn't know what to think at first. I mean, you're my sister! How could you be some sort of flower mage?"

Eris smiled. "I once called Lira a flower mage. Now I understand how wrong that title is."

"You deny you're like her?"

She shook her head. "I don't deny that I'm a keeper."

Jacen glanced back toward Eliara. "I returned yesterday to find a tree growing in the courtyard, a tree that hadn't been there only a week before, rising high above the others." He looked down and met her eyes. "And I heard what you did for Mother, how you used your flower magic to save her. Will she really live?"

"If she awakens and eats, she will live." Eris would like to have thanked her mother just once.

Jacen shook his head. "I've seen what the magi are capable of doing firsthand. The destruction they throw around. Seeing that—seeing *life*—gives me hope." He fixed her with his blue eyes, eyes that had once been gentle and happy but were now hard and filled with anger. For a moment that anger faded. "You have always been strong, Eris. I never gave you the credit you deserve. I can't say that I understand what you can do, but my men and I will fight with you if you'll help us destroy the magi. I will burn them the way they've burned so many of our men."

The hatred in his voice startled her. Would she end up like him? Was there anything she could do to help ease his anger? She wished she could bring back the brother she remembered, the brother with the easy smile and lighthearted laugh. The man before her was hard and filled with anger.

"I will do what I must."

Jacen studied her a moment longer and then nodded.

As the soldiers continued on, she turned to Terran rather than watching them pass. He looked at her and then pulled her close, wrapping her in his arms. Neither spoke as she sobbed against him.

# CHAPTER 25

*J*acen pushed the soldiers hard throughout the day. Eris and Terran followed behind, letting the soldiers lead the way. If they encountered Saffra troops, it would be better to have Errasn men to back them. Eris kept a distance from them, though; the constant hoofbeats hammering over the ground became jarring, building up tension within her. They didn't camp until late that evening.

"Do we rest?" Terran asked as the soldiers made camp.

Eris ran her hand over a handful of the grasses and closed her eyes. She delved through the grasses, pressing out and south, searching for what she feared she would find. The desolation, the emptiness, was closer now. Another day, and they would reach it.

And then what?

She hadn't thought about what she would do once they reached Saffra. But not even Saffra any longer, was it? The magi had pushed past the border and slowly destroyed the fringes of Errasn. Each day meant less of her homeland existed. Each day meant the magi claimed more.

But she didn't dare face the magi exhausted. She had little

enough control over her abilities the way it was. She could use the roots, trace them as she sensed the destruction, but more than that wasn't as predictable as what Lira wielded. Maybe it would have been better for Lira to come.

She let her eyes open, severing the connection to the plains. "I fear waiting, but if we continue on tonight..."

Terran nodded. "Then we camp for the night as well. Tomorrow we push forward."

She let him make the arrangements. Terran quickly cleared a small patch of ground and gathered a few dried branches for a fire. The air was warmer here than it was in the north, but as night came on, a chill still came to the air. Eris felt thankful for the cloak Imryll had given her. It had been comfortable during the warmer stretches of the day and kept her warm with the coming night.

Once settled, Terran tore off a few strips of salted jerky and handed them to her. She took them and chewed, glad he planned ahead. She'd grabbed only bread while Terran managed to bring meat and water and weapons.

He sat next to her and slipped an arm around her. Eris snuggled in against him and rested her head on his shoulder. She breathed slowly, enjoying the quiet crackling of the flame and the scent of the fire and how it mixed with Terran's scent. If only they could remain like this.

"I don't know if I can do what needs to be done," she admitted.

He laughed softly. "I think you're better prepared than you know."

"What if I'm not? What if we—" She couldn't say the words she feared. The idea of losing Terran frightened her more than losing herself.

"You have to do what's needed. You can't sit back and wait while the Conclave destroys everything you know, not if you're the Eris I know."

She let her eyes fall closed as she smiled to herself. Once, it had been so hard for him to say her name. He'd been too concerned about her station and the fact that she was princess. So much had changed for her—for both of them—that Eris no longer even considered herself a princess. Now, when Terran said her name, there was no hesitation, only affection.

Eris let herself drift, slowly delving into the grasses around her. As she did, an unsettled sense nagged at her, as if the grasses recognized the presence of the magi, almost as if understanding what would happen if they came. She tried pushing out reassurance but didn't know if it worked or mattered.

Connected as she was, she felt Terran move toward her. His mouth found hers, and she kissed back. They leaned back into the grasses, losing themselves together.

Eris tried not to think that it might be the last time.

She awoke to orange and red spreading across the horizon as the sun slowly climbed. The bright colors swirled together, looking nothing like any flower she knew. Still there seemed a distinct pattern she could almost discern.

Terran had already awoken. He cleared and buried the remains of the fire. His face looked lean and hard in the morning light, but he smiled when he saw she was awake. "I wish I had more to offer you to eat."

She smiled and pulled the rest of the bread she'd taken yesterday morning. "We have this."

"I could have hunted last night. Or at least set a trap. Plenty of hares out here."

"I preferred the way the night went." She flushed as she said it, uncertain how he would respond, but she turned to face him, meeting his eyes. "Last night was..." She couldn't finish. She wouldn't change anything about the night, a night so long in coming. And with facing the magi, she didn't know if they would

D.K. HOLMBERG

be able to share another night. He was her gardener and she was his keeper.

Now she felt connected to him in a way she hadn't before. Would he feel the same?

He touched her face and brushed a strand of hair back behind her ear. Terran kissed her lightly on the lips. "Me too."

He helped her to her feet, and she slipped back into her cloak. It had served as a blanket for them during the night, but they'd kept each other warm enough.

In the distance, her brother's soldiers already began moving, horses starting toward the south with steady precision. Metal gleamed in the sunlight, making them seem to glow. The banner at the front barely moved. From here, the thousand troops seemed so small, not enough to do much of anything against the Conclave.

Terran took her hand and squeezed. They watched the sunrise for a few moments, enjoying the peace that came with the new day. Finally, Eris took a deep breath and turned south, pulling him with her.

They moved quickly and outpaced the soldiers. After meeting with Jacen the day before, she had no interest in walking alongside them. She would do what she could to protect them, but she feared the anger in Jacen would seep into her.

By midday, the desolation drew near.

Eris had no other word for it. What she felt resembled the charred remains she'd found in the Verilain Plains, only spread over a much greater distance. The ground changed where the magi burned it, practically refusing to let anything grow.

Would her connection to the Svanth allow her to halt the spread of the desolation?

She didn't know. Sealing off even the small area in the Verilain Plains had taken huge amounts of energy. What this would require might be more than she could summon.

But she had to try.

Terran squeezed her hand, seeming to sense her unease.

212

The edge of Errasn appeared before them late in the afternoon.

It wasn't where the border should have been. The Loess River served as the traditional border of Errasn with Saffra, but even that wasn't entirely accurate. A wide swath of unclaimed land stretched from the Loess to the Kernig Mountains. Beyond that lay Saffra.

Eris knew little of Saffra. What little she knew came from books and her earliest lectures on geography. If only she'd paid more attention then, she might understand why Saffra worked with the Conclave.

She remembered Saffra to be an arid place, one where the sun shone hot and bright and little rain fell. The Kernig Mountains seemed to break any clouds attempting to make their way south, pushing rain into Errasn but keeping the other side of the mountains dry. Rocky shores were said to line the Dalish Sea, so different than the sandy beaches found in cities like Nasin and Asna.

"It's warmer here than I expected," Terran said.

Eris nodded. Heat shimmered in the still air. Thankfully, the cloak kept her comfortable and cool. "This is unnatural."

"What is?"

"All of it. I've never come this far south, but it's not supposed to be hot. None of Errasn is hot, not like this."

Touching the grasses, she sensed how they faded under the heat. Even if the magi didn't push farther, the change in climate would be enough to alter the natural landscape of Errasn. How much longer before the grasses died altogether? And then what? Would the Loess dry up, turning all of this into desert?

She sighed. Halting the magi advance was all she could hope to accomplish, but it still might not be enough.

They crested a slow rise. In the distance, the ground became hillier, the southern hills rolling toward the Kernig Mountains.

Water glinted distantly. Eris suspect that to be the Loess, though didn't know with certainty. Brown and dying grasses stretched toward the river, ending abruptly in places where it had been left charred and burning. Movement along the distant char was likely Saffra soldiers. Brown and black tents stood up from the ground. Flashes of color, mostly deep red and purple, moved, but otherwise, everything looked bleak.

Eris saw no sign of the magi.

"All of this is supposed to be Errasn," she said.

Terran nodded.

"Father thought the Loess would keep Saffra from advancing, but Saffra seems to have found a way across." Few bridges crossed the Loess, and those that did should have been easily guarded. Either her father's men had been forced back, or Saffra had come up with another way across.

"What now?"

Eris looked toward the east. The landscape looked much the same, blackened and burned away. Toward the west looked no different. How was she to stop it?

How had Lira held it off as long as she had?

Guilt settled through her at how selfish she'd been in healing her mother. Had she not spent the energy stored in Lira's garden, she might have held off the magi a little longer. Now, nothing slowed them.

Seeing the desolation made it somehow more real, more bleak. Even had Lira come, Eris doubted it would have made a difference. A dozen keepers wouldn't be able to make a difference.

And yet...if she did nothing, hope was lost. This close to the desolation, she felt it more strongly. With every passing moment, the grasses along the hills receded, burned away by whatever dark spell the magi wrought, steady and relentless. With enough time—days rather than weeks—the desolation would reach Eliara. Lira might be able to hold it off for a while, but the garden would eventually fail and fall into the same desolation as here.

She could practically see it in her mind.

Then it would move farther north. Through the Verilain Plains and onward until it reached the Svanth Forest. The forest would resist, but it could only fight for so long. Then it would fall, the memories of the first keeper falling with it, as the desolation spread north into Varden, eventually reaching Imryll and her forest. Nothing would remain to slow the Conclave.

"I have to stop this," she finally answered.

Next to her, Terran nodded.

# CHAPTER 26

*J*acen and his soldiers arrived later that evening. He frowned at Eris when he saw her already waiting for him and waved his men past. Sweat shone along his brow, and his helm rested on his saddle. A large water skin hung from his neck, and he took a long swallow.

"You knew it was like this," Eris said when he pulled up.

Jacen nodded. "It wasn't this bad at first. The Loess held them back."

"How did they cross?"

He shook his head. "Don't know. We destroyed the bridges, but they still managed to find a way. The Loess is too wide to cross without bridge or boat."

"Could they have dammed it?"

Jacen flashed a dark smile. "It flows out of the mountains before draining into the Dalish. No way to dam that much water."

Eris turned to look at Terran. He stood next to her, scanning the caravan of soldiers. He looked troubled, and his jaw clenched, but he said nothing.

"How many men remain?" Eris asked.

Jacen shook his head. "I don't claim to know about your ability, Eris, but do you think you suddenly have the key to defeating Saffra and its seemingly endless supply of troops?"

Eris took a calming breath. "You bring one thousand men to the battlefront. I simply wanted to know how many men were still here."

Jacen studied Terran as he nodded. "There were nearly ten thousand when I left. And I wouldn't have left had not Tholen come to tell me how near death Mother was. Even that wouldn't have been enough, but we needed reinforcements." He shook his head. "I left Tholen in charge of the men."

Eris found it strange to hear Jacen say that he left Tholen in charge of the men. So much had changed in the months she'd been away, but Jacen perhaps most of all. He carried a confidence he hadn't before, an aura of purpose and command, but it mixed with the blanket of anger he wrapped himself in. If he could not shed the anger, he would never manage to rule peacefully when their father was gone.

"How many men does Saffra have?" Terran asked.

Jacen glanced from Eris to Terran. With his deep green jacket and long-bladed knife tucked into his belt, he looked every bit the soldier as Jacen, only of a different type. No longer the gentle gardener, Terran had changed as well.

Jacen looked as if he debated answering. Then he shook his head. "It changes. They constantly have soldiers coming over the Kernig Mountains, but they move quickly through the passes, and our scouts think they lose nearly as many men as they send. And it's not the soldiers we fear." He fixed Eris with a firm look. "I'm hoping you can help with that."

She sighed. "I will do what I can."

Jacen nodded and spurred his horse forward to rejoin his men.

Terran watched the line of soldiers as it wound toward the east. "Why does this battle draw out so long?" he asked. "Your brother has plenty of men—well-trained ones at that. If it were all about the magi, they should have scattered the soldiers by now."

"Lira had been holding them off."

Terran turned and looked at her. "Her reach can't stretch that far. Her garden has limits." He shook his head. "No...there is something here that I'm missing."

"We should go," Eris said. "Find a place to camp before night falls."

He flashed a smile, but she shook her head.

"I think we'll need to stay near the soldiers tonight. If there's an attack..."

Terran nodded. "I know." He sighed and turned to her, sliding his hands onto her hips and pulling her close. "I wish there was something more I could do."

"I'm afraid there's going to be more than either of us can do before this is over."

She should have known something was wrong before they even topped the hill. Though the air was still, the grasses seemed to hold their breath, waiting for what would come next. As they followed Jacen, shouts and the sound of metal against metal greeted them.

Eris started running, but Terran grabbed her arm.

"You can't go running into battle. Even a keeper can take an arrow to the chest. I don't think your abilities would be of much use then."

She glared at him, but he shook his head.

"Let me take the lead here."

"You're not a soldier either."

He snorted. "No, but I've been hunting. And you're not the only one with gifts."

As they reached the top of the hill, Terran waved at her to drop to the ground. He crouched, lowering himself to the level of the grasses, only his head visible.

Eris dropped to her knees and sent a command to the grasses to obscure her.

Then she looked down.

She'd read about war before and heard old Tholen tell stories about when Errasn battled with Varden, but what she saw before her was nothing like the stories.

The Errasn camp lay in disarray. Tents had fallen and were trampled. Fires burned wildly, quickly catching the already dry grasses alight. The air stunk of char and death. Men collided with each other atop horseback. Sword clanged against sword. Blood spattered everywhere, staining the grasses a deep red.

How had Saffra attacked so suddenly?

She delved into the grasses, searching for signs of the magi but found none.

This was a standard battle.

The fires created a separation between the Errasn troops but seemed not to affect those from Saffra. Saffra soldiers moved ruthlessly. Most were mounted atop sleek black and gray horses that moved more quickly than any Eris had ever seen. Their dark armor had strange-shaped helms worked with stones across the forehead. Even the horses had armor, all with the same strange stones. The horses darted forward before retreating, attacking in groups and splitting the unprepared Errasn troops.

Errasn soldiers were being slaughtered.

Jacen rode tall atop his horse toward the battle, leading his men toward the Saffra soldiers. As she watched, his men formed into lines and crashed into the Saffra riders.

Terran tapped her leg.

She turned and he motioned at her.

Eris dropped to the ground. At some point during the attack, she had stood to observe.

"What was that?" he whispered.

"Stupidity."

Terran laughed softly. "I've never seen anything like this before."

She shook her head. "The battle? Me neither."

"No. The horses. I think the magi did something with them."

"What do you mean?"

Terran raised a finger and pulled the bow from his back. After nocking an arrow, he sighted. "I'm not sure, but watch the black stallion closest to us."

Eris followed the direction he pointed. A tall, black stallion flicked between a pair of soldiers, its rider slashing out with a wicked curved sword. Blood sprayed from the men, and they fell from the saddle. The horse moved with an almost ethereal speed. Even the well-trained Errasn soldiers struggled to fight it.

Terran loosed the arrow.

It flew straight, striking the horse in the middle of the ruby stone on the side of its armored helm.

The horse staggered, the helm protecting it, but the stone exploded.

All of a sudden, the horse slowed. It was as if Terran had severed a tendon. The Saffra rider was thrown, and Errasn troops converged, quickly dropping him.

"We need to let Jacen know."

Eris started forward, barely crouching as she ran toward the battle.

Terran ran after, shouting at her, but she ignored him.

With a silent command, she demanded the grasses protect her. An invisible barrier slid around her.

And then she reached chaos.

Horses and riders streamed around her, somehow sliding past without striking her. Jacen battled a pair of Saffra riders. She hesitated long enough to marvel at her brother's skill. Maybe her father had been right to trust him to lead the troops. Old Tholen wouldn't have been able to fend off two enhanced Saffra soldiers.

As she neared, an arrow exploded the stone of one of the riders attacking Jacen.

Terran stood at the edge of the camp, another arrow nocked. By the time she turned, it struck the other horse. The two men Jacen had battled were both down, trampled by Jacen's dappled stallion.

"Jacen!"

He turned and looked at her with an incredulous expression. "Eris? You shouldn't be here! Go with your man and wait until this is over."

She shook her head. "The stones. Target the stones on the armor." She didn't know which would help more—striking the stones the horses carried or the soldiers.

His face clouded. "What about the stones?" Too much space separated them, and he had to shout.

Another horse crashed toward him. Terran loosed another arrow, this one striking the helm of the rider. He must have had the same question. The stone exploded, and the rider dropped his sword, sagging from the saddle.

"The magi!" she shouted.

Jacen looked from her to the fallen soldiers. Understanding spread across his face with a widening of his eyes.

He kicked his horse forward, speeding through the line of his troops. "Target the stones in the helms. Horse or rider!" he shouted.

Eris turned, holding onto her connection to the grasses, keeping the silent command for protection as she did, until she reached Terran.

He crouched in the thick grasses, his quiver empty. "That was foolish," he said.

"He had to know."

"Might there not have been a better way to tell him?"

Eris sniffed. "If you know of one, I'll hear it."

The battle started to swing in favor of Errasn. Their numbers and the focus on attacking the stones turned the tide, but not quickly enough. Too many men—her father's men, men of Errasn —still fell. And Jacen rode in the midst of it. If she did nothing, he might fall as well.

She dipped her hand into the pocket of her cloak and pulled out the teary star flower. With the energy around her from the grasses, she hoped she could reach through the flower with enough power to shatter the stones.

"Doing this will let the magi know you're here," Terran said.

Eris looked at him and nodded. "They would learn soon enough. We need to do what we can to help the men."

Terran fell silent.

Eris pulled on the energy of the flower. While in the garden in Eliara, she had the sense of great power at the cusp of her aware- ness. She remembered how the energy stored in the forest responded when she needed it to heal her mother, and hoped to draw on that now.

But she felt nothing.

The energy of the grasses filled her, and Eris sensed that she could use it, but more than that—drawing on the energy from the distant Svanth—she could not. The teary star held some energy, but what it possessed was small in comparison to even that of the dying grasses around her.

"What's wrong?"

She shook her head. For her to be able to do anything to stop the magi, she needed to access the forest. Without that, with only the grasses to aid her, she wouldn't have nearly enough to force them back. The Verilain Plains, as expansive and alive as it was, had barely held out while she had attacked a few magi. The grasses here would not hold up against the entirety of the Conclave.

"I can't—"

She didn't get the chance to finish.

A rider wearing the maroon helm and armor of Saffra appeared next to her, sword flashing toward Terran.

Without thinking, Eris sent a surge of energy toward the stones on his helm.

They exploded, and he dropped from the saddle. His horse stomped on his chest as it started away, leaving the man dying with soft gurgling sounds.

Something shifted then.

Eris felt it around her, almost like the sun shining hot on stone.

The magi knew she was here.

# CHAPTER 27

*B*efore thinking more about it, Eris demanded the grasses send a surge of energy to the stones on the helms of all the Saffra soldiers.

The grasses resisted for a moment. She sensed how they already fought against the heat and the desolation the magi pushed upon them. Eris delved deeper and drew harder.

The stones cracked with a loud explosion.

Men shouted as they fell. Eris didn't bother to watch.

Heat pressed on her, hotter than before.

"What is it?" Terran asked.

Eris shook her head. "The magi. I feel them."

"Can you use it to learn where they are?"

She frowned. *Could* she use it?

Delving again through the roots of the grasses, she pressed out in a wide circle. She expected the magi to be to the south, probably past where the ground changed to char and the desolation marched forward. If they were there, Eris wouldn't have any way of sensing them. Where the grasses stopped—where the roots stopped—so did her ability to discover anything.

At first, she didn't sense anything other than the soldiers.

The heat pressed on her. As it did, she recognized it had a focus.

Eris used this and followed it, tracking it north and to the west. Behind her.

If the magi were upon the plains, she should have sensed them before. How had she not?

She shifted the direction she delved, tracing through the grasses as she listened toward the north. Once there, she felt a disturbance. More than that, she couldn't tell.

As she began to withdraw from the connection, there was something else, something unexpected.

The creature from the svanth forest prowled near the magi.

Eris severed the connection quickly.

"You found them."

She swallowed. When the creature had been gone from the Svanth, she hadn't given it much thought. The trees had tolerated its presence and it had never attacked them, but what did it mean that it appeared here now?

"I found them. But there is something else, Terran."

He frowned.

As she told him about the creature, her breath caught with another concern. Could it be working *with* the magi? Could the creature have been sent to the Svanth to watch her all this time?

"Now will you let me hunt it?" he asked.

She shivered at the thought of the creature. She'd never seen it—only caught flashes of it, barely more than streaks of darkness. Something that stealthy would be dangerous, even to her. But she couldn't fend off the magi if that creature attacked. Whatever it was. For that, she needed Terran.

"Now you can hunt it."

They hurried across the plains, leading away from the fading battle. Now that she'd destroyed the stones, the number of men at Jacen's command should be enough for him to fend them off. That was his fight.

But the magi were her battle.

Eris ignored the fact that she didn't have enough power at her disposal. What was stored in the plains—in the grasses and clumps of flowers and trees scattered around here—would have to be enough. If it wasn't…then she would have tried. And the Sacred Mother protect Eliara as the magi continued north.

Eris kept herself low as they approached where she'd felt the magi.

A small copse of trees—mostly oaks with a few elms mixed in— blocked her view, but they were like a taint upon the trees. Steady chanting rose from within. The leaves started falling, curling to brown and dropping. Much longer, and the trees would be gone.

Eris couldn't let the magi take anything more. "Go. Find the creature. This is my fight."

Terran nodded and started off, keeping himself low as he did.

Eris made her way down the hill, watching the trees. Near the base of the hill, she lay on the ground and pushed her feet into the soil, delving as she did.

Already the connection began to fade. As it did, Eris realized what the magi did, why they started with the trees.

Pulling on the energy around her, she pushed back, at first feeding the trees, pressing energy through their roots and up and out the limbs into the leaves.

She sensed relief. The oaks let her surge through them, drawing from them, and the elms followed. Eris felt strengthened by the connection. It might not be the Svanth, but there was power here, and she would use it.

The chanting stopped.

"She is here. The keeper."

"Destroy the trees and move back. We can't risk confronting

her yet."

A loud crack split the cloudless sky. Lightning streaked toward the top of the nearest elm. Fire danced briefly before fading. Whatever Eris had done kept the flames from hurting it. She wondered if it was the same thing Imryll did to keep a fire in her hearth.

Another crack and lightning shot down this time striking the elm. The elm was weaker than the oak, already damaged by whatever dark spell the magi worked on it, the desolation crawling through it. Fire licked the topmost leaves. Eris pushed against it. For a moment, she thought she might be strong enough, but then flames consumed the top of the tree.

Agony shook through the tree.

She pulled more strongly on the energy around her, using that of the plains, borrowing what she could from the oaks.

Lightning struck again, this time missing the trees. A familiar shout filled her mind.

Terran.

Her concentration faltered, and the flames erupted.

Soon all the trees were consumed. There was not enough energy along the plains to put out that fire. If Eris knew how, she would summon rain, but that was a trick she hadn't learned. Even if she had, the fire worked too quickly to do anything.

The magi scattered.

She felt them leave, moving south and to the west. Through the connection to the grasses, she recognized that the creature followed them.

Eris ran toward where she'd heard Terran scream.

He lay on the ground. At first, she thought him uninjured, but his chest didn't move.

A black streak burned through the front of his jacket, leaving the fabric singed and still smoking. The air around him smelled of hot fire and charred flesh.

Lightning had torn through him.

"Terran?"

She said his name hoping he'd answer, but he didn't move.

Eris touched his forehead. It felt warm. She rested her head on his chest, hoping to hear his heart still beating. There was nothing.

Tears streamed from her eyes, spilling out onto him.

Terran couldn't be gone. Not yet.

But he didn't move. His chest didn't lift, and no breaths came from his mouth.

Eris bit back a scream. The Sacred Mother wouldn't take him from her already, would she? Would Eris be a keeper like those in her visions, a keeper whose gardener had passed before her?

No. Not without doing *something*; trying anything to save him.

She delved into the roots of the plains around her. The sense from them already faded. Whatever destruction the magi had worked on the trees had already begun to spread. Desolation worked through here, dragging across the ground, making its way toward her.

"No!"

She pulled the teary star from her pocket and set it next to her. Connecting to the flower, she pulled through it, demanding energy.

None came.

"NO!"

Eris grabbed one of the svanth seeds and shoved it into the ground. The earth split before her hand, and she pressed the seed deep, far deeper than she had even at the palace. She placed the cutting of the teary star next to it, leaving only the teary star flower pressing out of the dirt.

The earth flowed back over the seed as she removed her hand.

Eris pulled on the energy of the plains, pushing it into the seed.

It came slowly, oozing through her, but it came.

But it was not enough.

Even if growing a svanth tree could save Terran, she didn't have enough energy to do so.

# CHAPTER 28

*E*ris rested her head on his chest. The teary star poked out
of the top of the disturbed earth, practically taunting her.
Terran's cheeks had cooled, and he still didn't move. She no longer
expected he would.

How could he be gone?

And how could there be nothing she could do?

A memory floated through her then, something Imryll said to
her when Eris had grown the teary star vine along her svanth tree.

*You draw too much, pull from yourself as you do.*

Could *Eris* feed the svanth seed?

Even if it meant losing herself, she would do it for Terran. She
had to try.

She shifted so she could touch the teary star again and delved
deep into the soil to where the seed rested. With a thought, she
tried drawing from the grasses, but they had little to give. Then
Eris pushed *herself* out.

Energy flowed from her, filling the svanth seed. Eris didn't
know what she did—or how she did it—only that her own energy
streamed away.

The seed swelled and burst.

As it did, Eris pushed more of herself, pressing into the young sapling, letting it mingle with the teary star vine.

As the svanth grew, she sagged, falling forward.

The tree caught her and pushed her away.

Still Eris drew upon herself. The tree grew.

As it did, the teary star vine wrapped around it, working around the trunk. Both grew quickly, somehow more quickly than it had in the Verilain Plains or the palace. And as it grew, the grasses welcomed the presence of the svanth and lent what energy they could.

Eris lay on the ground, eyes falling closed. She reached her hand toward Terran, wanting to touch him as the last of her energy left her.

Strangely, she felt content. Terran was lost, and she had given herself to this svanth tree, but it would stand as a marker to them, its strength would fight against the desolation the magi tried inflicting.

Maybe Eliara would survive. Maybe the Svanth would survive.

But she wouldn't be around to see it.

Eris took a breath, wishing she could see the Svanth one more time, but wishing more that she could have fallen beneath its trees. What better place for her and Terran to rest? She could nourish the next generation, maybe add her memories to those within the roots. If another keeper appeared, maybe she would serve better than Eris had managed.

Her breath came raggedly, and she let it out.

As she did, a glimmer of energy surged in her mind.

Eris frowned. Could she reach for it?

With the last of her strength, she delved.

This time she traveled the roots of the new growth. She followed them, tracing them deep beneath the earth. A great well of power, vast and oppressive, lay there, and she drew upon it.

Energy and power surged through her.

Eris gasped.

The tree surged, shooting toward the sky, given sudden life.

Eris pushed a message through the new tree she'd planted, sending the roots *toward* the desolation. With another command, she instructed the teary star vine to send a shoot toward Terran. It wrapped around him, winding him in thick arms of deep green. Eris summoned a swell of energy and pushed it over Terran, washing over his injury until she felt the damage.

Then she sent a pinpoint surge.

It struck him where the lightning had struck, moving through his chest and out his back, lingering in his heart.

And then Eris let the energy fade.

It hovered in the back of her mind.

The teary star vine slowly unwound until Terran touched the ground.

Eris ran to him. His skin was warm rather than cold, but he still didn't breathe. She placed her hands on him, forcing another surge of energy through him, but nothing happened.

She leaned toward him and kissed him. "You can't leave me yet, Terran. I need you too much. Come back to me."

Then she rested her head on his chest. She heard it faintly, the slow *thump* of his heart. Tears again streamed from her eyes, but different than they had before. Finally, he took a slow breath. And then another.

Only then did Eris dare let herself hope.

She held him until the sky turned dark and the moon rose in the distance. She held him as countless small campfires glowed from the Errasn troops. She held him as a chill came to the air for the first time since they'd made their way this far south, draping her cloak around them both to keep him warm. And she held him as the sun slowly started to rise, the pattern in the streaks of color giving her hope.

Finally, his eyes opened. He smiled weakly. "What did you do?" His voice came out as a croak.

She kissed him on the lips, pressing too hard, pulling away only when he started coughing. "Terran."

He blinked and looked up. A soft gasp escaped his mouth.

Eris followed his gaze. She hadn't looked at the tree she'd forced from the ground. Her focus had been on Terran, on doing whatever she could to see him live.

The tree towering over her rivaled any in the svanth.

"You've been busy," he said.

"You tried to die."

He started to cough. When it faded, he smiled at her. "You know I wouldn't do that to you. And I know you wouldn't let me." He turned and met her gaze. His deep brown eyes held flecks of green now. "How did you save me?"

Tears welled in her eyes again, and Eris pushed back the sob that threatened to overcome her. "I did what I had to."

"And the magi?"

She shook her head. "They destroyed the trees."

His eyes traced back overhead. "Not all of them."

She sniffed. "No, not all of them."

"This must have taken all the energy of the plains to grow. If you wasted it on me—"

"Not wasted, and not the plains. At least, not all of it."

He frowned.

"Once the tree sprouted, I felt the connection to—" To what? Something like the Svanth, but not the forest, at least not that she knew "To something like the Svanth. It helped feed the tree." She chose not to tell him how she'd nearly spent herself on saving him. "I don't know if it will work every time." In the back of her mind, she still felt the connection, but it was vague and more like a distant sensation. Nothing like the surge of power when trying to heal Terran or when she'd tried to heal her mother...

Each time she accessed the power since learning she was a keeper, she'd been healing. Even when battling the magi, she'd used it to keep them from destroying the Verilain Plains.

Could it be so simple?

Did it matter *what* she tried to use the energy for? Did the Svanth *care*?

If that was the case, would it help if she used the energy there to push back the magi? If it wanted her to use the power to heal rather than destroy, what better use could there be?

Terran laughed softly. "I see you've thought of something."

She shook her head. "I don't know. Maybe."

He nodded. "Then you have to try." He pushed off the ground, attempting to sit, but fell back with a grunt. "But it looks like you might have to do it without me."

She touched his forehead, his cheeks, and kissed him again. "I'm sorry, Terran."

"Do what you are meant to do, keeper," he said.

Eris nodded, then stood. She touched the trunk of the svanth tree and ran her hand over it. A long tendril of teary star vine wrapped around her arm. She clipped it quickly and tucked it into her pocket. "Keep him safe," she murmured.

The tree seemed to shudder in response.

---

Eris left her shoes off as she walked, delving through the grasses of the plains. The connection was better, more solid doing it that way. The svanth tree loomed distantly and stayed with her even as she pressed her awareness out and around her. If she closed her eyes, she could connect to it, to the energy now filling it. That energy—that distant, deep source of power—had to be the same source the Svanth accessed.

And now that she understood, Eris thought she could reach toward the tree growing in the palace in Eliara. Possibly all the way to the Verilain Plains. Each tree left a signal in her mind she could detect.

Eris used the awareness to track the magi.

She'd expected them to have moved back across the desolation where she would no longer be able to feel sense them, but as she used the grasses to listen, she recognized a patch of discord still on the plains.

Eris hurried toward it.

When she neared, she was not surprised to find the magi chanting near another small copse of trees. Much like the other, this was nearly a dozen oaks and a few maple trees. Through the chanting, the rising desolation worked through the trees.

There was something else, though.

The creature.

It crouched near the trees, unmoving.

A chill washed over her. Could the magi control the creature?

What would it do when she tried to stop them? Would it attack her, or would there be anything she could do to keep it from her? If Terran were with her, she would have someone else able to watch over her, but with him too injured to come along, she would have to find a way to do it on her own.

Eris lowered herself to the grasses, staying low. Anything she did now risked both the magi and creature realizing she was there. Once they did, she needed to be ready to push back.

At least this time, she had the energy of the svanth tree to draw on.

The thought reassured her.

Eris took a steadying breath and delved toward the trees near the magi.

The desolation pulsed through them, weak and thready, but growing strong.

Eris drew on the power stored in the new svanth and pushed out, letting it wash over the trees in the same healing spread she'd used on her mother. The chanting faltered, and with another push, Eris burned away the effect of the desolation.

One of the magi yelled something Eris couldn't hear.

The creature moved, and she readied a protection.

It wasn't needed. The creature moved *toward* the magi, not away.

Then the magi screamed.

A crack of lightning split the sky, striking the trees. Eris pushed against it, holding a barrier in place, and it fizzled out harmlessly.

Another scream followed by more lightning.

Eris pushed against this as well, drawing from the trees themselves, strengthened now that the desolation had been pushed out.

A third streak of lightning, but this struck the ground near the trees rather than the trees themselves.

A loud roar erupted, followed by a high-pitched scream.

Eris started to her feet before pulling herself back down.

She'd almost done the same thing she had when Jacen went to battle. There, Terran had been able to watch her back. She needed to be smart here.

Closing her eyes, she delved through the trees, uncertain what to expect. Jacen had told stories of the magi sending wild storms of lightning that would often catch the men of Saffra as often as it caught those of Errasn. What she sensed was different.

Lifeless bodies lay upon the ground. Without getting closer, Eris couldn't tell how many, but none of the magi still moved.

The creature still lived.

It didn't move. From what she sensed, she suspected it was injured.

Had the magi unintentionally *helped* her?

She started forward, needing to see, making certain to stay close to the ground and holding tight to the energy stored in the svanth tree. She had used some of it, but already it was replenished, more quickly than she would have expected.

As she neared the trees, the sight before her made her gasp.

Magi bodies lay strewn about the trees. The nearest had the top of his face missing, slashed through. Blood poured from his open wound, draining into the dry ground.

Had she done that?

The thought actually horrified her. She needed to stop the magi, but not like that.

Eris moved to the next tree. Another body rested there. Both arms had been pulled free from the body, leaving ragged stumps, almost as if chewed.

*What happened to them?*

It wasn't until she reached the next body that she understood.

This one had a large gouge through his stomach. Slashes opened rents in his flesh. Charred blood congealed around the wound. Breaths still came raggedly and slowly. Wet blood pooled from his lips with each slow breath.

The magi *had* been attacked, but not by her.

The creature from the Svanth had attacked the magi.

And now it lay wounded.

Without thinking what she was doing, Eris ran toward it.

# CHAPTER 29

*E*ris found the creature lying outside the ring of trees. She recognized it from the times she'd sensed it in the forest, the dark undertones to the way the grasses pressed against it. The creature was enormous. From a distance, it resembled a massive cat with a wolf-like head. Jet-black fur covered it. Long claws curled from huge paws. Standing, it would tower over her.

The head of the creature swiveled toward her. Deep yellow eyes stared at her.

Eris stared back. She had seen those eyes before.

"What are you?" she whispered.

The creature blinked. Eris recognized pain in the expression.

It was injured. Whatever the magi had done had somehow injured it. Eris wanted to touch it—to help it—but feared getting attacked.

Something about the creature seemed familiar, and more than simply its eyes. It had a smell, like the bitterness of the teary star mixed with the bark of the svanth tree...

Eris took a step toward it. This was a creature of the Svanth. She felt that with certainty.

More than that, she needed to help it. If she was right, and the creature had attacked the magi, she *needed* to help.

Eris summoned a surge of energy from the surrounding trees and tried pushing it over the creature, washing over it to discover its injuries, but it was as if the energy disappeared as soon as it struck the creature.

Did the trees not have enough energy to detect any injuries from this creature? Maybe the effect of whatever the magi had done to them—the desolation that Eris had only barely managed to heal—had not completely faded. In time, the trees would grow strong again, but perhaps they still needed that time, like Lira's garden after Eris had drained it healing her mother.

But she could call upon greater energy now that she'd planted the svanth tree.

Eris pulled through the trees, reaching toward the energy stored in the new svanth tree, and let that wash over the creature.

This held.

Energy filled it, draining away from the svanth tree. Yellow eyes brightened, and it blinked at her again.

As it did, there came a surge of energy in return.

It felt cold, practically burning into her mind.

She stumbled back and nearly lost her footing. She didn't dare take her eyes off the creature.

The sensation didn't leave. Instead, it grew stronger, filling her mind with a new awareness. It took a few heartbeats before she realized she felt the creature before her.

"What did you do to me?" she asked.

Harsh laughter rolled through her head, but Eris sensed no malice. Only vast strength. Pain mixed with it, an injury deep and sharp, but not fatal. The creature would survive.

"How can I feel what you feel?"

"It is the bond."

The creature didn't open its mouth but the voice filled her head.

"The bond?"

The creature laughed again, a low sound almost like a growl. "You have finally learned what you needed."

"What did I need to learn?"

The creature stretched. As it did, Eris realized its injury had healed. The connection to the svanth tree slowed, the drain of energy fading. As she reached for the energy of the nearby svanth, the distant power refilled it, whatever connection she'd forged binding them together.

Then the creature stood and began pacing around her. It stood nearly to her shoulder, a massive size Eris struggled to comprehend. She turned, keeping it in sight as it circled her, though there would be nothing she could do if it attacked.

"You had much anger when you first came."

Eris shook her head. "I only wanted to do what was necessary to protect my family."

That laughter echoed again through her mind. "You sought to destroy."

Eris pulled herself up and nodded toward where the magi lay dead within the trees. "And you didn't do something similar?"

"Only when attacked."

"You could have stopped them before they started attacking the trees. Why didn't you?"

It seemed to shrug and sat back on its haunches. "I am not the guardian here."

"Then why *did* you attack?"

It swiveled its massive head toward her and met her eyes. "You chose these trees."

"I healed them from what the magi did to them." Recognition came through the connection in her mind. "You can feel it, too. The desolation they have wrought."

"I am not the guardian here."

The guardian. She'd heard that phrase before but couldn't remember where.

Eris crossed her arms over her chest. "You could let the magi destroy everything before you would even bother doing something?"

It blinked at her.

"What are you?"

"I am the bond. I am the place between darkness and light. I am the shadows across the forest floor. I am of the deep." It turned to meet her eyes. "I am the guardian."

Eris shook her head. "Of what?"

The creature blinked again. "You." It stood and stretched. Even that movement seemed annoyed. "She should have instructed you about these things."

"Who? Lira?"

It flicked its ears as if annoyed. "The other."

"Imryll? She didn't tell me about anything. She thought me no more than a keeper of flowers, but Terran helped me realize I was both. That's why I can use Lira's garden, why the Verilain Plains listened when I first needed them. I still don't know how to draw upon the Svanth consistently, but I think I'm starting to understand." Eris turned, frowning. "Wait...how do you know about Imryll?"

It only blinked in response.

Eris remembered the flash of golden eyes in her visions after she'd been stabbed. The movement away from Eliara and the priestesses that saved her life. "Was that you?"

A low rumble echoed in its throat. "It should not have been me. We had no bond. I was not your guardian." It flicked its ears again.

"How? What did you do?"

It snorted, its breath steaming in the air. "Brought you where you could learn."

The beginning of understanding about what happened came to her. Imryll had mentioned a guardian. And she had a wolf who'd watched her with such keen eyes. Was this creature like that?

"How did you find me?"

It laughed again. "You make too much noise not to find you."

Eris didn't know whether to be upset or amused. "So we are bonded?"

She thought of Terran and the connection she shared with him. He was her gardener, but he was much more than that. They needed each other, they complemented each other. Without him, she *would* have grown too angry. When she'd thought she lost him, she had been willing to give everything of herself for the chance to bring him back. But her bond was nothing like the simple awareness she had with this creature.

The creature flicked its ears. "It has started."

"Do all keepers form such a bond?"

It snorted and stood. "Not all."

"All keepers of trees?"

"Such keepers form bonds."

"That's not an answer."

It looked at her. "It is all I know."

"You don't know why?"

A low rumbled echoed in its throat again and its eyes narrowed slightly. "I know more than you, keeper."

Eris didn't want to push. What did it know and not share? Could the first keeper have known? Had she bonded to a creature like this?

But Eris had no sense of that from her visions. Neither keeper had forged a bond like this. If they had, wouldn't she have recognized it during the vision?

Or was the creature the reason the first keeper planted the garden—the first svanth trees—where she had. The vision Eris had the first night in the forest where the first keeper and Therin referenced the great power beneath the surface. Could this creature be a part of that power, the same power she suspected she accessed by planting the svanth tree?

"What do I call you?"

It snorted at her. "You have no need to call. I will know."

Eris took a step toward it. The creature didn't move. She settled her hand on its back and ran her hand down the fur. The texture was familiar, though it took a few moments to realize why. It reminded her of the barbs along the teary star vine. And like the vine, the barbs did not pierce her hand.

"You must have a name."

It blinked at her and then let out a long breath of air, as if sighing. Then it turned away.

"No name?"

Through the bond, she recognized that it didn't. There was pain, a nagging ache.

"May I name you?"

She asked it carefully, afraid to upset the creature, but she wanted something to call it other than "creature."

It tensed, and then nodded its great head.

She thought of what to call something so massive. She knew little of it other than through the bond, and she sensed it held much back from her. Eris hoped she held as much back from it.

But what had it said?

It was the bond. The place between darkness and light.

Eris thought of the streaks of color at the sunrise, the pattern she could almost make out, as if a great arrangement worked across the sky, some meaning the Sacred Mother meant for her to see. In the forest, the massive canopy obscured the pattern from her, but other patterns existed, like swirls of shadow.

"May I call you Shadow?"

Eris waited, worried she might have offended it, but then it turned and met her eyes. It blinked and nodded.

Another surge of energy washed over her then.

"Now the bond is set," Shadow told her.

# CHAPTER 30

*E*ris stood, feet planted into the ground, delving deeply.

She pressed out, using the grasses to listen for anything that might tell her where the magi might be. Since she'd reached the border with the desolation—no longer did she think it the border with Saffra, now it was something different—she had come across the magi twice. Both times, they had been attacking copses of trees.

There could only be one reason they would need to do so. They knew there was a keeper of trees. But what did that mean?

Unless they understood the power stored deep beneath the earth.

She shivered. If the magi understood that power—if they could reach it—what would it mean for Errasn? Not simply Errasn, but beyond?

And what would it mean for the Svanth? Eris suspected the forest dipped into the same deep stores of power. If the magi pressed their dark spell, pushed the desolation deep underground, would they be able to destroy the Svanth?

More than ever, she knew she had to do something.

But she felt nothing.

Eris changed tactics. Pulling on the energy of this copse of trees and using the connection to the new svanth, she surged out, questing for trees. If they thought to attack only the trees, Eris would do whatever she could to stop them. Maybe in so doing, she could protect what remained of Errasn.

A larger grove of trees grew toward the west.

Eris started off, and Shadow followed. He—she'd come to think of Shadow as a he—looked at her occasionally but said nothing.

As they neared the trees, Eris realized there were no magi.

She thought of what she'd done with the other copse of trees. She'd used the energy there to protect them, giving them a similar sort of protection that had been built over the Svanth Forest. Could she connect these trees to the others and let them borrow energy from each other, even the energy deep beneath the earth, the same as the Svanth seemed to?

Eris walked to the nearest tree—a tall and slender elm—and laid her hand on its trunk. She delved, pushing deep into the roots. The trees stored much energy here, but would it be enough to push back the desolation if the magi came? Would Eris be able to link the trees together to help keep the magi from destroying everything?

She reached through the roots, drawing the energy of these trees with her. It came willingly, not fighting her as those within the Svanth had done. Eris stretched toward the other trees. Reaching the roots, she pushed them together, surging the energy from this larger grove of trees into that of the small copse. Then she waited.

"Will it work?" she wondered aloud.

Shadow sniffed. "You think to claim all this land?"

She shook her head. "I seek to protect as much as I can."

He sniffed loudly but said nothing. Through the bond was a sense of annoyance.

The linking seemed to hold. As she delved, she felt roots

reaching toward each other. In time, they would meet in the middle, tying together more fully than any linkage she could form. Doing so made both stronger.

The last thing she did was to send instructions through the trees to push back against the desolation. If it worked, she could make her way along the trees, doing what she could.

Shadow's ears flickered, and he darted away.

Eris followed him, using the shallow roots of the grasses to guide her.

He moved more quickly than she could manage, bounding across the ground and farther west. Another grove of trees grew there. Oaks and elms with a few poplar mixed in. Leaves wilted and curled, branches drooped toward the forest floor.

The desolation.

Eris paused, searching for any sign the magi might be there.

She found them within the trees. At least three, though whatever they did made it difficult for her to know with certainty. They chanted together like they had the last time, a pressure building in the air.

Eris urged Shadow to attack through the bond but she knew he would not. As a keeper, she was meant to protect—to heal and grow.

But the magi sought to destroy.

Could anything she did stop them?

Pressing her feet into the hard soil, she had to ignore the way the dried grass cracked under her feet. Eris delved, pulling from the distant svanth tree as she did, funneling energy toward the trees, sealing them away from the desolation.

The chant ended.

Lightning cracked from the sky, streaking toward her.

Eris raised a hand and pressed over her head. The lightning fizzled out.

Shadow attacked.

Through the bond, she felt it as he did. He leapt into the trees, jumping from the ground to the trees. With a broad swipe, he dropped the nearest magi. Another leap, and another magi went down.

Eris shifted her focus, pushing through the trees, drawing as much energy from the distant svanth as she could, using it to burn the desolation from the trees.

Shadow growled and struck again. The last magi fell.

He stalked from the trees and crouched next to her, waiting.

Eris pushed, drawing even more energy through her. The desolation was farther along than it had been in the other trees. She pushed harder, forcing more and more through her until it came out in a rush, washing over the trees as it overpowered the magi spell.

And then the trees were whole.

Eris staggered but caught herself. With another breath, she pulled the energy from the other groves of trees toward this one, linking them in the same way, tying them together. The energy between the trees built upon each other, creating a barrier she hoped the magi wouldn't be able to penetrate.

A sigh escaped her as she sat on the ground.

Shadow sat next to her, watching over her.

---

The sun crawled along the sky as she rested. When Eris recovered enough, she continued on. She searched for other clumps of trees, each time tying them together as she had with the others. By late in the day, she was exhausted from the effort.

Shadow trailed alongside her the entire time. They did not encounter any more magi.

Eris began to wonder at that. Would the magi know if others were killed? Could they sense what Shadow had done—and would they target him?

She'd already seen that he wasn't indestructible. A lightning strike—or any dedicated attack—would be enough to destroy him.

"Does it matter how far you are from the Svanth?" Eris asked.

His ears twitched. They rested near the most recent copse of trees. Eris crossed her legs over each other. The svanth tree she'd planted to help Terran seemed far away. Much farther, and she feared she might not be able to access its energy. Then she'd only be able to use that from the grasses and whatever she'd tied together of the trees. It wouldn't be enough if she came across more of the magi.

Something like a frown came through the bond. "I am stronger there," he admitted.

"What would have happened had I not healed you?"

His ears twitched again and his great head swiveled toward her. "That would not have been enough to end my existence."

Eris felt uncertainty from him.

"Does it help that I claim these trees?"

Shadow snorted. "You expand your reach, but it is not the same."

Eris wondered if that were true. Linking the groves of trees felt like a start, but it wouldn't be enough. And she didn't think she was strong enough to work as quickly as was needed. The magi could simply move around her, isolating her. And from what Shadow had said, the Svanth wouldn't lend her strength if she attacked.

She needed more strength. She needed the Svanth.

Could she at least *halt* the progression of the desolation? If she slowed it enough, she might give herself enough time to stop the magi, keep them from Errasn. And then...then she would have to learn what she could do next.

Shadow might know. The bond told her he knew something, but not what.

Eris started away from the copse of trees. Shadow followed her, moving easily alongside. She made her way south. Always before, she had moved east and west, searching for trees to link, creating an underground network of roots that would function like that within the Svanth. Doing so took time.

This time she went straight south. Toward the desolation.

"This place is unsafe," Shadow said.

Eris nodded. "That is why I came."

Shadow moved in front of her, blocking her from moving any farther forward. Eris turned to move around him, but he blocked her.

"I am the guardian. Beyond here is Nothing."

The way he said it made it clear he recognized the desolation. "That's why we must continue."

"You have no power here. You have not claimed this place."

Eris met his gaze. "But I intend to."

Shadow flicked his ears as he studied her. Eris felt something in her mind, a soft tugging sensation, and wondered if he could read her thoughts through the bond. A soft rumble came from deep within his throat, and he sniffed.

"You intend to heal this land?" he asked.

Eris inhaled deeply. "I intend to try."

Shadow nodded.

---

They reached the edge of dried grasses as evening settled around them. The sun neared the distant horizon, wide splashes of orange and red and yellow radiating from it, making it look like some massive flower. She stared at it, trying to see if there might be some pattern to the colors, but couldn't discover anything.

Eris had not seen anyone or anything else as they traveled. She held onto the sense of the grasses, delving as she walked and searching for anything that might signal the magi. She found nothing.

Shadow prowled nearby. Occasionally, he would range far

away before bounding back. As he ran, he seemed to stream across the land, moving in a blur, practically a shadow. More and more, the name suited him.

Eris stopped shy of the desolation. Part of her feared stepping across the border. Even the grasses receded from the edge of the desolation, letting it spread as it crept farther and farther to the north. Standing still, Eris had the sense of steady movement from the grasses, a constant crawling away from the desolation.

She couldn't continue linking copses of trees. Doing so did not stop what the magi had already done.

Shadow stopped and sat near her, watching.

Eris pulled one of the svanth seeds from her pocket. Would what she intended even work? Would it make any difference?

She had to try.

With a surge of energy, she pressed the seed deep into the ground. She pressed it deeper than she had with any of the others, pushing it all the way to her shoulder before releasing it. Energy flowed into the hard outer shell as she did, swelling until the seed burst forth, stretching toward the light.

Using the energy from the nearby trees, the connection she'd forged, she fed the sapling.

It grew steadily, drawing more and more energy.

When it reached her shoulders, she took a clipping from the teary star vine and added this to it. The vine drew more energy, unfurling like a flower before the sun. Eris coaxed the vine as it worked around the trunk of the tree. She pushed more and more energy into it as it grew, letting it rise ten, twenty, and then thirty feet tall.

As it grew, she encouraged the roots to grow outward, sending them south and toward the desolation. They dove deep beneath the ground, beneath the layer of what the magi had done, probing toward the distant stores she suspected there. Through it all, Eris sensed the ground was ready for healing.

Other roots she sent north, toward the neighboring trees,

winding around them and joining more fully with them. There was something like the shock from Shadow's bond when they finally touched.

Eris sighed and dropped to the ground.

Shadow looked down at her, and blinked.

"Will it work?" she asked.

His great head shook from side to side. "I cannot say. But it is a start."

# CHAPTER 31

*E*ris spent that night lying near the desolation.

The air remained hot, but a breeze gusted across the ground, as if starting from the tree itself. Eris rested against the trunk while Shadow watched over her. She slept, and dreams of darkness colliding with light filled her.

She awoke as dawn crept cracked the sky, feeling refreshed. The svanth tree towered overhead, having drawn even more energy throughout the night. Pushing to her knees, Eris looked out toward the desolation.

Something had changed.

She delved and felt the difference. The grasses no longer receded from where the desolation had been. They didn't push against it—not yet—but in time they might.

It was a start.

"Come," she said to Shadow.

He snorted at her, and his ears twitched.

Eris followed the line of the desolation, moving east. After a while she stopped. Something about the location and the nearby trees felt right. There, she planted another svanth tree, letting it grow and join the others. Power surged through the trees, creating something like a wall, a barrier she suspected the magi would struggle to cross.

When she finished, Shadow blinked at her. "He comes."

"Who?"

In answer, he flicked his ears and then bounded off.

Eris frowned. The bond told her where he'd gone. He sat on the other side of a small hill, stretched out across the ground, soaking in sunlight. In that, he seemed more catlike, but otherwise, he was nothing like any cat she'd ever seen.

Eris used the roots to listen for who came. A smile crossed her mouth, and she understood why Shadow had gone.

Terran.

He appeared atop a hill and paused. When he saw her standing next to the svanth tree, he ran toward her. Terran pulled her into a tight embrace as he reached her, kissing her firmly on the mouth.

"Something changed," he said, pulling away from her.

"What?" Could he feel the bond between her and Shadow? Would Terran understand or would he fear him?

Terran nodded toward the trees. "These. They..." He trailed off, as if uncertain what to say. "They push back whatever the magi have done."

Sometime soon she would have to understand what abilities he had as gardener. It was more than helping with growth. When they walked, he kept up with her easily. And he seemed attuned to the land nearly as much as she.

"If I plant enough of them, I might be able to hold them back."

Terran frowned, looking at her. "Just hold them back? You don't want to destroy them for what they did?"

"I think that's been my problem. I'm a keeper. I don't think I'm allowed to destroy."

"What do you mean?"

She shook her head. "My ability. I'm a keeper. That's why the power has worked for me when I use it to heal and grow. But for anything else, it fails."

"You fought the magi before using your powers."

"The forest was threatened. That's the only time, I think."

"It makes sense. You seem more at peace than you were before. I'm happy to see it." He kissed her again. "I was afraid of how I'd find you. Knowing that creature prowled here with the magi…" He shook his head. "I'm glad you've managed to stay safe. You can keep doing what you need, and I'll protect you while you do."

She smiled as she looked up at him, uncertain how he'd react. She had to know. "You don't have to."

He frowned.

And then Eris sent a summons to Shadow through the bond.

---

Terran sat on the stretch of flat ground, looking from Eris to Shadow while she leaned against the newest tree that joined the other five she'd planted throughout the day, creating the barrier and pushing the desolation back. It would take many more trees to complete, but Eris began to feel hope that what she intended might actually work. Another few days, and the entire border would be connected.

She could tell Terran still hadn't come to terms with Shadow. The way he sat, hand resting near the hilt of his knife, was as if he prepared for whenever Shadow might attack. As the day had gone on, Terran had grown a little more relaxed, though not completely.

"Can you talk to him?" Eris said.

She meant it for Shadow, but Terran frowned and stood.

"What do you want me to say? Does it even understand me?"

Shadow growled softly in response. "He cannot understand me as you do. Without the bond, you would not either."

Eris shook her head. And here she thought it would be easier for her with Shadow to help. Now she realized it might actually

253

make things harder, at least where Terran was concerned. And would Shadow be able to feel *everything* through the bond? Eris felt his annoyance clearly, but other emotions—like the simply pleasure of lying in the sunlight—came through the bond as well.

"I've already told you that he's my guardian, Terran. He will do me no harm."

Terran looked from Shadow to Eris again and nodded. The look on his face told Eris he wasn't completely convinced.

"I'm sorry—"

Shadow's loud growl interrupted him. The hair on his back stood on end. His ears stood tall and straight.

"What is it?" Eris asked.

"They come."

"Eris?" Terran asked.

"Who comes?" As she asked, she suspected she knew the answer and began delving.

"Bringers of Nothing."

Eris nodded. The magi.

"Where are they?" she asked.

Shadow's great head turned from side to side, and his ears swiveled. Frustration surged through the bond.

Shadow didn't know.

Eris traced along the roots of the tree, racing through them as she searched for signs of the magi. She found nothing.

How could they completely obscure themselves from her?

Terran watched Shadow, frowning at the low rumble emanating from Shadow's chest. He pulled his bow off his shoulder. Sometime since she'd left him, he'd refilled his quiver. He nocked an arrow. She wasn't surprised to see it was made from one of the branches of the svanth trees.

Shadow bounded away, streaking off in a dark blur.

Terran watched him go. "What is that about?"

Eris waited, wondering if Shadow had heard or smelled something, but the bond didn't reveal it to her. "Magi."

"Where are they?"

She shook her head. "I can't tell. The trees should keep them out..."

But they wouldn't keep them out entirely. Not until the barrier was complete. Now, all the line of trees did was funnel the magi in a certain direction. They could still get around them and into Errasn.

The magi must have discovered what she planned. And if they wanted to access the power deep below the earth, they would do nearly anything to stop her.

Eris ran west, hurrying after Shadow. Terran followed her silently.

She reached where the next svanth tree was needed and quickly planted the seed, surging energy into it. The sapling burst from the ground, and she sent the teary star vine swirling around it as it drew energy from the others.

Waiting only until its roots connected to the others—the others would feed it, drawing it upward as roots connected—she ran onward, moving west. She stopped long enough to plant the next seed, nurturing it as quickly as she could. Terran worked alongside her, and his hands on the soil helped her draw energy from the others more easily.

She looked at him, guilt working through her. "This should be you. You're the gardener."

He shook his head. "Not for this. This...this takes a keeper."

"I think it takes us both."

When the tree reached nearly fifteen feet, Eris ran on.

The effect of working so quickly drained her. Had she the time, she would have moved slowly, letting herself recharge after each new planting, but there wasn't the time.

Shadow hadn't returned.

As the fourth sapling planted since Shadow darted away climbed toward the sky, Eris sunk to the ground. She'd spent too much energy too quickly. She hoped it was enough for now.

She held her connection, pushing the roots out toward the desolation and binding them toward the neighboring svanth trees as others dug deep below the earth, solidifying the barrier when it joined with the others.

"Eris?" Terran looked at her, worry wrinkling the corners of his eyes.

"I'll be fine. I just need to—"

She didn't get the chance to finish.

The earth began rumbling. She looked around for Shadow but didn't see him.

Terran grabbed her hand, eyes darting from side to side.

And then the magi attacked.

# CHAPTER 32

*I*mmediately, Eris knew this was different than the other groups of magi. There, she had managed to surprise them, catching them off guard. This time, they surprised her.

The attack began with a surge of lightning.

It was nothing like she'd experienced before. Those had been single strikes, streaking toward the trees, trying to destroy the power within the trees as the desolation set in. But Eris could use the power within the trees to push back and against the magi.

This attack came all at once.

And she still couldn't see the magi.

Terran bellowed. For a moment, she thought something had happened to him again. Terror coursed through her with the thought. As tired as she was, she didn't know if she could protect herself, let alone Terran. She turned to him and realized he was unharmed.

He still shouted, but it was *at* her.

"Run, Eris!" he shouted.

She shook her head. She didn't have the strength to run.

Then the lightning struck.

It hit all around her, at first hitting earth and sending chunks flying. Each strike came closer, almost as if the magi used it to gauge where to find her. Dirt and debris flew around her. She barely had the strength to push away the ground as it exploded near her.

Terran yelled something else, but she couldn't make it out.

Eris pulled on the energy of the grasses, drawing strength from it. It helped somewhat, enough for her to look up as the next strike streaked from the sky. She flung her hand over her head. But the grasses couldn't provide enough strength to deflect the lightning.

She needed more energy.

Would the new tree be strong enough to aid her?

With the thought, there came the familiar surge when its roots joined the others. The sensation again reminding her of the bond with Shadow.

Where was he?

Eris drew through the svanth tree. Energy filled her, surging down the line of trees. Interconnected as they were, they drew massive amounts of energy, more than the smaller groves. But even those groves lent their strength with the others.

As she pulled the energy, she sensed a pattern to the way the trees were aligned but didn't have time to recognize it.

Eris pushed against the sky, forcing the lightning back.

Chanting started, low and steady, but rising quickly.

The sound seemed to come from all around her, but still she saw no sign of the magi. They must be here somewhere.

Shadow attacked.

His roar split the air like thunder. Someone screamed nearby. Blood sprayed, and Eris saw the magi appear on the ground.

When Shadow touched the earth, Eris sent a surge of energy through him.

She was rewarded with another loud roar.

And then he attacked, pouncing quickly. Magi appeared where

they had not been before, falling quickly as Shadow circled through them.

He moved like a creature out of a nightmare, flickering from one place to the next. Each time he landed, Eris pushed another surge of energy through him and he answered with another loud roar.

She and Terran struggled to stay on their feet.

Eris created a wall of wind, using the energy she drew from the trees to swirl the still air into a torrent that left them otherwise untouched. The magi chanting caught in the wind and faded.

Explosions of lightning crashed around them. Each strike tried to penetrate the protection Eris pressed over her. None reached her.

Then the attack shifted.

The magi turned their attention to Shadow. She drew upon the energy of the new svanth trees, on the newly linked trees throughout this part of Errasn, and fed that to him.

The attacks slowed, and then stopped.

Eris let the wind drop.

Shadow stalked nearby, ears twitching.

Magi lay dead or dying around them. Eris shuddered at how many there were. She counted at least ten, but the way Shadow attacked, tearing through the magi, made it difficult to know for sure.

Terran's eyes widened when he saw how many magi had fallen. He met Shadow's gaze. "Thank you."

Shadow growled low in his throat in response.

Eris made her way to the svanth tree and leaned against it. The attack had drawn much of the energy from the trees. Another attack like that might be more than she could withstand, at least without pulling from the deeper stores. She didn't know how to access that power directly.

Her eyes dipped closed, and she took a deep breath. She slipped into a light sleep. As she did, she delved, sliding across the grasses, questing out until she reached what she sought.

Her eyes snapped open. Jacen and his soldiers lived, but Saffra attacked.

"Magi," she breathed out.

Shadow's ears twitched, and he growled.

"Where?" Terran asked.

She shook her head. "Near Jacen and his men."

Terran nodded. "How many?"

Eris let her eyes fall closed again and listened, but couldn't tell how many magi were there. That alone frightened her.

She sighed and stood.

Terran hurried over to her and grabbed her arm. "You can't do this, Eris. You're too weak."

The thought of leaving her brother at the mercy of the magi made her sick. She couldn't leave him there, not without trying to do something. Even weakened, she could draw off the magi, give Jacen's soldiers a chance against the Saffra army.

"You know I have to."

Shadow looked at her.

The bond told her something made him uncomfortable. She could not use her ability to attack, not unless her garden—her trees—were endangered.

But if the magi succeeded, all of Errasn was in danger.

"I will claim them," she said to Shadow. "All of them."

His ears twitched again.

---

Eris ran toward the battle. Terran ran alongside her, keeping pace. Shadow ran ahead, scouting for danger.

More and more men of Saffra streamed toward the battle.

They moved across the ground, running with speed no man or horse should have. The magi fueled them. Were she closer, she might be able to destroy the stones. This time, Eris knew, would be different. The magi knew she was here. They would do anything to stop her.

And then they reached the battle.

Chaos spread in front of her. Saffra soldiers riding horses imbued with the magi stones crashed into Errasn men in silver armor. The Errasn soldiers seemed better prepared than when she'd seen them fighting before; they still had the numbers, enough to push back the Saffra troops, but for each man in maroon armor who fell, two men in silver dropped.

"They will know you are here the moment you attack," Shadow said with a low growl.

Eris nodded. She looked around, searching for anything that might help. During the last attack, she had been able to use the connection to the svanth trees to draw energy from. Here there was nothing but empty plains. Even the grasses were trampled and weak.

"Shadow," Eris started. She needed to ask, suspecting a way he could help.

He looked toward her, long ears twitching. His mouth opened slightly, revealing sharp, gleaming teeth.

"I will need to borrow from you for a moment."

She sensed a question through the bond but still pushed a surge of energy through her.

It filled her, a massive amount and more than she would have expected. How much could he store? When this was over—if they survived—she would have to learn.

Like a lightning strike of her own, Eris sent this out, splitting the energy as she targeted the Saffra soldiers and their armor.

Stones exploded, and men screamed.

Eris paused long enough to stab a svanth seed into the ground. With the remaining energy Shadow lent her, she slammed it into the seed, filling it until it burst. The sapling erupted from the ground and shot upward.

She almost didn't have enough time to plant the teary star vine.

The magi attacked.

Clouds blocked the sun, plunging the day into sudden darkness. The air grew hot and stale, burning her lungs with each breath. Thunder boomed, shaking through her bones. Lightning streaked from the sky. Eris barely managed to hold it off.

Shadow leapt away.

Somewhere nearby a magi shouted, "The keeper is here!"

"Access the Source, and she can do nothing!"

Eris shivered, suddenly fearful. The Source.

Could that be the distant power she sensed? The well of power feeding the svanth trees in the heart of the forest? If the magi reached it, her connection to the trees—the trees themselves—would fall. And she would fail.

She forced the teary star vine into the ground.

Terran plunged his hands near hers, scooping earth around the vine. "Let me. Save yourself."

His hands wove the vine across and around the trunk of the tree. Eris was amazed to realize how quickly they moved. For the first time, the barbs ignored him, letting him swirl the vine up the tree.

Eris let him work. With Terran focused on the vine, she could push more energy into growing the tree. She drew from everything she sensed—the grasses, herself, Shadow, even Terran—as the roots streamed deeper and the tree shot toward the sky.

All she needed was the roots to connect, to link to the others and join the pattern. Then she could draw upon the others.

The ground exploded near her.

Had she not been so close to the svanth tree, she would have been thrown. Terran gripped the vine of the teary star, holding tight as the explosion washed over them. He screamed.

A thunderous roar erupted, splitting the air.

Eris prayed Shadow was unharmed. If anything happened to

him, it would be her fault, especially if she had taken too much energy from him.

She clung to a branch. The connection let her press more energy into the tree. The svanth rose beneath her, pushing her into the sky with it as it grew.

Roots pressed out beneath the tree, spreading beneath the plains, reaching toward the other trees. And deeper.

A little more time. All Eris needed was a little more time for the roots to connect to the others she'd planted so she could pull on the power of the trees.

Lightning struck the top of the tree.

It was close—much closer than any of the other lightning strikes.

She had to shift her focus and sent a surge of energy up the tree and out the budding leaves. The lightning fizzled and failed. Another followed, and another. Too many in a row.

Her strength sagged.

She needed the roots to connect.

Gripping the branch, she pushed as much of herself into the tree as she could. She held tightly, but the tree jerked upward and threw her from the branch. The ground knocked the breath out of her. Lights swirled around her eyes, like the colors of the sunrise. Eris could almost make out the pattern there.

The ground rippled around her.

The hairs on her arms stood on end as lightning streaked toward her. She had failed.

And then the bond formed.

It thundered through her, filling her with more energy than was stored in the dozen or so trees she'd planted, more than the small groves of trees dotted across the plains could provide.

This filled her and overflowed out of her, the stores of a much greater garden.

The pattern it formed filled her mind, no longer a question. How had she missed what she created as she planted the trees?

Each grove of trees, connected together, bound by a svanth tree. This, the last, forming the pattern. The shape of the teary star flower.

Eris delved deeply, connected by the new svanth tree. Terran hung in the tree, cradled in a bundle of vines. Shadow leapt through the magi, attacking, an injury leaving one leg useless. He still moved in a blur. When he landed, Eris pushed power through him, filling him with it. It was the power of the plains, but it was more than that. Power greater than she should be able to reach filled her.

The power of the Svanth.

Shadow's roar filled the air.

Eris stood. Wind swirled around her. She sent it up, scattering the darkness the magi summoned. Sunlight pierced through them with a bright ray. Eris basked in it a moment, filling herself with a warmth so different than what she felt near the desolation.

She knew what she needed to do. She must protect the land— her people—from the magi. As she had told Shadow, she had claimed them.

A deep breath, and she moved toward the magi.

The connection to the Svanth told her where they were. Someone screamed nearby; Shadow's work. A magi sent the earth rumbling but she settled it with a wave of energy, the roots of the tree catching it. Swirling wind sent the magi south, away from her.

Chanting began, the awful sound somewhere nearby.

The building pressure of their spell pressed the wind from her lungs. Through the bond, she summoned Shadow. She sensed him pause and then leap in the direction of the chanting. It died suddenly.

A flurry of lightning attacks streaked toward her.

Eris drew through the trees, connected somehow to the Svanth and deeper, and waved the spidering fingers of electricity away.

She advanced further. Magi surrounded her. They were a blight on the grasses, their simple presence tainting where they stood. A gust of wind swirled around her, summoned to lift them away.

The wind protected her but failed to throw the magi.

She stopped. "Shadow!"

He ran toward her, but not in time. More magi joined the others, nearly two-dozen now in all. More than she could stand against.

Eris dropped to her knees. She pressed her feet as deep into the soil as she could, solidifying the connection.

The ground tried to ripple under her, a great tremor threatening to split the earth apart. It took all her effort to hold it together, leaving her with barely enough strength to stop the stacked lightning strikes coming.

If she failed here, the magi would access the Source. They would move openly toward Eliara. The Svanth would fall, and everything would fall behind it.

All because she wasn't strong enough.

Eris closed her eyes, begging for more energy.

One hand reached overhead, pushing above her. The other gripped the ground.

Shadow appeared next to her. Resignation shone in his eyes. She wasn't strong enough.

Eris was thankful she wasn't alone for this.

When Terran appeared at her side, she nearly sobbed. She'd never been alone, not really.

And now they would all die together.

"I'm sorry I pulled you here."

Shadow answered with a sorrowful growl. Terran grabbed her hand.

Eris pulled the last of the energy she could find, pressing it down to hold the earth together and up to shield them from the lightning. Already, she knew it wouldn't be enough.

She tried pulling more, knowing the trees had no more to lend.

If she could access the deeper stores, she might be able to push them back…

And then it was there, filling her, foreign and strange and feeling of oak and elm and pine, like that of Imryll's forest garden, a sense somehow familiar.

Deeper than that, she felt the enormous energy, ancient and buried.

It terrified her as she pulled on it.

Shadow growled and streaked away.

Eris sent all of the energy rippling out of her in all directions. The lightning broke harmlessly over her head. The ground settled. Magi screamed, though she didn't know if it was from what she'd done or from Shadow's efforts.

And then everything fell silent.

As she collapsed to the ground, wind swirled around her. The connection to the trees was there, but weak.

Terran helped her, holding her as she fell.

Shadow appeared next to her. Blood stained his jaw and streaked down his flank. She reached out to touch him, and he made a low rumble deep in his chest.

"Are they gone?"

Shadow's ears twitched, and his deep yellow eyes searched the land around them. "They are gone for now, keeper."

Eris let out a long sigh and dropped her head to the ground. Exhaustion overwhelmed her, and she found a dreamless sleep.

# CHAPTER 33

When Eris finally awoke, sunlight filled the sky. A cool breeze blew in from the north, refreshing and scented of earth and rain. She rested against the svanth tree, her back pressed against the rough barbs of the teary star vine. Terran held her head, running his fingers through her hair.

She blinked up at him. "You're here," she said.

"I wouldn't leave you."

Eris swallowed, thinking of the other keepers from her visions, the way the first keeper had lost Therin, living the last of her days without him. Or the next keeper, regretting the loss of Heath. More than anything, that seemed the legacy of the keepers.

"I…" She swallowed, unable to continue.

Terran touched her hair, running his hand along her face. "I know."

Eris pushed herself up and looked around. "Where is Shadow?"

Even as she asked, she sensed him nearby.

Terran nodded toward the tree.

Eris looked up at the massive svanth now growing high over-head. Wide leaves spread out from thick branches, filtering the light. A dark shadow spread across a pair of upper branches. Shadow's low growl rumbled softly, carrying to her ears.

"How long have I slept?"

Terran smiled, the lopsided smile she remembered returned. "Only a day."

"And the magi?"

Terran's face clouded briefly. "They are gone. Once he knew you were safe, Shadow followed them. I do not know what he found."

Eris nodded. It was a question that could wait for later.

She sighed. Awareness filled her, much like within the Svanth Forest. She had no need to delve to learn what she needed.

Grasses pushed back against the desolation. The barrier made by the svanth trees would hold, pushing back whatever the magi had done. More work remained to complete the barrier, but there was no sense of urgency, not as before.

They had won.

It seemed impossible to believe. How had she managed to push back the magi by herself?

But she hadn't, she realized. Without Terran, she wouldn't have been strong enough to make the journey. Without Shadow, she wouldn't have survived even the first attack. She couldn't have done it by herself...and she didn't have to.

Eris let out a long breath.

"What of the soldiers?"

She managed to stand. She was weak, but the awareness of the trees pressed on her, lending her strength. Eris drew from the trees to fortify herself. The svanth trees gave to her freely, buoyed by their deep connection to the Svanth Forest.

And something deeper. The Source. With more time, she would have to learn what that was and why the Conclave wanted it.

For now, she was content knowing her garden had grown, expanded by what she had done. Eris knew there would be consequences. Hopefully Lira would be able to answer and explain. If not, she would seek Imryll, especially now that she knew she'd borrowed from Imryll's forest during the magi attack. Without that reservoir of strength, she would not have survived.

Terran took her hands. "I am sorry, Eris."

He tried pulling her toward him, but she resisted. "What happened? Where's Jacen?"

Terran glanced up at the svanth tree before leading her away.

Carnage spread out before her.

Men in maroon and silver armor lay dead and broken. Blood-stained faces and shattered limbs splattered about them. The stink nearly gagged her.

But others still lived. Men wearing Errasn armor moved through the battlefield, taking what they could. Eris searched, looking for signs of her brother.

She found him surrounded by a half-dozen Saffra soldiers. He lay, eyes staring toward the sky, peace finally worked across his face.

A sob caught in her throat.

"I'm so sorry, Eris," Terran said.

She took a shuddering breath and turned away. "He saved us. Without him…"

She didn't want to consider what would have happened had Jacen's men not forced the magi into an attack. What would have happened to her had the soldiers come across her while she expanded her garden?

At least Jacen had finally found peace.

"What will you do?" Terran asked.

She looked south, feeling the desolation still pressing against the barrier, but the barrier was incomplete. She needed to strengthen it before the magi returned.

Eris had been mistaken. She thought the magi only intended to destroy, but they had been after something. The desolation had a purpose, a dark one.

Through the connection to the new svanth trees were glimmers of the power they sought to claim, the same power buried deep beneath the Svanth. Had the magi managed to access it here, they could have destroyed the Svanth without ever stepping foot in it.

With everything she learned, she still knew so little about her abilities. The first keeper had not known everything, but she had the foresight to tap into something greater than a keeper of flowers would access. But it meant there was an older order, maybe something even more than the keepers. And the magi knew of it.

"Eris?" Terran asked.

She blinked, tearing her eyes away from the image in her mind. "I must finish what I started," she began. "The magi have scattered for now, but the desolation pushes on without their help. We will finish the line of svanth trees and extend our garden as far as we can. And then I need to return to Eliara and speak with Lira."

The palace looked different than the last time Eris had come.

It was more than the towering svanth tree rising at the center of the garden. The palace itself seemed changed. Or maybe it was her that had changed even more. Either way, she did not feel like she was coming home.

She walked ahead of the column of riders, making her way to the palace with only Terran at her side. Eris hadn't wanted to be with the soldiers, not while they carried her brother's body back with them.

It hadn't taken long for Eris to catch up with the army. She'd spent the last two days continuing her plantings, and now a long row of svanth trees stood like sentinels near the edge of the desolation. The connection to them was strong—stronger even than her connection to the Svanth itself. She wondered if planting them herself made the difference, or if the trees dug more deeply into the ancient energy—the Source—she sensed there.

When that energy had filled her, she had felt afraid. It was vast and powerful and uncaring about who used it. Were the magi to connect to it...

She shook away the thought. For now, she'd kept the magi from reaching it.

"You don't seem happy to return."

Eris sighed and turned to Terran. She fingered one of the svanth seeds still in her pocket. After she returned to the palace, she intended to continue planting. If she was right, she might be able to push the desolation back toward Saffra, back beyond the border of Errasn. A nagging worry told her she needed to reclaim the Loess River.

"There is much to do," she answered. And much more to learn, but Terran knew that. Worse, Eris had no idea where to start.

Shadow would help.

He ranged off away from her. He was her guardian, but he knew she was safe here.

"Your family will need you," Terran said.

She nodded. It was the reason she had returned.

They said little more as they passed through the outer city. Eris bypassed the huge iron gates—still closed, she noted—and made their way through the servants' gate. Inside, the renewed energy of the garden washed over her, and she smiled.

The energy within the garden was different than the last time she had been here. Then, the flowers focused and funneled every-thing they could, storing it for Lira to access. The flowers still did that, but the svanth tree created another source of energy that mingled with the flowers. Rather than competing, they comple-mented each other. She wondered if Lira even felt it.

Eris made her way into the palace and toward the throne room.

Lira stopped her outside the room. She wore a flowing lavender dress made of a thick fabric. Her hair was rolled neatly atop her head, and her hazel eyes took in everything as she looked from Eris to Terran. Her lips pursed and then split into a smile. "You succeeded."

Eris noted the surprise in her tone. "For now. Much darkness remains of what the magi did. I have begun the healing, but it will take time."

"I feel..." Lira paused, as if searching for the right word. "Echoes of what you did."

"I would like to show it to you." A part of her still wanted Lira's approval, even though there was little Lira could teach her that applied to what Eris did. She was simply a different kind of keeper.

Different. Always different.

Only this time, had she not been different, the magi would have succeeded.

"I would like that," Lira said.

"We will need to prepare."

Lira's eyes narrowed. "For what?"

"For when the magi return. I won't be able to do it alone."

A moment of fear washed across Lira's face before fading. "You think to rebuild the gardens."

Eris hadn't given it much thought, but standing here, seeing Lira and knowing how different her skills were, she had fleeting visions of the help she would need. "I think we must find the keepers. All of them."

She still didn't know who had left the messages in the flowers. Had it been Ferisa and the priestesses...or had there been someone else? Another keeper? One arrangement held flowers from the Svanth, but who else could reach them?

Terran squeezed her hand. Other than Lira, Eris knew of only Imryll, but she doubted Imryll had left her forest. There were other keepers, though. Were she to delve deep enough, she suspected she could find them.

Lira nodded slowly. "Perhaps you are right. The time for hiding is past."

As Lira turned to go, Eris caught her arm. "What of Ferisa?"

Lira took a deep breath and shook her head. "Gone. And from what I can tell, so are several others, all priestesses of high rank. Those who remain will not speak against them, but I suspect they all were part of the sect."

Terran stiffened. His jaw clenched slightly.

Eris only sighed. More things to worry about. Not only did she have to fear the magi returning, she had to learn what this sect of the church intended. Why had they tried to kill her? A nagging worry told her it had something to do with the Source as well.

Lira patted her hand. "Go. Be with your family as Jacen returns home. They will need your support."

Eris turned away from Lira and made her way to the great doors of the throne room and pushed them open.

She should have felt anxious or relieved or *something*, but all she felt was a strange sense of calm.

Her family waited. Runners sent ahead of the soldiers had sent word. Eris wished she had been the one to share the news of Jacen's death, but perhaps it was better this way.

She nearly stumbled when she saw her mother.

Her golden hair had returned, but it was streaked with hints of brown. Her bright blue eyes carried flecks of green, much like Terran's now did. She sat atop her seat, smiling at Eris. Her father sat next to her, his hand reaching across the distance, their fingers entwined. He looked healthier than he had, more like his old self.

Her mother stood and hurried to her, throwing her arms around her. Terran stepped to the side, letting them have the moment together.

Had it only been days since she'd left? In that time, her mother had regained much of what she'd lost. Strength and vigor that hadn't been there only a week before. She carried a regal air about her again, a queen once more. She should not have regained so much vigor so quickly...unless it was something of the healing Eris had done.

"Thank you," she whispered. "You have become so much more than I ever hoped."

Eris blinked back the sudden tears. Hearing her mother speak of pride about her meant more than she imagined. "I'm sorry I couldn't save Jacen."

Her mother held her, and tears fell from her eyes as well. "I fear Jacen has been lost since the magi first attacked him."

"I could have saved him, too. Had I only known how."

"You did what you could. I pray he found peace at the end."

Eris thought about how Jacen had looked up toward the sky, the way tension had finally left his face and eyes at the end, and knew that he had.

"You knew what I could become," Eris said.

Her mother pushed away and glanced back at her father. He smiled at her with a mixture of sadness and love. When she turned back to Eris, she nodded. "You are much like her, you know."

"Like who?"

Her mother smiled again and ran a hand through Eris's dark hair. "She would have been so proud of who you've become."

"Mother?" Eris asked.

Her mother's lips tightened, and she nodded, as if coming to a decision. "You weren't the first keeper in the family, Eris."

As she said it, Eris thought she knew what would come next.

She was wrong.

"Rochelle always was different. When she learned what she could do, she finally understood why. And then when she had you...she feared for your safety, especially after what the magi had done to Elaysia."

Eris shook her head. "What are you saying?"

Her mother swallowed. "Eris—it's time you know the truth. I did what I had to do to keep you safe. Hanrik doesn't even know. He was away in the north, settling the battle with Varden when she came to me. She was so frightened...I had to do something."

"What? What did you have to do?"

"Rochelle was a keeper like you."

Like her. Maybe Eris wasn't as different from the rest of her family as she'd always thought.

Her mother took a deep breath and sighed. "Not just a keeper. It is time you know everything." She glanced toward where her father sat. "Eris—you have been a daughter to me. I love you as much as I love the others. But Rochelle is your mother."

Eris gasped. "My what?"

Her mother nodded. "I—" Her mother couldn't finish.

Eris looked away. Rochelle was a keeper...and her mother.

All the years she'd felt different—all the years she'd felt as if she didn't fit into her family—but all that time she *had* been like her mother, only she hadn't known. Had she never been different? Could Rochelle have taught her what it meant to be a keeper? But why had she left? Why would she abandon Eris here, uncertain whether she would ever learn to use her ability?

Eris swallowed. Did knowing change anything? Would it mean Jasi and Desia were no longer her sisters? Did it mean she shouldn't grieve Jacen? Or feel angry that Ferisa had betrayed her?

Or should she not feel relieved her mother—at least the only woman she'd ever known as her mother—still lived?

Eris sighed.

If anything, she should feel relieved. Though she didn't know what had happened with Rochelle, she still had a family. And now she no longer needed to fear that she was different, because she *was* different. But that difference had saved Errasn. She should feel proud.

Except...Eris didn't know how to feel.

She looked at her mother. Tears streamed from her mother's eyes. Eris put her arms around her and hugged her. Her mother stiffened at first, but then hugged her back. She sobbed softly onto Eris's shoulder.

Eris would figure out how to feel later. For now, she would grieve with her family.

Book 3 of the Lost Garden: Keeper of Light

*Eris must rebuild the lost Gardens of Elaysia to stop the coming darkness, but doing so risks the life she desperately wants with Terran.*

In the aftermath of the recent attack, Eris wants nothing but peace and the chance to enjoy her life with Terran as she learns what it means to be a keeper of both trees and flowers. But when she finds a message with a strange and powerful flower, she learns a threat greater than the magi has reappeared.

Understanding this threat takes her on another quest, this time to convince the only remaining keeper of trees to teach her. She travels to the one place her magic cannot, dragging Terran and her mysterious guardian Shadow with her. If she fails, much more than her life will be lost, but all of Light will be lost.

Looking for another series? Grab Shadow Hunted, book 1 of the Collector Chronicles.

Carthenne Rel is born of shadow magic. Gifted with the power to control the flame that burns within her. A master strategist. All will be tested by the mysterious Collector.

As she travels south, wanting to solidify her growing network, word of attacks in the south leads her to a distant city with a strange past. While searching for answers and attempting to establish a presence as she has in countless other cities, she finds power that rivals her own and a challenger who might be not only more powerful than her, but an even more cunning strategist.

Carth must save her friends—and the city—before the plan set in place by the Collector succeeds.

---

Check out the first in a new series: The Dark Ability.

Exiled by his family. Claimed by thieves. Could his dark ability be the key to his salvation?

Rsiran is a disappointment to his family, gifted with the ability to Slide. It is a dark magic, one where he can transport himself wherever he wants, but using it will only turn him into the thief his father fears.

Forbidden from Sliding, he's apprenticed under his father as a blacksmith where lorcith, a rare, precious metal with arcane properties, calls to him, seducing him into forming forbidden blades. When discovered, he's banished, sentenced indefinitely to the mines of Ilphaesn Mountain.

Though Rsiran tries to serve obediently, to learn to control the call of lorcith as his father demands, when his life is threatened in the darkness of the mines, he finds himself Sliding back to Elaeavn where he finds a black market for his blades - and a new family of thieves.

There someone far more powerful than him discovers what he can do and intends to use him. He doesn't want to be a pawn in anyone's ambitions; all he ever wanted was a family. But the darkness inside him cannot be ignored - and he's already embroiled in an ancient struggle that only he may be able to end.

# ALSO BY D.K. HOLMBERG

*The Lost Prophecy*

The Threat of Madness

The Warrior Mage

Tower of the Gods

Twist of the Fibers

The Lost City

The Last Conclave

The Gift of Madness

The Great Betrayal

*The Teralin Sword*

Soldier Son

Soldier Sword

Soldier Sworn

Soldier Saved

*The Cloud Warrior Saga*

Chased by Fire

Bound by Fire

Changed by Fire

Fortress of Fire

Forged in Fire

Serpent of Fire

Servant of Fire

Born of Fire

Broken of Fire

Light of Fire

Cycle of Fire


*The Endless War*

Journey of Fire and Night

Darkness Rising

Endless Night

Summoner's Bond

Seal of Light


*The Shadow Accords*

Shadow Blessed

Shadow Cursed

Shadow Born

Shadow Lost

Shadow Cross

Shadow Found


*The Dark Ability*

The Dark Ability

The Heartstone Blade

The Tower of Venass

Blood of the Watcher

The Shadowsteel Forge

The Guild Secret

Rise of the Elder


*The Sighted Assassin*

The Binders Game

The Forgotten

Assassin's End


*The Lost Garden*

Keeper of the Forest

The Desolate Bond

Keeper of Light


*The Painter Mage*

Shifted Agony

Arcane Mark

Painter For Hire

Stolen Compass

Stone Dragon

www.ingramcontent.com/pod-product-compliance
Lightning Source LLC
Chambersburg PA
CBHW020244180626
46810CB00006B/2364